Macedonian Gold

Michael Seraphinoff

Sydney/Shtip/Greenbank 2004

Macedonian Gold by Michael Seraphinoff

While this work is fiction, the Republic of Macedonia and its language, history, people and culture are real. Names of characters, some places and incidents are the products of the author's imagination or are used fictitiously. Any resemblance to actual events, locales, or persons, living or dead, is entirely coincidental.

For information on ordering books in the USA, please contact by phone 1-360-678-4168 or email *mjseraph@whidbey.net*.

Publishers:
Nettle Hollow
3830 S. 530th E., Greenbank, WA, 98253 USA
And
The Macedonian Literary Association "Grigor Prlichev" Sydney
P. O. Box 227, Rockdale, NSW 2216, Australia
For the Australian publisher, Dushan Ristevski

National Library of Australia card number and ISBN 0 9581162 6 1

Printed by "2nd of August- S" – Shtip, Republic of Macedonia

Cover design and layout by Susan C. Prescott and Michael Seraphinoff

This book is dedicated to the present-day living, breathing, struggling Macedonian people.

This book is also dedicated to the memory of the Veneti, Pelasgi, Brygi and Paeoni who are every bit as real as all of the other peoples mentioned in this story. But they apparently disappeared into the Balkan stew a long time ago. Or did they?

The ancient Macedonians are among the most famous people in history. Several famous figures in history were of Macedonian heritage. These include Alexander the Great ...and his father, Philip II of Macedon, ... One of the greatest philosophers of all time, Aristotle was also a Macedonian (by his father), and so was the Egyptian Queen Cleopatra VII. (She was a distant grand daughter of the Macedonian General Ptolemy. ...There are those who believe that the Holy Evangelist Luke, as well as a number of Byzantine emperors, were also of Macedonian heritage.

– from *The Descendants of Alexander the Great of Macedon,* by Aleksandar Donski,

Chapter One – the story begins

When you happen to be the center of attention, lecturing to a classroom of rapt college students, you notice someone who disrupts that attention. But then it would have been just about impossible to overlook the big ape in the expensive suit who stepped into the middle of my class that morning.

He had olive skin and close-cropped, jet black hair and one of the broadest foreheads and thickest necks I had ever seen on a man.

I was thinking, mafia bone-crusher? But I couldn't imagine what he wanted with me.

"Allo, are you the archaeologs?" boomed the deep voice of the visitor.

Bearded chins, shaggy heads and bespectacled faces of several graduate students and a small brood of eager undergrads turned as one toward the newcomer.

I frowned slightly at this interruption and glanced down at the Middle Woodland etched clay pot in my hands, then at the visitor. "That would be me, Professor Jack Starkweather, but..." I waved the clay pot in front of me, as if to say, can't you see I'm busy with this at the moment? I couldn't believe how rude the man was.

Professor Boris Milevski, visiting lecturer on Slavic antiquities from the Republic of Macedonia, as I would later learn, didn't hesitate for a single moment, as he grandly announced, "I am looking for an American archaeolog who it would interest to be a party to discovery of the tomb of Aleksandar Makedonski, the one you know as Alexander the Great."

One of the students said, "Man, wouldn't that be far out." Others nodded their heads or grinned. My first thought was, who did he think he was coming in here and making wild pronouncements in the middle of one of my lectures? But my next thought was, yeah, sure, what "archaeolog" wouldn't give his left... but I simply said, "Of course I would. That is, if it's reasonably possible that you're not just leading us on some wild goose chase."

Dr. Boris Milevski appeared puzzled as to what chasing wild birds had to do with it, but he got the drift. I would want more than a good story before I packed my picks and trowels.

The lunatic then disappeared about as quickly as he had appeared, but only after depositing a packet of papers on my lectern and saying, "Read this and think about it. Then you call me."

At the close of the workday, after everyone else had left the building, I remained in my office. My hand trembled slightly as I studied the packet of information that Dr. Milevski had given me. Even if this all proved to be total B-S-, I'd been looking for some ticket out of this cow town for a while now. I was beginning to feel as stale and musty as this office. And when did I become an office worker? I asked myself. One of the "suits," as we used to call them.

I stared at my soft, smooth hands, that had once been calloused and sun-burned, like those of any farm boy, and then at the grey tweed suit coat that hung on a rack near the door, and my leather briefcase. Then my eyes returned to the page in front of me.

What to make of this claim. The credentials of those involved from the University of Skopje in the Republic of Macedonia, formerly of Yugoslavia, looked legitimate enough. If the words and diagrams and photographs didn't lie, then maybe...

"I've got to get out of here," I muttered, as I looked around me at the dingy little office in the museum basement that I had occupied for nearly twenty years now. Grayness permeated the room. Mouse-gray overcoat. Whitewashed walls in need of a paint job. Gunmetal gray cabinets. And the dim light that filtered in the narrow slit of a window from an overcast sky, all seemed determined to mock my efforts to rise above my chronic lethargy.

What have I been doing? One term's set of lectures blur into the next, and the local summer excavations begin to merge into one another in my memory.

I stared at the notes from the last faculty meeting. There seemed no end to all the petty bickering in the department. My eyes were drawn to the picture of my family. The kids were grown up now and their mom was on an enthusiastic career course of her own these days.

"Hey, what do you think of my spending the summer in Macedonia looking for the lost tomb of Alexander the Great?" I said to my wife, Jo, during our after work check-in call.

"Sure, and hey, why don't you go look up Cleopatra while you're over there too," she laughed. "Don't forget to pick up the groceries."

I tried to figure out where the reference to Cleopatra was coming from as I searched my pockets for the grocery list. "Okay, I've got the list. See you in an hour," I said and hung up.

I dialed the number of the head of the department, while I composed my speech, proposing to suspend other projects and put together a crew to go to Macedonia. "By God, yes, to Macedonia to find Alexander the Great." It sounded better each time I said it.   I actually let the phone ring once before I hastened to hang it up before anyone could answer at the other end.

At dinner that evening Jo and I were both rather quiet. Neither of us brought up the subject I'd mentioned over the phone earlier that day. She'd probably forgotten all about it by now. Just another one of Professor Walter Mitty's little pipe dreams.

I wanted to ask her about her comment earlier over the phone about "Cleopatra," but I didn't. After all, it was just a little wise crack. But what had kept me from making my phone call to the department head earlier in the day? Maybe the whole thing was just too crazy.

My heart was pounding and I was drenched in sweat. This time a deadly, blue-black viper, thick as my wrist, had wrapped itself around my chest. It was slowly tightening the ring, so that I could barely breathe.

With a tremendous effort of will I eventually managed to stir my fear-paralyzed body. I thrashed from side to side, the way I had seen a hapless African wart hog do once in the death-grip of a snake in a nature film. That broke the nightmare's spell over me. I awoke to a peaceful night at home in my bed. Jo's rhythmic breathing beside me was proof that all was normal in my world.

It was the third time in the past month that I'd been visited in my dreams by this particular snake. What did it want from me? Or me from it, maybe? Was it a manifestation of a mid-life crisis? So what's new? Everyone I knew was grappling with that one.

No fan of snakes, I was beginning to weary most literally of this one in my dreams, as it deprived me of the rest I needed in order to go back in the morning and face another day at the U.

But now, something tucked way back in some innermost recess of my brain, that had thus far evaded consciousness, began to surface. Tomorrow, first thing in the morning I resolved to call the head of my department again, and I wouldn't hang up before he could answer this time.

Three weeks later, much to my astonishment, to the high-pitched whine and the thick, oily smell of a jet's engines, still in a daze, I climbed aboard a flight to Zurich at Detroit's Metro Airport. I was accompanied by a hand-picked crew of assistants and by Dr. Boris Milevski. The photos and the reports from Skopje University's Archaeological Studies Department, plus the personal letter from the Macedonian President, had opened doors and cut through bureaucratic red tape like a Swiss Army knife through butter. Such was the effect of this information on all who saw it.

Too good to be true, I thought as I peered out at the green, rolling farm country of southeastern Michigan as it receded into the distance down below. But mighty damn good to be on a flight out of here for a while. The thought also crossed my mind that maybe that dreadful nightmare would not be following me out of the country.

After a brief time in Zurich our party boarded a second plane, this one a Palair Macedonian Airliner bound for Skopje, Republic of Macedonia. During the flight I pulled out the report from the archaeological team from the Museum of the Republic of Macedonia. This was about the tenth time I had reviewed it. I seemed to need to do this, if for no other reason than to reconfirm for myself that this wasn't all a dream from which I would soon awake.

Borko, as Dr. Milevski preferred me to call him, sat in the seat next to me. He was beginning to get on my nerves. It was bad enough that his substantial bulk spilled out of his seat and over into mine, but I really wished the guy would just shut up and let me think.

At the moment he was peering over my shoulder at the open pages of the report. "I couldn't quite believe either, when first I received this report," he said. "But after the discovery of Philip, Alexander's father's tomb at Vergina in Greek Macedonia twenty some years ago, there has been renewed interest in exploration of *nekropol* sites in Macedonia. This is further goaded by discovery awhile back of a Macedonian commander's helmet similar to that found in Philip's tomb."

I frowned slightly. Borko wasn't going to take the hint and let me read in peace. Hadn't we already had this conversation several times already?

I set the report down on my lap and adjusted my glasses, as a way to exercise my cramped right arm that had been pressed into Borko's side for the past hour. "But Alexander's tomb wasn't really expected to be in Macedonia at all," I said. "Ancient accounts explain how the body was transported in a grand procession to its final resting place in Alexandria in Egypt."

Now I've done it, I thought. He'll go on for half an hour before I can get another word in edgewise. How did I ever let myself get saddled with an inconsiderate boor like Borko?

"However, there is logic to the return of Alexander's remains to his homeland," responded Borko, his speech slurring only slightly after more than enough airline brandy. "After Aleksandar's death in 323 BC in Babylon, there was division of the empire that he conquered. His generals divided among them the vast territory, stretching from Greece to India and the shores of the Caspian Sea to Babylonia and Egypt. To avoid conflict it would have made sense for the great leader's body to eventually be returned to his home, and land of origin of all of the Macedonian generals."

I turned to face Borko now. The man could certainly hold his liquor. I'll say that for him. The glass he was raising to his lips had to be his seventh shot of brandy. I began to weigh what Borko had just said, and to my astonishment, he actually let me finish a thought for once. "But that's not what history tells us. The Macedonian General Ptolemy, who somehow got his hands on the prize of Egypt, manipulated things to also gain possession of Alexander's body," I finally said.

"If you think that ancient Macedonian politics was filled with intrigues, wait until you meet present-day Macedonia." He quickly responded. Though Borko surprised me by what he left unsaid this time. He just fixed me in a steady stare that rattled me slightly. I was reminded that the Balkan pot boiled over periodically, and recent history had shown that that meant right up to the present day.

An hour later the plane touched down at the airport on the outskirts of the Macedonian capital, Skopje. There was the familiar whine of a small electric motor lowering the landing gear into place. Then the double bump of contact with the tarmac, and the blurred images of scrub oaks on the edge of the runway flitting by. A cloudless sky emitted painfully bright sunshine.

My body rejoiced as I pried myself out of the narrow, cramped plastic confines of my plane seat. My tall, lanky, greyhound-lean body traveled poorly enough on any passenger jet's standard class seating, but sitting next to Borko had considerably compounded my misery.

Borko was strangely oblivious to his surroundings. Or perhaps not so strangely, considering the amount of booze he had consumed during the flight. He slowly raised his humid bulk out of the seat, and now he filled the aisle as he gathered briefcase and bags of consumer goods out of several overhead compartments. The guy definitely takes up a lot of space, I idly observed while waiting my turn at the overhead compartments.

A small bus from the University of Saints Cyril and Methodius transported our American team to temporary quarters in a university-owned apartment complex. We feasted on a sumptuous dinner of stuffed peppers and potatoes at a local cafeteria before assembling at an outdoor cafe adjoining the complex for some beer and conversation.

Birds sang in the upper branches of the tall, spreading plane trees that sheltered the cafe from the bright Mediterranean sun. Spring had sprung even earlier here than back home, judging by the thick green foliage that surrounded us.

My two grad assistants, Joel and Deb, were busy knocking back glasses of beer at the moment rather than supervising our work crew made up of four of my undergraduate students. I had always liked to think that while, of course, each was a distinct personality in their own right, that my students were one in their deference and devotion to me, their mentor. Was I ever naive back then.

Not far into our second round of the good locally brewed *Skopsko pivo*, printed like most things in this land in Macedonian Cyrillic that made it appear as **Скопско Пиво** on the label, our colleagues from the State Museum arrived - like a spring storm. "Welcome, *dobro ni dojdete*, as we like to say it here," boomed the darkly-tanned mountain, Borko, as he again seized my pale, white hand in a vise-like grip that made me flinch. "You are not to believe what you will be seeing tomorrow. Thank your lucky stars for being chosen to be part of something we archaeologeests spend all our lives dreaming about."

A beaming crowd of young faces surrounded Borko. The newcomers, a surprisingly well-matched Macedonian mirror-image of our American team, included his assistant, Sasho, and three devoted "post-diploma" students. The Macedonian students all spoke excellent English, perhaps a prerequisite for this crew. With their Gucci jeans and short, stylish haircuts, and practiced cool, they felt cosmopolitan enough to seem right at home among the hippest crowds in the world's capitals rather than provincial Balkan Skopje.

Of course, Professor Borko continued to captivate everyone. "Built like a brick out-house," Joel whispered to me. Even hefty Joel must have felt a bit puny next to this burly Balkan giant.

"*Na zdravje*! To health!" the professor shouted the toast in his rich baritone and downed his glass of clear, fruit-scented local firewater known as *slivovitsa*, in one gigantic swig. "Tomorrow morning we go to Marvintsi, and history!"

Tomorrow, I thought, a sudden electric chill passing down my spine, man, could it really be possible that I was about to be "party to the discovery" of more exotic goods than arrowheads and pottery shards for a change?

The next morning everyone assembled, ready to go by seven am, despite last night's drinking bout and our American team's jet-lag. We piled into the museum's dusty old workhorse of a bus and set off for the southeastern corner of the Vermont-sized Republic of Macedonia. The road out of the capital followed the muddy, gray course of the spring-swollen Vardar River as it meandered its way south to the Aegean Sea at *Salonika*.

"So I assume that you are aware of the reasons why we have chosen to make you a party to this historic find," said Borko, who sat next to me as our two teams mingled in the seats behind.

Ad nauseum, I had heard those reasons. My throbbing head begged for mercy. I continued to sip from my mug of American-style coffee. I was still avoiding those thick, sweet little cups of black coffee favored by the locals.

I always hate myself the next day after I drink too much. Besides the headache, my tongue felt like sandpaper and my gut churned with each swerve of the van. I thought I might puke my breakfast up any moment now, hopefully not on my esteemed colleague.

Finally I ventured to say, "Not altogether, but I now know enough about your problems with Greece - their dispute over your right to the historic name Macedonia, to know that the discovery of Alexander's tomb in the Republic would bolster your country's claims to this ancient name."

Borko clapped a strong hand on my shoulder, spilling a little of my coffee. "*Da*, I mean, yes," he said. "And that is exactly why you must be present at the excavation. So that no one will be able to question the science of our work." He paused momentarily and daubed ineffectually at the spilled drink on my shirt, with his handkerchief. "Though, to be honest, I did not wish to share glory in this discovery with anyone. The decision to include you was made by others, over my objections."

I shifted uncomfortably in my seat. Was I about to let go of that delicious cheese pie I'd had for breakfast an hour ago? I had no ready answer to Borko's assertion. Who in our field would rush to invite another archaeologist to share in a discovery?

It occurred to me, however, that Borko had left out one humiliating reason for the presence of our US team. The Republic of Macedonia was flat out broke after years of living under a Greek economic embargo, accompanied by loss of trade with their chief trading partner, Serbia, during the wars over the break-up of Yugoslavia. Macedonia was the only former Yugoslav Republic that had managed to bow out of the federation without a single shot being fired, but the price in economic terms had still been devastating.

"Oh, is that so," I finally murmured. I held a hand close to my mouth in case my condition should suddenly take a turn for the worse.

"I don't blame you for being here," Borko continued. "I would have answered such invitation as readily. It is just the shame that politics should enter into our work at all."

I frowned slightly at this. "So how did you make this incredible discovery, Borko?" I asked, growing less concerned at the prospect of this morning's meal landing in my neighbor's lap.

Now Borko looked uneasy. His face clouded momentarily, then he smiled. He knew that I knew that Borko himself hadn't found beans. Grave robbers, farmers or the lowliest, most ignorant of archaeology paid laborers on a dig usually made the major finds. The chief archaeologist on an excavation, in any event, got all the glory, as the one in charge and the one who would get to explain the significance of the discovery to the world.

"It was the grave robbers of Marvintsi," admitted Borko, "who guided us to the entrance of the tomb. They were chased off by the local politsia before they had a chance to do more than clear most of the debris from the entryway. We have, thus far, only completed the removal of obstructions and entered only as far into the tomb as the pictures that brought you here."

I smiled at the answer that I had wanted to hear. We both knew full well now that Borko got called to the site, before he invited me to join him in the work.

The spring greenery of the Skopje plain gave way to dry uplands with spotty stands of scrub oak. The road continued to follow the winding path of the broad canyon carved by the Vardar River. Conversations started up in various parts of the bus, some simply continuing the topics of the night before.

The two hour bus ride passed rather quickly this way, for everyone but me. I swore I would never touch another drop of that devil's brew as long as I lived. All conversation came to an abrupt halt, however, when Borko suddenly shouted, "There it is, Marvintsi!" A village appeared off in the distance by the bank of the river. Pyramid-shaped orange tile roofs contrasted with the graying whitewashed walls of village houses.

A few minutes later he bellowed again, as all eyes followed his pointing hand. "And there is the necropolis!"

The Macedonians are mentioned in the Holy Scriptures, the Bible, in relation to the mission of Saint Paul to Macedonia, where Christianity began its expansion into Europe. For example, in "Apostles" (16:9):

"Over night Paul had a vision, a man was standing before him, a Macedonian, begging him and saying: 'come over to Macedonia and help us.' "

– from *The Descendants of Alexander the Great of Macedon* by Aleksandar Donski

Chapter Two – Alexander's tomb?

Neither Marvintsi nor the necropolis quite lived up to Borko's dramatic announcements. All I could see was one more sleepy little village with narrow lanes with shade trees, albeit set in a picturesque region of broad valleys and green rolling hills. The necropolis occupied a dry, stony hillside, dotted with spindly stalks of chicory and thistle, not far from the river.

Several large green canvas tents clustered at one end of the site, which was about the size of a football field with a series of rectangular holes forming geometric patterns across it.

"Welcome to the ancient Macedonian city Idomene, or Isarot, as it was known in even earlier times," Borko again announced for all to hear as the bus pulled into a parking area. God, how that booming voice reverberated painfully in my tender skull this morning.

"There are three such major centers of ancient Macedonian civilization located in southern reaches of our republic," he continued in the same bone-jarring voice. "Besides Idomene, ancient chroniclers mention the cities Gortinija or Atalanta and Europ. We're fairly certain that this necropolis is on the outskirts of what was once the city they called Idomene."

After depositing all of our supplies and equipment in the tents, our team reconvened at a smaller, roped-off section of the site, where a crew of six were busy digging, sifting and then sorting artifacts.

The crew chief, a stolid, cheerless woman with black hair beginning to streak white, Dr. Misirkova, paused in her work long enough to offer a frowning nod in acknowledgement of our arrival. With a certain amount of prodding from Borko, she grudgingly produced three bronze coins from the day's finds from her pocket. Each was about three-quarters of an inch in diameter. She drew our attention to one with the figure of a classic Macedonian war helmet stamped onto it and with the letters MAK-DON-- clearly legible alongside the helmet.

Everyone smiled and then oohed and aahed over the coin, despite the understanding that we had bigger fish to fry. It was still a taste of that delightful sense of discovery that fueled archaeological excavation. Professor Misirkova, however, remained stone-faced.

Then Borko urged us to follow him along a narrow donkey track on up and over the ridge top. As we descended out of sight of Dr. Misirkova's crew, Borko gestured in their direction and said to me, "Many are called, but few are chosen. Poor Jovanka Misirkova," he said with a smirk. "She is committed to the completion of her work at that site, and it will also help divert public attention from our work site. You know, Professor Misirkova is not the only one to miss this opportunity. We've had an American team work with us here in previous years, but, fortunately for you, they lost interest in us and went off in search of Trojan gold somewhere off the coast of Asia Minor."

After receiving permission to pass from the two guards posted at the trailhead, we continued along the narrow, winding footpath through several shallow ravines and up and over a series of low ridges covered with scrub oak and the occasional stone pine.

At one point in the trek, Borko shouted back over his shoulder, "watch out for the *smoki*, that snake has very nasty bite."

I would indeed watch out for "smoky." No need to tell me twice, with my feelings about snakes.

After a half hour of hiking, we came to a large boulder alongside the path, about the size of a volkswagen bug automobile. It was engraved with strange symbols, there was a series of crosses, many decorated with additional lines and some had small cupolas etched at the ends of the lines that formed the crosses. There were other symbols as well, mainly circles, dots, and squares arranged in some organized pattern.

Borko could see that I was intrigued by these petroglyphs. "Ancient Macedonian rock art," he said. "Many thousands of such rocks occur all over our country. They appear to be thousands of years old, and the symbols used are, as you see, somewhat simple, but they give us hints about the beliefs of the ancients. With obvious symbolism of earth and heaven and the unity of the cosmos. But mainly they and their makers remain a mystery."

After we'd gone maybe only another 50 paces, Borko raised his hand in a gesture of attention. He paused, and once he was sure that he had everyone's full attention, he said, "Look across the ravine, do you see something not altogether natural about the ridge ahead?"

We all studied the wooded hillside where he pointed. The lowering sun cast a speckled light across the green leaves rustling softly in the breeze. A little gray bird set up a twittering alarm cry as it skittered among the nearby oak boughs and the spire-like crowns of pines.

Finally, Joel broke the silence. "I see a formation in the rocks, there to the left of that lone pine!" he shouted.

Everyone peered at that point on the ridge that he had just described for us. "I see something, maybe..." said Sasho.

"Yeah, there's definitely something there...I think," added Joel.

Sasho squinted, then shaded his eyes with one hand. "If you follow the contour of the rocks, they form an arching vault over something, I would say," he ventured.

"Yes, indeed, my young falcons," Borko pronounced, as he again led the way down into the wooded ravine.

The path met a small stream at the bottom of the hill and followed the course of the waterway as it tumbled down the slope. About two-thirds of the way up the side of the ridge the stream had its source in a small, rock-lined pool fed by several small fingerlet springs. A cairn consisting of hundreds of soccer-ball sized dark basaltic rocks covered an area of hillside about twenty by twenty five feet, just beyond the dark waters of the pond. A section of this rock face about twelve feet above our heads had been cleared away to reveal a carved stone facade. It was about four feet high and twelve feet in length. This frontispiece rested upon a series of columns that framed a marble set of doors. All but six inches of the doors was still buried by rock. Two armed guards, who lazed in the shade near the entrance, rose to greet our archaeology team as we approached.

I eased my way past Borko to become the first of the team to stand before the great marble doors of the tomb. "Well, I'll be damned if it isn't just as reported!" I called back to the others as I raised my arm in a sweeping gesture over the chiseled letters that ran the length of the facade.I could make out most of them. ALEIANDROE__MAKEDO__. A wave of excitement passed through me as I struggled to pronounce the inscription.

"Alexander of Makedon, eh?" Borko couldn't resist saying it.

Dapples of late afternoon sunlight played over the marble doors and the tantalizing words. No one moved or spoke for several minutes. Borko moved to my side, facing the assembled crew. "Tomorrow we'll be back, at dawn, to complete the clearing of the entrance," he announced.

"We'll need to spend the evening getting everything together that we'll need for our work," I added. No way in hell was Borko going to run things by himself, I resolved.

After a few more minutes spent savoring the scene, we started back the way we had come. None of us would sleep very well that night, I thought as we hurried along in an effort to beat the setting sun back to camp. Anticipation would wreak havoc on everyone's equilibrium. Yet, it was highly unlikely that I would need to waken any of my crew when the first light of dawn crept into the tents.

When we returned to the camp we were greeted by several journalists from Skopje and one from Thessaloniki. The reporters from the Skopje dailies mainly concentrated on trying to pry something out of the Macedonian team. Borko simply dismissed them with a wave of his hand. "There will be no discussion of the new site until we have completed our initial survey," he announced regally for all to hear. End of subject.

The lone Greek reporter focused his attention on me and my American crew. Following my Macedonian colleague's lead, I urged the reporter to interview Dr. Misirkova about her crew's latest finds.

This, however, only served to further pique the reporter's curiosity about the work of the joint Macedonian-American crew. The Greek reporter, a dapper, handsome young fellow with thick, jet-black hair, named Mavros, followed me around the camp making small talk. Eventually he asked, "Couldn't you tell me what it is that has brought your crew all this way?"

"It's no use, Mavros," I replied. "You'll just have to wait until we're ready to talk about our work."

His smile abruptly turned into a hostile frown. It sent a slight chill down my spine, seeing how quickly his charm gave way to hostility. It was a short-lived show of anger. Almost immediately he smiled at me again. He would be sticking to this story like a bee to spilled honey, in any event, that was clear.

After supper the crew sat around a campfire together and drank coffee and beer and shared some of their excitement over what tomorrow might bring. Borko and I and our lieutenants met in his tent, to plan strategy and see to all the last minute details for tomorrow's work.

Once we had completed our planning for the morrow Borko brought out a bottle of <u>mastika</u> , the local equivalent of the Greek ouzo. No, I said to myself. I don't need any more liquor rotting my gut and splitting my head. But it only seems fitting that we celebrate a little today, I immediately relented.

The fiery, sweet liquor soon had us as giddy as some of our students over the prospects for the coming day. Deb, a serious researcher and almost a doctor of the science in her own right, was the first to confess, "You know, part of me just wants to rush at the door of that tomb with the abandon and wanton gluttony of the lowliest grave robber and get my hands on whatever is in there." She paused, then continued. "I'm just glad I have all of you dispassionate scientists along to keep me in line." And she winked.

"Yes," Borko said as he refilled camp mugs all around with *mastika*, totally ignoring my protestations that I'd had enough. "We will engage ourselves in rigorous scientific investigation of this site. You may be sure. Though I too would love to go for an immediate look at the contents of the tomb."

I raised my glass to the group. I admit, I get tipsy rather easily. My face was beginning to flush and my ears were feeling warm. "May this be the discovery of an ancient treasure trove to match our fondest archaeologist's imaginings," I shouted. Even if I have to share the glory with Borko the blowhard, I said to myself.

"Gold and riches like way beyond our wildest dreams!" shouted Joel. "Better us to get our hands on it than your average grave robber," he chortled as he waved his glass at us.

I lifted my eyebrows slightly while struggling to suppress a frown. So typical of my grad assistant, Joel Martin. I stared momentarily at the tipsy, bespectacled, heavy-set clown. He was a bit burly, but rather more on the pudgy side, with a short-cropped beard and short black hair that kinked slightly, as African hair will. I sometimes wondered if he would ever mature into a meticulous and exacting scientist. He always seemed a bit too frivolous, and far too interested in life outside the archaeology lab and work site.

I glanced over at Deb, with her almond-shaped eyes and silky black shoulder-length hair. She was always a welcome sight, petite and polished in contrast to Joel, and attentive to all things. Perhaps I was being overly hasty in my dismissal of life outside the archaeology lab.

The party eventually began to break up as each of us succumbed to the fatigue of a long, busy day. Borko clapped a burly hand on my shoulder, nearly toppling me over, as we prepared to part ways for the night. "Well, Jack. Do you have any misgivings so far about coming all this way to join us in our investigation?"

I took it all in stride, or should I say, in sway, since everything seemed to be swaying all around me, including my own body, as I struggled to regain my balance.

Borko giggled. "Not to worry, my friend. There will be plenty enough glory to go around for everyone before we're through here."

I nodded humbly and wondered if Borko really had read my mind. Was I really that obvious? "Pleasant dreams, Borko."

I tried to extricate myself from my colleague's shoulder grip. Borko peered up at the star-studded sky, where the sparkling constellations slowly wheeled through the night time. He seemed entranced by those magic tiny embers of light that had moved the ancients to elaborate myth-making. "It's a great moment to be alive and to be us, here and now, eh Jack?"

After finally getting away from Borko, no easy task even when sober, I wasn't quite ready to go off to bed. I heard the sounds of voices and saw the light of the campfire that the crew had built. I approached their circle and heard a couple of them call out, "Hi, Doc." Which I answered with the most clearly enunciated "Good evening," that I could manage in my present condition.

My arrival created a temporary lull in their conversation. I always seemed to have that effect on these kids. Throwing them a bit off-balance and making them self-conscious. I liked that in some ways, because it was evidence of my high status. But it wasn't long before the students again focused attention on each other rather than me.

I studied my students who had had the good fortune to be chosen for this expedition. I glanced at each one in turn. I tried not to be too obvious as I studied the lone female among them, Deb. Hey, even our Sunday school teacher ex-President Jimmy Carter admitted to lusting after an occasional woman in his heart, I rationalized, so how was I to ignore one so precocious and pleasant to look at? It crossed my mind that Jo's reference to Cleopatra in our conversation before my departure might have had something to do with my grad assistant.

I also couldn't help but notice the tentative mingling of my crew with Borko's students. Joel had already latched onto one of the females on Milevski's crew. Couldn't fault his taste. The Macedonian student, Rada, sat rather proudly erect, tall and slim, with short-cropped black hair and intelligent brown eyes.

The students resumed their conversation. As I listened to their smoke-husked voices flow from the dark outer circle into the lighted center, I imagined that I was an anthropologist out in the field studying some exotic nomad tribe gathered around their campfire. If I squinted and didn't look to the occasional gleam of an aluminum beer can or the glow of a cigarette, the image was almost convincing.

Joel was giving Rada particular attention. He had twisted his torso and head slightly in her direction in order to better see her as he spoke. "I can't believe you guys are really Macedonians. Are you sure you're not from Pittsburgh and you're just faking an East European accent?" he goaded her.

Rada's eyes sparked. "You should believe it," she said. "*Ako sakash, nie kje zborime makedonski*. If you want, we'll speak Macedonian. But I think you'll understand me better if I speak English."

Joel leaned toward her. "The Bulgarians say that you're all Bulgarians, but you just won't admit it."

"The Bulgars can say whatever they like. I know who I am. That's all that matters," Rada answered in an icy tone and then turned away from him.

Joel leaned back in his seat now, but he wasn't ready to break off their conversation. "So do you think it's really the Big Mac, Alexander, buried out there where we're going tomorrow?"

She merely shrugged. So Joel continued. "And if it is him, do you think Alexander the Great is really your Macedonian ancestor? I understand that you Slavic Macedonians arrived on the Balkan Peninsula around 600 AD, about 900 years after Alexander's time."

Rada took the bait this time. "Maybe, who knows," she said. "The Slavic language and culture of present-day Macedonia can only be traced back to the fifth or sixth centuries. But perhaps the ancient Macedonians spoke the proto-Slavic of our ancestors. And even if the Slavs came later, why wouldn't they intermarry with the natives, and simply because of their superior position, their language and culture came to predominate. In which case we are still related to Alexander."

Joel raised his eyebrows at this, as if to say, 'that's a stretch,' but he only said, "That's all just a guess though."

Sasho, Borko's sandy-haired, clean-shaven young assistant, looked up from the book he was pretending to read by the dim firelight and in his rather proper British-sounding English, he murmured, "Was it mere speculation that led to the murder of Oikonomides?"

My ears perked up at this. "Yes," Rada chirped in. "In 1988 the Greek archaeologist Oikonomides wrote that 5000 texts in the ancient Macedonian language were discovered by his colleague Andronikos during his 1976 excavation of the tomb of Philip II. He claimed that these texts were immediately taken to Athens under police guard. All access denied. He threatened to publish portions of the texts, but immediately after his arrival in Athens, he was found dead in a hotel room. All very suspiciously."

Sasho could no longer contain himself. "So what are the Greeks afraid of?" His shrill voice revealed his passion. "Could it be that those texts would show that the ancient Macedonians spoke a language similar to ours and not the Greeks, maybe?"

In a bid to claim some space in this conversation, Deb asked, "Do you think we're gonna find some of those texts in this tomb?"

"Perhaps," Rada ventured.

Joel snorted. "I'm sorry, but you've got to be kidding. The Greeks couldn't hide a major find like that. Oh-koino-whatever-he-was could have just gone off the deep end, and then met with some bad luck."

Rada folded her arms and stared straight ahead of her. She turned to Joel again. "You don't know the Balkans. Politics mixes shamelessly with religion, with culture, and with science here."

Welcome to the real world, I thought. I'm often amazed at how naive some of my students can be.

Deb shifted in her seat. "You talk about politics rearing its ugly head in our science," she said. "Do you remember when Professor Imre Boba wrote his book about the Moravian mission of Cyril and Methodius?" She looked from face to face for confirmation. "Did he ever piss off the Czechs when he suggested that the mission might have been in Slovenia instead of Czechoslovakia. The Czechs had a national holiday around that event. Czech scholars weren't satisfied until they'd silenced the poor old professor and his supporters."

Rada poked her face close to Joel's. "And what about the Dead Sea Scrolls?" she demanded. "Do you think it was pure science that kept them from the public for so long?"

Joel appeared to enjoy having her this close. He peered in her eyes as he said, "It's still a stretch from that to murder."

She poked him in the shoulder for emphasis as she said, "A Greek anthropologist received death threats awhile back after she wrote a book about the Macedonians of northern Greece. Cambridge Press was even frightened out of publishing it by similar threats."

"Well, a lot of people make a lot of threats," Joel muttered.

Deb took advantage of the pause in their debate. "Lame, Joel, really lame," she said. "If it really makes you feel better to think that people don't really do each other in around here over stuff like that, that's fine. But I think we should watch our backs while we're working here!"

I could feel my own back quiver slightly, exposed to the black night that surrounded us.

The crew sat in silence for awhile, staring into the licking flames of the campfire. Eventually though, Deb yawned and shook her head to get some of the sleepiness out. "A while back I saw the Greek traveling exhibit featuring Alexander in St. Petersburg, Florida," she said. "The pieces from Philip's tomb were really great. Though I didn't learn much new about Alexander. There was a rehash of some of the old tales from around the world - it's pretty amazing that stories of Alexander are told as far away as Ireland and China."

Sasho seemed to follow Deb's every word carefully. This attention appeared to stem from more than an interest in her ideas. "From what I understand, the Greeks made their usual claims on Macedonian history. To bolster claims to possession of over half the territory of old Macedonia, the Greeks have insisted that Macedonia was, is, and always will be Greek land. No other evidence is allowed," he said.

Deb rolled her eyes at this. "If the evidence exists, it'll be accepted by the Greeks, except for maybe a few loonies who would also argue that the earth is flat."

"You don't know the Greeks," he stated flatly. Sasho had stiffened and raised his chin. He peered out into the dark night.

"Hey, I know my parents and my aunts and uncles and grandparents and their friends," Deb bristled.

I raised my eyes from the fading embers of their fire. "Meet Deb Economou, Sasho," I said.

Sasho stared at her now. "You are Greek?" he asked.

Deb frowned. "Greek-American," she answered.

A slightly chastened Sasho croaked, "I'm sorry. I try not to be prejudiced, but it just seems so unfair that other peoples can take pride in their connections to their ancient ancestors on the same territory they live on today- no one questions the Italians' right to take pride in their ancient Roman ancestry, or the Chinese connection to their ancient civilization, or the present-day Jews' connection to their ancient Hebrew ancestors, or the Greeks' connection to their ancient ancestry, but they refuse to grant us that same right to take pride in our ancient Macedonian ancestry. So sometimes my anger with our neighbors to the south gets to be too much."

"I'm sure that they have some anger too," she said.

I suppressed a smile. My scholarly nomads slowly began to struggle to their feet. The fire had faded into a barely perceptible orange glow. The pinhole lights of the thousands of stars above our heads loomed brighter in contrast. I stayed on, alone for a time, with my dreams.

The next morning our crew began the removal of the remaining stones from the entrance to the tomb. We worked slowly and carefully. We cleaned and examined the exterior thoroughly before venturing to get inside the tomb. Our first full day at the site passed this way, and everyone marveled at our patience and equilibrium as the moment of truth drew nearer.

That afternoon upon our return from the site the reporters were again waiting. They were no longer making active efforts to pry information out of our crew. Like vultures who had determined where their next meal would come from, they simply waited. And while they waited they made small talk. They chatted with each other and with members of the archaeology team.

It was inevitable that the Greek reporter, Mavros, would eventually become acquainted with Deb Economou, the Greek-American. Deb had been no more forthcoming about our work than anyone else, but she couldn't resist the opportunity to use her Greek. After all, she had had to listen to incomprehensible Macedonian conversations for several days now. If it raised a few eyebrows among her fellow crew-members, that was their problem.

That evening after supper everyone again gathered around the campfire. Together we watched the sky go from pale shades of orange to red and the stars rise and the cooing of doves give way to cricket song. I simply sat back and enjoyed it all while the students continued their games with each other.

Joel tossed a new piece of wood on the fire, causing only a momentary panic among us as the red firefly sparks shot past our heads and mingled with the fixed sparks of starlight. "Do you think we'll have trouble cracking that door? It looked really solid," he said as he sat back down.

Rada held her coffee mug in both hands to warm them against the growing coolness of the late spring night. "I suspect that we will spend several days simply learning the details of the tomb's exterior before we ever try to 'crack the door.'" She wrinkled her nose as she pronounced the last few words, to suggest just how crude and unprofessional Joel had sounded, as if we were robbers cracking a safe or something rather than scientists involved in a scientific investigation.

We saw the headlights of a car in the distance and heard the chug of a slightly out of tune engine as it approached. Deb stood up at the sound of the car motor.

Everyone had seen her strike up the conversation in Greek with the smooth-talking Greek reporter earlier that evening. Now she announced to us all that she had agreed to join him for an evening at a club in nearby Valandovo.

Borko gave me a questioning look as Deb and Mavros drove off in Mavros's volkswagon. I only shrugged and said, "She's a big girl, Borko." Though I too felt a twinge of what? Disapproval, or was it simply jealousy of some sort? But I quickly turned my thoughts to more important matters.

Borko and I retreated to his tent in order to further plan our strategy for opening the tomb. Once we had settled on the tools and how we would use them, I pulled out a flask of Kentucky bourbon and two small tumblers. I set one down in front of Borko and the other in front of myself and poured us each a shot. If I was going to ruin my liver, by god, I wanted America's best to do the job.

We sat there like that, for some time, neither saying a word. Borko finally broke the silence. "You know, Jack." He always pronounced it more like "Jeck," which only added to my irritation with him. "Tomorrow is liable to be the most memorable day of our lives."

He paused to knock back the whole shot of whiskey, refilled his glass, and topped off mine before continuing. "When you are young you imagine that nothing will ever match your youthful adventures. As one grows older, perhaps, fortune or fleeting fame matter most. But I tell you, in the end it is discovery, that is most satisfying and leaves the deepest impression on one."

I swirled my drink, not daring to drink any more, knowing that the Bor would refill it to the brim again if I did. And it was my whiskey, that I'd been hoarding away for a special occasion. "Discovery, eh? Could be," I finally said. But inside I knew that Borko had hit it right on the head. There was nothing, absolutely nothing in life that stirred me quite like the prospect of finding 'the Big Mac' in the tomb tomorrow. Though I didn't need to endlessly pontificate about it like some people I knew.

After a time we rejoined the rest of the crew, who were still seated around the campfire. No one seemed to want to sleep that night, so we continued to drink beer and talk late into the night. It was well past midnight when Deb finally returned from her evening in town.

There was a pause in the conversation as everyone listened as Mavros' slightly out of tune Volkswagon again pulled into the parking lot. We heard Deb as she and Mavros exchanged a final "*kali nikta*," Greek for "Good night." The car door slammed and he drove away. A hint of exhaust fumes and stale cigarette smoke floated in the aftermath.

As Deb approached the circle, smiling to herself, no one looked up. Nor did anyone bother to greet her. I sensed that the crew was conveying a subtle reproach by this, but she tried not to show any concern.

After a time the circle broke up as each of us sought out tents and beds. The mood among us that evening had seemed rather subdued. There had been no loud or raucous behavior. It was as if we had finally exhausted our ability to wax enthusiastic over the prospects for grand discovery in the days ahead. Even Borko had restricted himself to the briefest parting "*Dobra noch,*" before retiring for the night.

... there are a number of historians in the United States, led by Professor Eugene Borza, who is considered one of the most knowledgeable scientists on the subject of ancient Macedonia, who clearly state that ancient Macedonians were not Greek. Historians with similar positions have also appeared in other countries.

– from *The Descendants of Alexander the Great of Macedon,* by Aleksandar Donski

Chapter Three – the tomb's secrets revealed

Most of the crew stood in a semi-circle around the marble double doors of the tomb and watched as Borko wedged a thick steel bar with a chisel-like head into the crack between the doors. As he slowly applied increasing pressure to the bar, Joel was pressing on a similar pry bar near the base of the door. I stood balanced on a ladder above them, poised with a long wooden slat in my hands, prepared to slide the board into any space that might appear between the doors. Deb held the ladder in place.

"Watch it, Borko! You're going to chip the marble. Get that wedge in there deeper!" I barked.

"It's okay. I think it's moving," Joel groaned with the effort. "You just be ready to place that board in!" Borko shouted back at me. "There it goes! It's moving. Get ready, now..."

Borko leaned further into the bar and nodded at Joel to follow his lead. Borko's big hands were now trembling with the effort. "Can you place it in?" he rasped, nearly out of breath.

Suddenly there was a sharp thwack and Borko bounced away from the door with the bar still clenched firmly in his hands. Sasho caught him from behind.

Dammit, Borko! I told him to get that tool in there deeper. Now he's almost chipped the marble, I grumbled to myself. "I thought we'd determined that there were no further locking mechanisms and that the doors should be free to open now," I said to him. "But something must be wrong."

"No, I don't think so. We almost had it. Let me get another grip on the edge," Borko said.

There was very little edge for him to catch the pry bar on, but Borko gamely set himself to prying once more. Though once again, before I could even get the wooden wedge into place, the pry bar gave way, sending Borko sprawling.

"We'll have to try something else," Borko finally rasped, still trying to catch his breath from the Herculean effort.

We took a break and discussed our options. Both Borko and I were beginning to feel unsure of ourselves. As we talked it out, we began to realize that we would have to proceed more cautiously. Obviously there was some problem that we hadn't figured on. Something was blocking the doors that the experience of others and our own understanding couldn't account for. I finally suggested a course of action. "We've got chisels. So let's work our way all the way around the perimeter of the doors and loosen everything that could possibly be interfering with their movement," I said, and Borko nodded his assent.

Soon several members of the crew were busy tapping away with hammers and chisels. Slowly and laboriously they cleared away all material in the crack both between and above and below the doors. Gradually they made their way completely around both doors.

"Alright! That's enough!" Borko finally shouted to them. "Stand back and let me set the bar again."

This time the pry bar did not give way, but still Borko was unable to pry the door open. He motioned for help and Sasho and several others rushed to his side and sought hand-holds on the bar. Deb and Rada took up similar positions on the bar that Joel was struggling with at the base of the door. They all heaved at the bars with all their strength. Still, nothing gave way.

"There's something wrong here," gasped Borko. "We've got to study this further, though I would've sworn there was no lock."

"No, " I countered from my precarious perch. "I think it moved a bit that time. Give it another try."

Borko looked up at me and grimaced slightly, but he moved back into prying position, as did the others. "Alright everybody, push!" he commanded.

The bars shifted slightly in their hands, but there was little evidence that the doors had loosened at all. I shook my head as I stumbled down the ladder. "Well, this obviously isn't working," I said to no one in particular.

We decided to break for lunch and consider our options. After the meal the work went no easier. We tried prying at the slabs from alternate edges. Finally Joel muttered, "We ought to just smack that door with a sledge."

"Yes, that's exactly how you would do things," Rada scolded him. "So bright idea!"

I never quite knew how to take things that Joel said. You never knew if he was being serious or not. Borko and I looked at the door. Then at each other. It was now late afternoon. We decided that we should call it a day and come back tomorrow for a fresh start.

I was totally bushed. My back and shoulders ached from the horrendous efforts we'd made to open the tomb. I felt gritty and my clothes were thoroughly soaked with sweat. It was a relief to get back to the camp and shower and turn in early that night.

At dawn the next morning we were back at the entrance. This time we had brought along some small hydraulic jacks to ease the work along. Joel and Sasho set them up at several points along the front of the tomb and with the aid of some specially molded wooden beam lengths we managed to get the jacks to raise the frontispiece above the doors ever so slightly.

Borko and I slowly set wedges in place and began once more to pry at the heavy marble doors. Yet, we had no more success than we'd had the day before. "It's not working, Borko," I finally said.

"You're right," he answered in a resigned tone of voice. "So I suppose we'll have to proceed as we decided last night."

"Okay, everyone, go get your shovels, " I called out, and the crew members went to retrieve them from our tool cache.

After several hours of laborious digging, we finally managed to undermine much of the foundation stone at the bae of the doors. The heavy stone appeared to be settling slightly, increasing the gap beneath the doors.

"This is not standard procedure, mind you. And I wouldn't normally suggest it," I said to the crew as Borko strode off in the direction of our tool cache and returned with a large pry bar. He set the bar in place and once again began to slowly apply pressure to it. I was once again perched on the step ladder above him, and promptly conveyed any evidence of movement to him.

"Look out, Doc! It's coming down!" Joel shouted in an earsplitting voice,

The heavy stone frontispiece shifted slowly in its place. Joel grabbed Borko's shoulder and pulled him back from the entrance. I leapt from the step ladder and fell sprawling on top of Borko and Joel as the whole frontispiece of the tomb crashed only inches from us.

Deb released a quiet little gasp and the guards rolled their eyes slightly, but no one said anything. They watched silently as Borko lifted himself up and helped Joel and me to our feet. A last piece of stone came tumbling down and landed with a thud on the ground at our feet. But now the doors swung wide and the tomb lay open to us.

It all happened too quickly for me to take fright at the collapse of the door. And my colleagues had provided such a soft cushion for my landing that I had barely felt the effects of the fall.

Borko and Joel must have fared as well, because immediately the three of us rushed to the opening to peer into the dark beyond, our recent brush with death already forgotten. The rubble in front of the doors made us look more like grave robbers than proper scientists at the moment, but no one cared. Everyone's attention focused on the opening.

Borko called for a flashlight. He stuck his head through the opening and waved the beam up and down, then to the sides, with Joel pressed up against him, trying to see over his shoulder.

"We don't have time to do more than make a brief survey of the tomb's contents today," I said.

Borko looked back out over his shoulder at the eager crowd behind us at the door, and added," You'll all get a chance to take a look, but nothing will be disturbed."

Several lanterns were lit and Borko led the way into the dusty interior. The archaeology team members now shone their lights this way and that across the barrel-vaulted interior. Everything was covered with a layer of dusty grime that served to obscure all we saw.

The room was no more than twelve by twenty feet in size and maybe eleven feet at the highest point. The first thing to catch our attention was a colorful mural that spanned the far wall. Even after twenty three centuries of slow deterioration the figures were still discernible. "The first frame appears to show the birth of a child of a man-god union," said Deb as her flashlight beam swept over the wall painting. "And this next one must show the taming of the great war horse, Bucephalus."

Sasho swept his light on ahead of hers and said, "Those are probably some of his military conquests."

"These wall paintings are in style with the monumental narrative Greek wall paintings found on the walls of the tombs at Vergina," added Borko.

"Somebody pinch me, so I'll know I'm not dreaming all this, please!" shouted Joel.

The several flashlight beams began bouncing from wall to wall and object to object in rapid succession. "Here's his armor!" someone shouted.

"Look over here, there is a set of metal wreaths. I think they must be pure gold!" shouted Rada.

"What's this? Is it a bronze lantern? And some clay pots. That's probably what he was supposed to snack on on the way to the next world," said Joel.

Borko and I stood side by side now in the middle of the chamber. Borko held a lantern high above our heads. Both of us were momentarily speechless. We stood staring at a large object that occupied most of the floor at the far end of the room, obscured by the dust and faint lighting.

"It is, isn't it?" I finally said.

"What else could it be?" asked Borko.

The others joined us in staring dumb-founded at what appeared to be a four-wheeled cart about seven feet long with a curved, gable-less canopy-like roof perched on a series of three foot high columns. Precious gems sparkled with each sweep of a beam across the delicate gold leaf-like shingles of the roof. Panels between the delicately-carved ivory columns depicted scenes of marching soldiers with elephants and others with kings and queens paying tribute to an emperor-god figure. Gold embroidered banners and bits of tapestry glittered in the pale lantern light. There were bronze, silver and gold statuary of winged figures and emblems with the Persian royal palm.

In the center of the cart lay a richly decorated casket that appeared to be made of pure gold. It contained a body, embalmed in the Egyptian fashion, wrapped in royal purple cloth with gold embroidery. A golden diadem lay across the king's forehead.

"Ancient writer Diodorus Siculus wrote about Alexander's fabled funeral cart, based on an eyewitness story he got from Hieronymos of

Kardia. Although the cart he described was much larger, his story does not begin to match the magnificence of the real article," declared Borko.

Something in the corner of the room caught Deb's attention and she separated herself from the crowd around the cart to investigate. "Oh, my," she gasped, as she knelt over something in the dark corner. "This is incredible!"

"What is it?" Sasho asked. He approached her kneeling form. Soon he too was hunched over a clay canister set on its side on a low metal stand.

"What do you make of this, Sasho? I've never seen this script before. Have you?" she asked as the two of them carefully examined a pale yellow roll of parchment tucked inside the clay container. They didn't dare try and unroll it for fear that it might crumble in their hands.

"No, I can't say that I have. There is something a little familiar about this alphabet though, but I can't quite figure out why," he said.

"Alright everyone!" Borko's voice boomed through the chamber. "We've had a chance to survey the contents of the tomb, and now it's getting late. We'll be back tomorrow to begin the proper examination and eventual retrieval of the artifacts. But we must tear ourselves away for now."

Joel completed an initial set of flash photographs of the chamber from various angles around the room, and Deb and Sasho carefully placed the canister with the scroll they had been examining back onto its stand. Soon everyone had emerged from the tomb, blinking in the light and shaking the dust from our clothing and hair. The guards helped us reseal the entrance to the tomb as best we could, and our crew set off for the base camp.

The excitement of the returning crew made it clear to all who saw them that something big had happened that day. Only Professor Misirkova, who had remained rather sulky and withdrawn since our arrival, continued to ignore us and our camp. Her crew kept their distance as well. It struck me as somewhat odd behavior, but I was too caught up in our find to pay it much mind.

Borko and I had talked it over on our way back and had decided not to issue a statement quite yet to the journalists covering our work. Although we were almost a hundred percent certain that we had discovered the final resting place of Alexander the Great, and one of the most remarkable archaeological finds of the century, we preferred to remain cautious in our comments.

Our obvious excitement at the day's finds, however, was obvious to the representatives of the press. They clamored to join us when we returned to the site to continue our work the following day. Borko was gentler than usual in his refusal of the journalists' request. They had been waiting impatiently for some shred of news from us for many days now.

Mavros apparently tried his best to get something out of Deb. He cornered her after supper. They had a conversation in Greek for the better part of an hour, before he too finally must have decided that he would have to wait until tomorrow to learn about our find.

That evening everyone, including Borko and I and our assistants, sat in a circle around the fire and watched as the surrounding ridges faded in the night and the sky filled with stars. We talked and laughed and joked with each other and drank beer or wine until late into the night. It was a celebration, and Borko presided over it. "Sometimes life has great hopes that cannot be realized, and sometimes, like today, it gives more than hoped for," he pronounced, and he raised his glass in a toast. "*Na zdravje!*"

Now it was my turn. "I hope that the youngest among you, in particular, will be able to forgive us your elders for exposing you at such a tender age to what will probably be the high point of your bright careers. Will you ever top this find in the long and distinguished careers that await you? Not likely, my friends," I said, and concluded with the salutation, "Cheers!"

Joel took a swig from his beer and looked over at me. "Doc, why do you think Alexander ended up way out here in the wilderness instead of in Aegeae in Macedonia or in downtown Alexandria, where most people figured he'd be?"

I studied the fire and said, "It certainly raises as many questions as it answers."

"Some scholars suggested all along that Alexander was as likely to have been returned to his homeland as buried in a foreign land that he never had more than a passing acquaintance with in his lifetime," said Sasho.

"This Macedonian wilderness, as you call it, was once a thriving center for ancient Macedonian civilization," added Borko.

Rada leaned forward, so that she could see and be seen by all in the circle. "But Macedonian royalty was always buried in the centers to the south."

"Alexander was not your average Macedonian king, nor did he give much to tradition during his life. He adopted new customs wherever he went. So why should he be any different in death?" asked Borko.

"I think that the tomb is going to yield some answers," I said. What I didn't share with the others, however, was my uneasiness at the possibility that the giant stone block that almost crushed Borko, Joel and I that day had been designed to fall on anyone who forced the doors.

The mood shifted again from thoughtful to jubilant as someone suggested a song. The Macedonians first regaled their guests with one of their favorite folk songs. It was a lively, joyous song that put me in mind of certain Mexican village tunes I'd heard in the past. Their voices blended in a most splendid harmony, as if they'd been singing together for years as part of some choir.

"Makedonsko devojche, kitka sharena,
vo gradina nabrana, dar podarena,
dali ima n'ovoj beli svet
poubavo devojche od Makedonche?
Nema, nema, ne kje se rodi
poubavo devojche od Makedonche."[1]

Joel led the vigorous applause as he nodded and smiled at Rada, after someone explained what the song was about.

Joel led our American crew in a soulful rendition of "Summer Time," which drew as much applause from the listening Macedonians when it finally ended.

Deb peered into the flames and said, "I can't wait to get back into the tomb to see what else is there. I'm dying to know what all else is in there."

Joel, who was also staring at the flickering yellow flames, simply answered, "Yeah."

Sasho turned his gaze from the fire to the starry sky above. "Of course, that's true. But we'll need to be sure and do our work right. We don't want

---

[1]   "Macedonian girl, a lovely bouquet,
gathered in the garden, a gift bestowed.
Is there in this wide world
a more beautiful girl than the Macedonian?
No, nowhere is there born
a more beautiful girl than the Macedonian."

to damage anything." He paused as he peered back into the fire, then went on. "There are people who would like us to make hasty conclusions after a quick and careless survey of the tomb's contents, such as those reporters who visited today." He glanced over at Deb and Joel as his voice trailed off.

Joel's gaze swept over the faces in the circle now, finally coming to rest on Rada. "Look, folks, I want it understood that I am as serious a student of archaeology as anyone here. And I don't sleep through any of my classes. If my style sometimes suggests otherwise, I'm sorry. And I don't want to feed anybody's stereotypes about African-Americans either."

The circle of young men and women became particularly quiet for a few moments. Then Deb said, "You mean to say you're not into knives and guns and jivin' white folks?"

Joel mock-scowled at her. "Cut the crap, Deb."

This seemed to relieve some of the tension. Deb's gaze returned to the fire. "Boy, did that tomb look loaded with gold."

Rada stared intently into the flames. Her eyes gleamed with fiery sincerity as she said, "Yeah, it really did!" The "yeah" was a bit drawn out and distorted as her first attempt to imitate her American colleague's speech-type.

Sasho remained fixed on the fire too, as they all were now, as he said, "I feel so lucky to be on this project. It could be one of the rarest and greatest archaeology finds of all time."

Rada vigorously nodded her head in agreement. "That it could, yes, it really could be," she said.

I felt the excitement in their voices. It ran through each of us like an electric current. I knew that I was every bit as excited as "the kids," but I felt more restrained about expressing it around them. I probably just spent more time smiling and giggling than usual that evening.

A time came when we could barely keep our eyes open and our minds focused. We would soon be drifting off to cots and sleeping bags back in the tents, but no one could quite bring himself to be the first to leave the circle.

Deb and Sasho sat next to each other by the fire. Weariness and a bit too much beer had loosened Deb's tongue. "Sometimes I feel like you expect bad things from me, just because you know I'm Greek, Sasho," she said to him. "You say that you're not prejudiced, but I see it every so often in your looks," she said.

I raised my eyebrows slightly at this, but said nothing. It wasn't for me to play camp counselor to my young charges.

Sasho looked at his hands, then peered up at the Milky Way, the Godfather's Straw as an old Macedonian legend would have it. The bright specks of straw litter left in the aftermath of passing of the Godfather's hay wagon. Anything rather than look in her eyes at that moment. "No, I don't think so," he finally said.

Borko, who was seated nearby, couldn't resist a comment. "Since you're an American, I don't think you can understand the bad blood between the Greeks and our people," he said to Deb. "It goes way back and it isn't all that easy to put behind us, as ancient history."

Deb shifted in her seat on a smooth boulder near the fire and grimaced slightly as she spoke. "It's true that I haven't studied that history, but why should I, if all it does is feed grudges?"

Borko looked more closely at her now, I knew he was about to make one of his lectures. "Perhaps we should forget ancient wrongs, ancient Macedonian Tsar Philip and Aleksandar's conquest of the Greek city states 2300 years ago, or my ancestors' invasion of the Byzantine Empire 1500 years ago. And no one really wants to remember the awful lesson the Byzantine Emperor Basil decided to teach his troublesome neighbors in 1014, over by the Strouma, in a valley to the east. But there are still people alive today who remember the day they were chased from their homes and villages across the border in Greece. To this day they are not allowed to return to lands they were forced to flee, or have they been offered any money for what was taken from them during the civil war in 1948."

Deb glared at him now. "Is this all you Balkan people can do? Nurse your grudges and wait for the chance to take revenge? Like the Bosnian Serbs?" she demanded.

Now it was Sasho's turn to scowl. "Maybe you would not be so quick to judge us if you'd been on our end of things. Maybe Joel could tell you something about the subject, or maybe one of your American Indian neighbors."

She looked at him even more intently now. "No, I feel for the suffering and injustice done to others. But I won't be guilt-tripped or made to hate like you Balkan men!"

Could I have answered as articulately when I was twenty three? I wondered.

"All good," Borko conceded, as I thought to myself, 'please shut up, Borko.' Which he did, fortunately. Even Borko seemed too tired to engage in his usual long-windedness.

Deb continued to fix Sasho in her gaze. She was obviously more comfortable with him than she was with the Professor, Borko. "We Americans have put right some of the wrongs of the past," she finally said.

"That's all to the good," Sasho nodded his assent. Obviously Sasho was no more prepared than Borko for long-winded argument at this late hour, or perhaps with such an effective debater.

No one spoke further. Everyone watched the fire and the stars in silence for a time before they finally got up one by one and drifted off to bed and sweet dreams of tomorrow. I watched a bit uneasily though as Deb and Sasho exchanged a few final words as they rose to leave the circle. Sasho fixed her in a stare as he announced, "Now the Greeks will never again be able to say we have no right to call our land an equal part of old Macedonia, with equal right to the ancient name."

Deb frowned. "Did you really ever need vindication from ancient history to call yourselves whatever you please?"

"I'm glad that you think it is so easy. Now if you could just convince several million Greeks who have wanted our heads for years now for using the ancient name, maybe things will be a bit happier here for everyone," he said as he stood up to go.

"Look. I was never part of your ancient feuds and I don't care to begin now," she said as she also rose a bit unsteadily from her seat.

Sasho looked from the fire to Deb, his eyes darting somewhat nervously now. "I'm sorry to bring up such things on a night of celebration. Sweet dreams," he said as he turned to go.

"Sweet dreams to you too," she murmured back as she stumbled off in the direction of her tent.

For some reason their conversation had evoked an uneasiness in me, a vague foreboding. I looked from the one to the other as they each made their way to bed.

I thought that I would go off to bed myself, but I realized that I couldn't, not until I had done one thing more. I cautiously made my way in the dark across the camp to the parking area. I was still a little spooked by Borko's earlier warning about snakes. I climbed into the van and fumbled around in the dark for a while until I found the ignition and got the engine up and running and turned the headlights on. As I drove along the narrow asphalt road, mesmerized by the flickering images of bushes and trees caught momentarily in the glow of the headlights, I began to think back to another happy time in my life. Jo was tall, slim and athletic. She had the loveliest silky, smooth slightly tanned skin, and flowing blonde hair. The kind I suppose that Yeats was talking about when he wrote: "Who could love you for yourself alone and not your yellow hair?"

I remembered back to an evening when we rode around the campus on our bicycles together, one warm, fall evening. Up and down parking ramps. Down sidewalks and through grassy courtyards with elm trees with leaves that glowed magically in the soft light of the street lamps. We wove intricate patterns around each other in the broad empty parking lots in some cyclists' mating ritual. Then we raced playfully on to explore some new pathway together. The energy and enthusiasm of youth bore us along on a tide that eventually led us back to her apartment and bed.

It wasn't a particularly passionate night. Kisses and embraces were somewhat tentative, more affectionate and playful than lustful. We were new to each other after all. We were still in the process of getting acquainted. And the discovery was so pleasant.

I finally arrived in Valandovo and found a hotel where they allowed me to use my credit card to call the states. On about the third ring, Jo answered. "Hello," I said.

"Oh, dear, how are you?" she asked. "How is everything?"

"Fine. I just wanted to call and tell you that we found it."

"Found what?" she asked through a yawn.

"What we came all the way over here for," I answered, a bit petulantly.

"Oh, you mean Alexander the Great?" she said, with more interest now.

"Alexander the Great's tomb," I mumbled, though I had thought that when the moment came I would be blurting the words out in grand style, perhaps adding, 'the greatest archaeological find of the century!'

"Oh, is that right," she said. "Will you all be famous now, and I'll get to read all about you in tomorrow's newspaper?" She quipped in her usual way. Which I never quite knew how to take.

"Maybe," I said.

"Would you like to hear about what I've been up to since you left?"

she asked.

"But don't you want to hear some of the details about our find?"

"Why, of course," she replied.

Just then I glanced over my shoulder and saw Mavros standing no more than five feet away, studying me silently.

"Something just came up that needs my immediate attention. I've got to go now," I mumbled into the phone. "I'll call you again real soon. Love you. Bye for now."

"Love you too, bye," she answered and hung up.

I turned to Mavros now.

"Well, is it true?" he asked.

"What?" I asked in reply, in a deliberate act of denial.

"You know, what you just said about Alexander."

"We'll talk about it some other time," I said.

"I'll pay very well for an exclusive on this," he said as he moved to partially block my exit as I began to head for the door.

"Not now," I said brusquely as I gently nudged past him and strode out the door into the street and hopped back into the van.

That night for the first time since I'd left the states, I was visited by the dreadful snake of my dreams. On this occasion it chose to make its appearance as I lifted the lid of the case that held Alexander's mummified body. Sweet anticipation suddenly turned to pure terror as I spied the menacing head of the serpent where I had expected to see the linen-wrapped corpse of the world conqueror. I recoiled in horror, slamming the lid shut before the snake could strike at me.

It is known that the great Athenian orator Demosthenes, in his work "Phillipic," made the following insulting remark about Philip II of Macedon:

"That man Philip, not only is he not Greek, but he does not even have anything in common with the Greeks. If he were only a barbarian from a decent country – but he is not even that…"

Why did Demosthenes name Philip a "barbarian" and what did this term mean in antiquity? Scientists are almost unanimous that the term "barbarian" chiefly referred to people who spoke a language unintelligible to the Greeks, and contained a dose of disrespect for those peoples' culture.

– from *The Descendants of Alexander the Great of Macedon* by Aleksandar Donski

Chapter Four – a strange turn of events

We had the guard detail increased so that there were now sentries posted day and night at every possible point of entry to the site. We also had a set of heavy metal doors constructed for the entryway, that we could lock securely behind us at the end of each work day.

As the time drew near for us to tackle the examination of Alexander's casket, I grew increasingly uneasy. I was haunted by the terrifying image of the snake in my dream. On the one hand, it made me want to get the casket opened as soon as possible and have it done with, while on the other, I recoiled from the thought of peering inside the case.

However, before we could even get to the mummy-case, somewhere into the second week after opening the tomb, we began to sense that something wasn't quite right at the site. Joel was the first to mention it. "Doc. Take a look at this," he said, as he held up a pale, gray-green oxide encrusted bronze urn from among some artifacts in one corner of the antechamber.

"Joel! What are you doing!" I snapped. "You know better than to handle artifacts before we've had a chance to do a thorough 'in situ' analysis."

"Yeah, I know, Doc," he answered. "So tell me why this urn doesn't have the coat of powdery dust on it that everything in the tomb had on it when we opened the place up?"

"It would seem that someone wanted a closer look at it," I said as I examined the bronze vessel.

"Alright," he said as he carefully set the piece back onto its iron stand. "But take a look around. It's not the only artifact that's looking tidied up."

"So someone on the crew has been dusting items off in order to get a better look at them."

"Yeah, I suppose that's all it is," he replied.

But later that same week Joel approached me again, but this time with the opposite complaint. "Where is all this dust coming from that's settling on everything?" He drew a finger across the layer of fine grey powder that had settled on the funeral cart.

All that his action drew from me though was a frown, since he'd already been warned not to handle the artifacts.

The following week though, it was Rada who reported something amiss in the tomb. She drew our attention to the small table that held gold wreaths. "There is something not right about those wreaths," she announced. "I don't know what it is. But they don't look right to me."

"How do you mean, not right?" asked Borko.

"I've been looking at them now for several weeks," she answered. "And I know that they have been changed somehow."

"I took some pictures of them on our first day in the tomb," said Joel. "Those pictures have been developed and made into prints now. I could bring them out with us to the site tomorrow for comparison purposes."

That evening back at camp we continued to share our concerns about tampering with artifacts in the tomb. Borko and I and our lieutenants sat around a small camp table in his tent. We were sipping from small glass tumblers filled with rakija, home-brewed plum brandy that Sasho had obtained from his folks.

"So you also believe that things are not right in the tomb?" Borko asked Deb in response to something she'd just said.

She nodded, and he looked around at the rest of us. "Anyone else?"

"I have suspicions too," said Sasho. "But we have been so careful with security, that I can't imagine that anyone has managed to gain access to the tomb."

Deb winced slightly and looked away. I acted on a sudden hunch. "Do you know something, Deb? That you're not sharing with us?"

She hesitated, then said, "Well, yes. Mavros has visited the site without us. And he told me something."

"What?" shouted Borko. "How could that be?"

"He's lucky he didn't get shot," I said.

"So when was this?" asked Sasho.

"A few days ago," she replied.

"And what did he manage to see?"

"Not much really. If what you mean is, did he manage to get into the tomb. What he did was sneak through the woods to a place above the tomb, where he could see the site fairly well, at least with the help of a set of binoculars."

"And?" Sasho urged her on.

"He said it was near sunset, just after we had gone home for the night. And he told me that he was surprised that we hadn't sealed the doors to the tomb when we left."

"Did he report seeing anyone in the vicinity of the tomb?" I asked.

"Just the usual guards we always see there in the morning."

"Why didn't you share this with us sooner?" asked Borko.

Deb shifted uneasily in her chair. "I didn't want to say much. But when Rada mentioned her concerns today, I thought maybe it would be enough if I just added a little to her suspicions. That is, instead of having to say what the source of my suspicions was and get Mavros into hot water."

"If you would rather not reveal to him that you've shared this information with us. That's fine," I said. "But please urge him not to risk his neck trying to snoop out a story again. We'll fill him in soon enough."

"Yes," said Borko gruffly. "You make certain he knows not to do anything so stupid again." He wagged a finger in Deb's face as he spoke, for emphasis.

"You'll need to have a talk with the guards," I said.

"I'l talk to their chief as well," said Borko.

"Maybe Mavros just thought the doors looked open from that distance," suggested Joel.

"Maybe," said Sasho, without much conviction.

The next morning Joel brought his photos along to the site. As we studied them, clustered around the table with the wreaths, our sense of alarm grew.

"They are almost the same as those in the photo," said Borko. "But see how the shapes of some of the laurel leaves is different."

Sasho crouched down in front of the table so that he could examine the wreaths as closely as possible. "Yes, they do not look right," agreed Sasho. "Do I have permission to send one of the wreaths into Skopje to the museum for some analysis?" he asked.

We let Sasho box up one of the wreaths and take it with him that evening when we returned to camp. Borko's questioning of the guards about open doors after our departure was met with firm denials from them. Though the chief of security later assured Borko that he would investigate the matter further.

Two days later we got a call from the museum confirming what we had suspected. Sasho announced the bad news, in a slightly hoarse voice, "The wreath is a fake. It was of recent manufacture. So reports the lab technician. It is composed of lead painted with cheap gold paint and then subjected to an aging process. To add insult to injury, the technician said in his report that it was such an obvious fake that he was surprised that we had needed him to confirm it!"

The next morning was overcast. Dishwater gray clouds hung low over the green landscape. It was the first morning in Macedonia that I needed a sweater. The chill in the air might have hastened our steps, if that were possible, as we hurried down to the site. I already had a gut feeling that everything would be wrong when we got there.

Upon our arrival we raced from object to object. Every item that we had identified to contain precious metals - either gold or silver, proved to be a fake.

"We appear to be victims of a well-organized and highly-skilled band of thieves. They've infiltrated our site security and succeeded in replacing dozens of artifacts with convincing replicas," I announced what was obvious to everyone.

"Not all that convincing once you remove some of the dust and grime from them," said Joel as he held a small golden statue of a horse and rider up to the light and wiped away some of the grime with his thumb and forefinger.

"It was Joel who first noticed some items were being tampered with," I said in an attempt at some fairness toward Joel.

"Is there really anything left to protect at this point?" asked Sasho.

"There is the funeral cart," said Borko.

We all turned to stare at the cart. It appeared intact. It was the real prize from an archaeologist's standpoint.

"So how can we protect it from these thieves?" asked Sasho. "They have access to the tomb somehow in our absence. Which means that they obviously have friends among the guard detail."

"Not to mention the possibility that they have friends on this archaeology team," I added.

"No one on my crew could possibly be involved!" insisted Borko.

"Nor mine!" I shot back.

"It's great that you have such confidence in all of us," said Deb. "But somebody close to this archaeology project, in security and maybe in excavation is involved."

"I wouldn't be surprised if that old maid, Professor Misirkova was," said Joel.

"So how do we create security around the cart?" I asked.

"I will volunteer to spend the night tonight on the site," said Sasho.

"I will too," said Joel.

Borko and I exchanged glances. "So what do you think, Borko?" I asked.

"For tonight, at least, that would make sense," he answered. "While we get the help of the security forces."

Sasho and Joel returned to camp and came back with a tent and their bedrolls. They set up camp directly in front of the doors of the tomb. So now we had our young colleagues there to watch the guards, who were supposed to be watching over the tomb.

Borko and I put in a call to the chief of security, who immediately ordered a full replacement of all of the guards on the site. Both the day and night shifts. He assured us that the guards would be thoroughly interrogated. "It is not surprising though, that some of them prove to be less than reliable, seeing how little the state security pays such men," he added at the end of the conversation.

"The thieves must have access to a broad range of resources to have pulled off such a sophisticated heist," I said to Borko. "They've enlisted skilled forgers of art objects. They've infiltrated security on the site. And they appear to have someone who can pick the lock on the doors as well."

For once, all that Borko could manage was a grim nod in reply.

I was visited again that night by "my snake." This time, however, when I lifted the lid of the casket, the massive snake's head that reared out at me broke into a hideous cackling, mocking laugh. I fled in terror from the tomb, without a look back.

When I awoke from my nightmare, I immediately began fumbling in the dark for my clothes. I stumbled out the tent door in the middle of the night with a terrible sense of foreboding. The whole damn crew of us should have camped out around the funeral cart, was my first coherent thought.

I stood there in the cool night air for several minutes, until I could no longer stand the waiting for dawn. I slipped back into the tent, and once I'd located my flashlight, I set out for the tomb.

The sky was still filled with glittering stars at that hour. The night was silent except for the occasional song of a cricket or the distant call of a night bird. I drank in the sweet, fresh, slightly damp night air in large gasping breaths as I hurried along. I was so familiar with the path by then that even in the dark I was able to make the trek to the site in less than half an hour.

As I approached the site I was immediately aware of the absence of any lights or sounds. Where were the guards? Why hadn't Sasho and Joel left a lantern burning in front of the tomb entrance? I immediately grew wary. I shut my flashlight off and began to walk more slowly and quietly, while willing my breath to no longer come in loud panting gasps from my recent exertion.

I felt the approach of someone from behind, but before I could react I was engulfed in total blackness and hurled to the ground. My arms and legs were pulled behind my back and tied firmly in place with a rope. I was also apparently enclosed in some sort of cloth sacking. I was tempted to call out for help, but something told me that the effort would be pointless, and it might even result in further assault. So I remained silent, waiting and listening for whatever would come next. My bruised and tortured shoulders plagued me less than my thoughts during those long hours.

I lay like that, on the ground, a short distance from the tomb, until full light and the arrival of the rest of the crew. After freeing me and listening to my rather unhelpful description of how I came to be laid out there like a rodeo calf, everyone hurried on to see what had transpired at the tomb itself.

We all stood and gaped in silence for a moment before rushing to the aid of our colleagues. Sasho and Joel had been bound, gagged and blindfolded and the doors to the tomb hung wide open. The guards were, as one might expect, nowhere to be seen.

After our initial shock wore off, members of the crew rushed to the aid of Sasho and Joel, who couldn't have been happier to see us after so many hours lying helplessly bound. Once they had been freed from their bonds and had regained some circulation in their cramped limbs, Sasho rasped, "A group of masked thieves managed to surprise and overpower us during the night."

Unfortunately, they could offer few more details about the thieves than I had. They were, however, able to tell how the new guard detail, when they had arrived, had on ski masks and that they were the ones who had done this to the two of them.

Borko immediately rushed to the tomb entrance with me only a step behind. Everything inside the tomb appeared as we had left it, but when I heard him bellow out a Macedonian word, delivered with more force and conviction than usual, I just knew that our thorough examination of the funeral cart would reveal yet another forgery. Only the faded, peeling interior wall paintings and the lettering on the tumbled down exterior facade remained - mere hints of the authenticity that had once been here.

Just about then, Borko noticed Mavros among the crew members, poking his head into the tomb and peering around. He must have somehow managed to follow us out to the site that morning. Borko turned a furious gaze on the Greek journalist and the American student Deb Economou, who, as usual, was right by his side. "You! You're responsible for this, aren't you! The girl told you all about the site and you had your friends come somehow and steal everything they could carry!" he shouted.

Deb turned to me, but I gave her a stern look. She shook her head in vigorous denial of all Borko had said.

"What garbage!" Mavros muttered as he backed away from him. He wasn't all that interested in a toe-to-toe discussion of this with an angry bull like Borko. The journalist's hand trembled slightly as he tried to light a cigarette under Borko's menacing gaze. Eventually he flung the unlit match at Borko's feet and strode away.

"It's not true! We talked about a lot of things, but not the site!" Deb shouted at Borko.

Borko turned his gaze on her now. His face remained stony as he said. "Come, Jack. Despite remoteness of the site, there is obviously some other way onto it, and the bastards have several hours ahead on us. So let's get busy, searching for it. There has to be a pretty obvious trail left by a party carrying that much material. Let's go look for it!"

Deb was almost in tears now. She looked from crew member to crew member. I could tell that she wanted to bolt and run and maybe catch up with Mavros and get as far from our accusing eyes as she could. But something must have told her that that would be a mistake. She had to tough it out.

Finally, Sasho, of all people, said to her, "Come, if you had nothing to do with this, then you'd better come along and help us find the thieves."

I felt sick to my stomach. A hangover was nothing compared to this. In my gut I just knew that the marvelous find that had been dangled in front of our faces had been irrevocably snatched away now. I admired the nobility of Sasho's gesture, but I was too devastated to see beyond the loss.

The crew members began to try and piece together the story in the dusty trail at our feet. Donkey tracks were everywhere. A well-beaten path that led over the ridge top, however, seemed the likely path of the thieves' escape.

The donkey track led us through rugged, mountainous terrain. The trail switched back frequently and rose and then dropped precipitously a number of times as it traversed the ridges. Our crew followed this trail for more than an hour before the entire panting, sweat-soaked party collapsed at a watering stop along the trail.

We sat clustered at a place where the trail switched back up a ravine. Donkey droppings that still had the power to twitch noses littered the area around us, near a small stream that cut across the path.

"So what is it exactly we're doing?" asked Joel, waving a sweaty hand at the swarm of flies attracted by the fresh dung. "Say we catch up with the thieves. Are they armed and dangerous? Why didn't we send someone back to camp to alert the police? Get them to chase after the thieves, who must be in league with the guards who have been watching the site."

Borko and I looked at each other. Each hoped the other would come up with a good rationalization for our impulsive pursuit. Finally Borko said, "No, we don't expect to catch up with them. It's enough if we can simply find the route they followed."

The initial shock of the theft had by now worn off. I tried my hand at explaining what we were doing. "Considering the quantity of goods that they carried, especially the funeral cart, there is no way the thieves could travel in this sparsely-populated region inconspicuously. There are bound to be shepherds or hunters or woodcutters who will have seen a party of that size. We need to make contact with such people as soon as possible," I said.

"Well, wouldn't it still make sense for someone to go back and alert the authorities?" asked Deb.

"Yes, that's a good idea. Why don't you and some of the others do that," suggested Borko as he rose to push on.

"Alright," replied Deb, and she turned in the opposite direction to retrace the path back to camp. She was joined by most of the others. Only Sasho, Joel and I moved to follow Borko.

———————

That evening the group that had returned to camp with Deb clustered around their returning colleagues.

"Did the police find you? And did you find anything?" Deb asked as we drew near.

The weary, downcast appearance of the returning group provided much of the answer even before anyone spoke. Even Borko, who normally had more than enough to say on any given topic, sat hunched over, peering into the fire for a time, not saying a word.

I was bone weary by then. I'd had almost nothing to eat all day and only a few hours of sleep the night before. My body and brain were barely functional. I too sat there by the fire and gazed out into the black night with an unfocused zombie-like stare.

Finally I mustered the energy to respond to Deb's questions. "The police caught up with us on the trail which eventually led us to a remote mountain village. The authorities have begun an investigation. They'll let us know as soon as they learn something."

There was little to do but wait for some word from the police investigating the theft. For the next several days the crew busied themselves studying the interior of the tomb, its construction and wall paintings. Everyone remained rather subdued and almost morose at times as we went about our work.

The presence of the replicated burial items only served to remind us of the extent to which we'd been suckered by the thieves. I was particularly puzzled by the fact that they had gone to such additional trouble to dump a faked funeral cart on us as well.

When I mentioned this to Borko, he said, "Maybe they were originally hoping to slip it into the tomb completely undetected. But when they had to change their plans, they decided to give it to us anyway, since they'd gone to such trouble to construct it."

On the third evening after the theft, Borko reported to us on his latest call in to police headquarters. He frowned and kept his eyes fixed on the ground as he said, "The investigation is stalled. The police report that no one in the village could be found who had seen or heard anything about the stolen things." He paused and lifted his gaze to the first stars appearing in the gathering darkness above. "I urged them to continue their search, particularly the search for the guards who disappeared from the site the night of the robbery, as well as those who had been hired earlier, and their chief. But he told me that he has questioned their chief thoroughly, and the man claims that he had received a call from someone on our crew on the evening of the final theft, ordering the removal of all of the guards from the site, because our own crew members wanted to take over security.

"Did he say who called him?" I asked.

"He said that the man did not remember," he replied.

"I'll bet he's lying," said Joel.

Borko's face took on a particularly grim expression as he added, "The chief of security told the investigator that he suspected that we had faked the robbery in order to cover the fact that we had been made fools of by someone. An elaborate hoax, a tomb of Alexander the Great, in the first place. The investigator told me that for now, he considers their work done, unless new information should come to light."

He paused again and took in the entire crew in a sweeping gaze, and then Borko slumped forward and stared at the fire as he murmured in a hoarse and pained whisper, "So now we know why the thieves bothered to give us with a replica of the funeral cart as well. So that people will think everything was a hoax from the start."

The smoke from our campfire swirled in all directions. Its thick, gray fog stung my eyes, burned in my nostrils, and tickled at my throat. But I made no move to avoid it.

Finally I spoke again, though my smoke-teared eyes remained fixed on the several feet of ground between me and the fire pit. I just couldn't get myself to look at anyone. It was all too awful. My voice cracked slightly as I said, "I suppose it doesn't matter by now whether the police continue their investigation or not. The thieves have had plenty of time to shift their plunder to a whole network of crooks who deal in stolen art, jewelry or precious metals."

No one else spoke for the longest time, and Borko offered no further information than the brief report he had just delivered. Word was out that the American crew might soon be returning to their work in the states and the Macedonians to their work at the museum in Skopje.

It grated a bit that Professor Misirkova wore a slight smirk whenever I encountered her. I began to wonder if she wasn't part of the conspiracy against us. But when I suggested this to Borko, he merely snorted and said, "Jovanka? No. She is just ungenerous about our good and now our bad fortune."

For the next few days our crew worked on final preparations for the return to Skopje and the Americans' return to the US. We catalogued what few artifacts remained to us and then packed all of our equipment for the trip home.

We sat around the campfire for what was to be our final evening together. No one had much to say, it seemed. I studied the preliminary photos of the tomb that Joel had taken weeks before. Although they were quite impressive, I instinctively knew that, in the absence of the artifacts, no one would believe in their authenticity. It was almost painful to look at the photos now. They were such a powerful reminder of what could have been, should have been, if only... Mistakes were made. Yes, dammit. Mistakes were made. Nothing worse in the world than regrets, I thought, as my fingers mechanically pressed themselves into the glossy plasticine coating on the photo paper.

The expedition that was to have been the pinnacle of my career was ending in anti-climactic disarray. And we would soon be slinking out of here with our tails between our legs.

I looked around me at the youthful faces of the students who had accompanied me. They too registered disappointment, but they would rebound in ways that I never could. Some things are once in a lifetime opportunities. But at least if you're young enough you can still hope, I thought to myself. If for no other reason than because you don't have enough experience of the world to know when you've encountered a once only chance. And the wreckage from my personal life was about all that would be waiting for me when I got off the plane at Detroit-Metro.

It was at that moment that Sasho interrupted my somber thoughts with an announcement. He straightened his shoulders and thrust his head forward into the circle, so that he could see everyone and all could see him. "I think it would be hasty for us to abandon all hope of retrieving the stolen artifacts," he said. He paused to see if he had our full attention, then continued. "I have a small confession to make. I couldn't resist the temptation to begin study of the scrolls found in the tomb. Though, of course, much more thorough examination will be required to verify what I've learned, I believe that they contain a remarkable message that may bear on our problem."

"*Zoshto ne kazhish nishto do sega*!" Borko blurted in Macedonian before he could catch himself.

"I didn't say anything because I didn't know enough til now to have anything to report," replied Sasho.

Borko merely grunted at this.

"Well, tell us what you've learned," I said.

"I don't have a complete translation yet," Sasho answered, "but from what I've been able to..."

"Where is the scroll?" Borko interrupted him. "Go, bring it out for us to see!"

Sasho went back to his tent and returned shortly with the scroll, still wrapped in protective plastic. Someone brought out a lantern and set it down in front of Borko. He then carefully unrolled the sheet of pale, creamy yellow parchment onto the sheet of plastic laid on the ground. Soon everyone was clustered round him and the manuscript with its mysterious script in an unfamiliar alphabet.

"At first I didn't know what to make of the text," said Sasho as he held the scroll open with his two hands. "But there was something familiar about the alphabet. Then it hit me. The text is written in something like the glagolitic alphabet that has long been believed to be the invention of the Slav enlightener, the ninth century monk from Salonika, Kiril. It was used in his early translations of Christian texts for missionary work among the Slavs."

"Some recent research suggests that the alphabet may have older roots in the Black Sea region," added Rada.

"That wouldn't surprise me, considering what I've been able to determine so far," said Sasho. "Anyway, once I was fairly confident about the phonetic values of most of the letters, I then had to make some sort of linguistic sense of it all. Again, it was not easy, but, fortunately, it proved to be written in a language with most of the features of the proto-Slavic that it is believed that our ancestors spoke."

"Does this mean that the ancient Macedonians spoke the ancestral tongue of we present-day Macedonians, and that we are their descendants, after all?" asked Rada.

"Not necessarily," replied Sasho. "Since we don't know for certain how old this text really is, nor has the language been properly studied to know its linguistic relation to our own language. There are a number of possibilities, but it certainly suggests our kinship. Though not necessarily direct, but maybe as a result of successive waves of migration of early Slavic peoples to the Balkan Peninsula who spoke languages related to the present-day Slavic languages of the region, rather than one single migration in the 6th century. The Veneti, for example, are one of the peoples cited by some authorities as a possible ancient link to the modern day South Slavs."

"So what have you been able to make of the text so far," asked Borko, leaning his broad shoulders over the scroll and effectively blocking the view for everyone else.

"Well, this portion," and he pointed to a section of the text with his index finger, "clearly refers to a cult dedicated to Zeus-Amon, the Greek-Egyptian god or gods," said Sasho. "Though I can't make out all of the words, look, here is the name Olympias, Alexander's mother's name. And this - *baeudati* - seems to refer to preservation, protection or something like that, of the tomb of Alexander," he said as he pointed to another portion of text.

"What do you think it says, then?" I asked impatiently.

"I can't be totally certain," he answered. "Some of the words have me puzzled. The language appears to be essentially proto-slavic, but with influence of what may be North Iranian or maybe Scythian - *Zeus-Amon bogos baudaet_olympias vaezaet __aleksandrom_ __xvala bogoi dionisu*."

"But what is your best guess, based on what you have seen?" asked Borko, nervously fidgeting in his seat, now that he was no longer hunched over the mysterious scroll.

"I would say that Alexander's mother conveyed his remains under the protection of her own dionysian cult with ties to the cult of Zeus-Amon."

"So would that be to suggest that Alexander's mother was able to get possession of her son's body away from the generals and kings who would have used it for their own purposes?" asked Borko.

"Yes, so it would seem," replied Sasho. "But what makes me curious is this line that follows - *Olympias velaet venetoi _ mesta measkumcu xsatriti _ g'panoa svarogom Aleksandrom.* What I understand it to say is that `Olympias instructs the priests of this cult,' and then there is something I can't make out. Then it says 'In the place called *Measkumcu,* to protect the tomb of her son the god-king Alexander,' and there is more that I haven't yet made sense of."

He paused at this point and looked up at the circle of faces that surrounded him in the pale lamplight. "Do you know what the name of that village is, where we lost the trail last week? Meshkom. The name could have easily been derived from Measkumcu."

Borko gasped. "Are you suggesting that this cult has somehow survived all these centuries intact, and continues to exist there to the present-day?"

"I'm not suggesting anything. I'm only reading from this ancient text," responded Sasho as he carefully re-rolled the scroll and wrapped it in its protective plastic sheeting.

"Well, it may be rather fantastic, but this whole expedition has been," I said to no one in particular, while edging away from the gritty, smoke-filled center of the campfire circle.

"There are secret cults that have survived in this part of the world for many centuries. Some truly do date back to ancient times, protected by secrecy," announced Borko.

"So perhaps we have been too quick to put this to grave robbers," he added, as his eyes traveled momentarily to Deb, and then his gaze quickly dropped to his feet.

She glared at him. I read righteous anger in her look, the anger of one who's been wrongfully accused. Sasho, who was seated next to her, gave her the slightest wink, with the hint of a smile, I suppose to suggest that he was pleased that she was proving less likely to be a party to the crime.

"Would you like to delay your return to the USA until we can visit Meshkom?" Borko asked as he put one heavy hand on my shoulder and peered intently into my eyes, with his usual flare for the dramatic.

I considered my options. To return home with little more than a few photographs of one of the greatest archaeological finds of all time. Photographs, I might add, that few, if any, reputable scientists would even be willing to look at. Or to stay a little longer and see if something might yet be salvaged from the rubble of this expedition. "I think I can delay our departure by a few more days, if you think there's any chance..." my voice trailed off.

"There's little chance," said Borko. He paused for effect. "But there's some," he finally added.

"Alright," I said, taking another step away from the fire and out of his physical reach. "Then we'll go in the morning to Meshkom." I glanced around me at the members of my crew. "What about the rest of you?" I asked "Would you rather go home?"

"No," Joel answered and shook his head. "We need to see this through."
The others nodded their heads in agreement.

"Alright, we'll all visit the village together," said Borko, in keeping with his usual need to have the last word, always.

We sat on together in silence for a while. I could sense the relief among the members of the crew, that they weren't going home just yet, and nearly empty-handed at that. The fire had nearly died down. Only a few red, glowing embers remained. A sliver of moon had risen in the black, star-sprinkled sky. Crickets sang from hidden places in the surrounding woods. Mysteries surrounded us. Beckoned us to their unraveling.

As the crew members dispersed among their respective tents for the night, Deb caught my attention. "Professor Starkweather," she began as she looked around her furtively. "I want to say a few things."

Sasho had taken a few steps towards his tent, but now he lingered, just out of obvious sight, out of the circle of firelight.

"Do you really believe all this?" she asked.

"What do you mean, all this?" I replied.

"I mean this whole expedition," she said. "This could all be some elaborate hoax arranged for our benefit. You've seen how much these people want to demonstrate that they're direct descendants of Alexander the Great."

"So what are you getting at. What's your point?" I asked wearily.

"Could somebody be setting this whole thing up?" she asked. "Doesn't it seem at times as if we're being played along like fish on a hook? First we're shown tantalizing photos of a tomb entrance that lures us over here. Then just as we're about to begin our study of the tomb's contents, everything we thought was real conveniently disappears, including the guards assigned to watch the tomb. Why can't anyone from the local police identify the thieves? And why trust Sasho and Professor Milevski about the meaning of the scrolls, providing they even are real?"

I frowned. "I agree that some of it certainly seems a bit far-fetched, but.." I paused and fixed her in my gaze. "Did you come up with this theory all by yourself?"

Deb shrugged and looked down at the fire pit. "Who cares whose theory it is. Does it sound at all plausible to you?"

"It's too early to say," I answered.

I glanced off into the shadows, where Sasho stood, the least bit visible to me. Deb followed my gaze and stiffened a bit as she spied the dark form silhouetted against the slightly less black of the night.

"We'll talk about this more, some other time, ok?" I said.

Deb nodded and looked again in the direction of Sasho, but now he was gone, and we too departed for our beds.

Stefan Verkovich... left... records of Macedonian folklore with ancient Macedonian elements, which he came across during his lengthy stay in Macedonia. He noted that a large number of such narratives, passed down from generation to generation. ...This folklorist also recorded that in the southwestern part of Macedonia the people declared themselves to be pure Macedonians, descendants of Alexander the Great.

– from *The Descendants of Alexander the Great of Macedon* by Aleksandar Donski

Chapter 5 – paying a visit to the neighbors

Borko guided the museum's micro-bus along the winding, hilly road, really little more than a donkey trace that passed as a road, to Meshkom. His passengers lurched forth and were thrown back in their seats repeatedly as he ground the gears in search of the right one for a particular grade.

We received a cold, silent stare from a wild-looking shepherd tending his flock, and again from a boy and an old man with a staff, tending a small herd of scrawny cattle, out to take advantage of the spring grass that had sprouted between the scrub oaks that dotted the hillsides. As we approached the village the trees grew thicker, and willow and cottonwood replaced the oaks, and the stares from the people we passed seemed to grow stonier still, if that were at all possible.

On the outskirts of the village just a few feet off the side of the road, I spied another stone covered with ancient runes, similar to the one we had encountered as we had approached the site of the tomb of Alexander that first day that we had walked the trail there from our camp. Then we entered the village by a narrow lane between stone-walled courtyards and houses. Through an occasional open gate we could see elderly women hand spinning wool or preparing food on outdoor wood cook stoves, while grandchildren played nearby.

It took a few moments for it to register that I no longer had to tense my muscles for the next wild lurch of the van. The village reminded me of countless other villages I had seen in my time here. There was really nothing unusual about it, other than that there didn't appear to be a square meter of flat ground anywhere. It was the sort of place that there were jokes about, how the cows had two legs shorter than the others so they could stand on the hillsides without falling over.

Borko pulled the van up in front of what appeared to be a village administrative center. It was a chalky gray stuccoed building with a weathered orange tile roof, suffering from neglect.

Sasho jumped out and approached the door. He tried the door handle, but it wouldn't open. He tapped on the door, then louder. Finally he called out. Still there was no response.

Sasho got back in and he and Borko exchanged a few words in Macedonian. Borko continued on through the village until we came to a small grocer's shop. Everyone piled out as the van came to a halt out front. We were all eager to stretch our legs after a long drive.

A balding, heavy-set shopkeeper in a blue work jacket and a couple of elderly men in baggy, worn-looking suit coats sat on sacks of grain out front of the store. They puffed on cheap Balkan cigarettes and drank beer from brown half-liter bottles as they eyed us suspiciously.

Borko called out, "*Dobar den*!" Good day. The shopkeeper returned Borko's greeting with a tentative nod of his head.

The conversation between the archaeologist and the shopkeeper that followed appeared decidedly one-sided to me, even given that any conversation with Borko tended that way. The shopkeeper restricted himself to an occasional "*Da*" or "*Ne*," to Borko's lengthy questions.

The shopkeeper eventually waved Borko away and went back inside his store. Even I could read his gesture to mean something like, 'enough of this, pal, time for me to get back to work'.

"So what did he say?" I asked.

"Not much," said Borko, as if I hadn't noticed that already. "But he did suggest that the village <u>kmet</u>, or mayor, could perhaps be found at the building we visited, but if he was not there, he was not sure where we might find him."

"What do you propose we do then?" I asked.

"Since we've come all this way, I say we wait here, and send one of the boys over to occasionally check the village office for return of the *kmet*", replied Borko, shading his eyes with one hand, as he looked off in the direction of the village office.

"Fine with me," I said. Some of the crew, upon hearing this, went into the shop to buy soft drinks or beer.

The afternoon wore on. Everyone drank their fill and studied the dusty road out front of the store until we knew every rut and fly-infested pile of animal dung by heart. The weather took a decided turn toward the hot. The Mediterranean sun burned bright and searing hot in a cloudless sky. We all grew increasingly listless as the day advanced, vacated earlier by the old men, who had disappeared shortly after our arrival.

"Couldn't someone go to the mayor's house?" asked Deb, in a yawning voice, her back leaned against the shady side of the parked van.

The shopkeeper said he wouldn't be there at this time of day," answered Borko from his own perch on one of the feed sacks by the shop door.

Sasho had also tried to engage the shopkeeper in conversation, but the man would say no more to him than he had to Borko. When he had also tried to talk to the old men, it was then that they had all remembered important work that they had neglected back at home and had hurried away.

Eventually villagers started to return from the fields or from jobs. A man in baggy blue coveralls passed by the storefront on his tractor. Two women with broad colorful head scarves, carrying wooden pitchforks on their shoulders, passed by on foot. A husband and wife drove by in a horse-drawn wagon. A few villagers stopped in at the store to pick up supplies on their way home, but no one showed any interest in conversation with the outsiders.

Borko finally cornered the shopkeeper alone behind his counter. "*Kade e kmetot sega*!" he demanded. But the man just shrugged in response to what I suspected was a demand to know where the mayor was.

Borko glared at the shopkeeper now, but the man simply returned the look with a bit of interest added on.

"What do you expect to do, Borko, bully the man into submission?" I asked as I approached the counter beside him.

"I'm tiring of his game!" he shot back, never taking his eyes off the shopkeeper.

"Ask him to tell you where the mayor lives," I suggested. I was anxious to steer Borko away from a pointless confrontation.

"I'd rather break this ones neck!" snarled Borko.

"It might provide you with some temporary satisfaction, but it won't get us any closer to some of the answers we're looking for," I said. Although I too was feeling increasingly annoyed with these people.

"And a good thing it is, for this one," Borko said, as he nodded in the shopkeeper's direction. When he asked my question of the man, he received a terse one sentence reply.

Borko motioned for me to follow him. We all piled back into the van and Borko drove off with a squeal of tires.

He raced the van up the street about a hundred yards and slammed on the brakes, hurling everyone forward in their seats. When I'd recovered from the shock, I could see that he had parked us out front of a big wooden gate nearly opposite the village office building. Sasho jumped out and banged and called at the gate until finally a woman dressed all in black emerged from the house and approached.

They talked briefly and Sasho returned to the van, shaking his head.

"Well, what did she say?" Borko asked.

"She said that her husband wasn't home, and she didn't know when he would return."

"So where is he?" asked Borko.

"She said she couldn't say. He could be anywhere in the village," said Sasho.

"We'll wait then," announced Borko.

"Can we go get something to eat while you wait?" enquired Joel.

"Go wherever you wish!" snapped Borko. And the crew members dispersed into the village, after promising to be back at the van before dusk. It was now late afternoon.

Only Borko and I remained in the van parked out front of the mayor's house.

"How much you want to bet that he's in there right now, with his feet up on a cushion and a beer in his hand, watching the latest news from the capital on tv," I ventured as I peered in the direction of the house. Even with the windows rolled down, the van felt like an oven. These poor Macedonians couldn't afford air-conditioning in their vehicles. Trickles of sweat slid down my chin and dripped into my lap.

"While we sit here in this broiling metal box and wait for him," said Borko, scowling in the direction of the mayor's house.

A few minutes later Borko grabbed the handle to his door and threw it open. "Wait here! I'll be right back!" he said and hurried off down the street on foot.

He returned shortly with several bottles of cold beer. He urged me to open my door as Borko slid the van's side door wide open. Then he turned the van radio up full blast and handed me a beer and opened one for himself.

A face immediately appeared at a window of the house. Borko held his beer bottle aloft. He grinned broadly and downed a swig of beer. The face disappeared from the window. Not five minutes later the mayor himself appeared at the door and motioned for Borko to turn off the radio and come up to the house.

Borko shut off the music and approached the mayor's house. I watched from the van as the two men shook hands. They talked for well over an hour, standing out front of the mayor's house. Once again it appeared that Borko carried much of the conversation. Unlike his earlier exchange with the shopkeeper, however, Borko came away from this meeting looking slightly subdued.

"Well, did you learn anything?" I asked as Borko climbed back into the van and the mayor retreated back into his house.

"I'm not certain," Borko replied, as he sat staring out the window of the van at the street beyond.

"So what did he say? What did you talk about?" I asked impatiently.

"I didn't really get to ask him that many questions. Mostly he asked the questions," said Borko. He continued to stare out the window, blinking as if he had just awakened from a nap.

"What do you mean, he asked the questions?"

He turned to face me now. There was an unfamiliar, strangely subdued look about him. This was not the usual, full of himself, bombastic Borko that I had come to know. What had happened to the man?

"He wanted to know about our work. And about our backgrounds. Where we studied. With whom. He was particularly interested in what we knew about ancient Macedonian language, literature, history and culture. He kept asking me detailed questions about all these subjects. One after another. I could barely keep up with his questions, let alone to ask him anything!"

"Well, didn't you at least manage to ask him the obvious question?"

"You mean, did I ask if his interest is due to some ancient cult?"

"Yes, I suppose that's what I meant," I replied, though the question sounded a bit odd when Borko actually said it aloud.

"He never gave me the chance to ask such a question," said Borko. His eyes grew wider as the meaning of what he'd just said became clear.

"What? You've got to be kidding!" I said, shaking my head in disbelief. "Call him back out. This is absurd. You have got to get some answers from him."

"I know," replied Borko, though he made no move to leave.

"Well then, call him!" I ordered. What in the devil was the matter with the man? I asked myself as Borko remained in his seat, as if frozen in place. It was still hotter than hell in the van, even with all the windows and doors open. I simply wanted to get what we came here for and get out as quickly as possible.

Finally Borko sheepishly returned to the gate and called toward the house. The mayor again came out to him and they exchanged a few words. Within a couple of minutes Borko was back in the van.

"He will say no more. Answer no questions," he said without looking at me.

"It's that simple?" I asked. "You ask and he refuses to answer and that's that?" I stared at Borko in disbelief. The voluble, garrulous bull, Borko, was rarely at a loss for words. How had he been cowed into such submission by a mre village mayor?

Borko continued to stare out the front windshield, unwilling to meet my gaze. Finally he said, "The mayor did say one other thing." He paused and turned to look at me now. "He said that people in such a hurry as we are shouldn't bother asking questions. Because we don't have the patience to stay and listen to the answers."

Try me, I thought. But I hesitated to say it. That response didn't sit quite right. Too quick, too arrogant somehow. Yet, my professional training had prepared me to be a careful listener. I had recorded long interviews with informants in cultural anthropology studies. Why didn't it feel quite right though to say that?

"We shouldn't just leave it at that," I said.

"I know, I know," snapped Borko. Again it was as if he were emerging from a fog, and as it dawned on him just how little he had accomplished, he banged on the steering wheel in frustration.

Our students and assistants began to trickle back from the village. Once everyone was in the van, Borko headed us back in the direction we'd come. The crew began to talk rather animatedly as soon as we were underway.

"Did any of the rest of you notice some of the odd speech those people used among themselves?" asked Rada.

"Yes, I did notice some very strange words," said Sasho.

"What do you mean?" asked Borko.

"It wasn't exactly that they used strange words as much as the fact that they gave words an odd sound," answered Rada. "At first I thought maybe they were *Shiptars*."

"Don't use that word, Rada," Borko said. "You know they insist that we call them *Albantsi* now."

"Who?" I asked.

"The damned Albanians! That's who!" snapped Borko.

I rolled my eyes slightly. I'd had other intimations of the ethnic tensions here, but I hadn't expected such an outburst from one of the intelligentsia.

"But it wasn't Albanian they were speaking," said Rada.

"No, it wasn't," added Sasho. "Nor Vlach."

"Who are the Vlachs?" asked Joel.

"Another of our minorities," said Borko.

It wasn't long before the entire crew sat sprawled against each other, nodding off to sleep in their seats.

It grew quiet in the van. The drone of the engine and the occasional shudder of the tires on rough pavement were all we could hear. Neither Borko nor I said another word during the rest of the drive home.

When we arrived back at camp, a weary crew quickly made their way to bed. The two of us lingered in the van.

"So what next?" I asked eventually, to break the silence.

"Why do you expect me to have all the answers!" snapped Borko.

Now I peered over at Borko's dim form seated next to me in the dark van. Normally Borko loved to run things. Obviously he was floundering. But wasn't I myself helpless here without Borko to translate and pave the way for me? All the more reason, it seemed, to be frustrated at Borko's inability to cope.

"Let's sleep on it then, and see if we have any better luck tomorrow," I finally said.

"Alright," answered Borko. He rose abruptly from the seat and strode off toward his tent without another word. I simply followed his movements with my eyes, puzzled at his strange behavior.

The next morning we were no more certain about our next move than we'd been the night before. We ate our breakfasts slowly and deliberately.

Finally I said, "I say we return to Meshkom and simply 'hang out' for the day again. The whole crew." And I gestured in the direction of the others, spread out along the camp table, finishing their breakfasts. "That we disperse into the village. Stroll the streets. Visit the shops. Loiter and watch people at their work. Try to engage them."

Borko set his espresso cup down and waved the large chunk of bread in his hand at me as he spoke. "Loiter? Is that some kind of trouble-making? Throwing things around or something?"

I suppressed a smile. "Well, it could be interpreted that way, but it more literally means spending some time somewhere with no particular business or purpose."

"But we would have a purpose!" said Borko. To which I merely gave a small, noncommittal nod.

The ride home that evening passed in near total silence. The visit had been a dismal failure. No one had succeeded in establishing the least measure of rapport with the villagers. After a day of being stared through, stepped around, and generally ignored, no crew member seemed to have anything to report.

We persisted in our visits, however. Day after day we returned to the village. But nothing changed. Day after day the village people worked and played around us. They didn't try to drive us away, but no one would engage any of us in conversation either. Finally after a week of this, Borko and I gathered everyone together to discuss our options.

"We're getting nowhere," I announced.

"It's true," agreed Borko.

"We have got to somehow break through the wall of silence these village people have set against us," I said.

"Now I know how the Jehovah's Witnesses must feel when they come to my door," said Joel.

"Things are made more difficult by the fact that they often speak some strange dialect among themselves," added Rada.

"I have yet to hear this strange speech you keep talking about," said Borko, standing now and shifting restlessly from foot to foot.

"Haven't you heard them greet each other with an odd form of our hello?" asked Sasho. "Instead of the usual '*zdravo*,' it sounds more like '*zadravu*' to me. I'm beginning to suspect that it is, in fact, related to the language of the ancient text. The one we retrieved from the tomb. I've noticed an ancient form of this word in the text - '*s'dravu*,' which could be closely related to their word," said Sasho.

"Our own language is also related to that of the text, isn't it?" asked Rada.

"It is, but obviously not so very closely as their speech," he answered. "I'm beginning to suspect a very close connection, though I've been exposed to too little of either, so far, to make any kind of real comparison."

"They seem like ordinary enough villagers to me," said Deb. "I don't see anything so special about these people. Are you sure that their speech is so unusual? Based on a couple of examples?"

"Since when did you become such an authority on our Balkan peoples?" Sasho frowned as he demanded to know.

"Since when have we ever had more than your own speculations to guide us in our search for, as Joel likes to call him, the Big Mac," Deb quickly responded, glaring back at him.

"Well, unlike Deb, who has only her skepticism to offer us," announced Sasho, as he surveyed the crew members. "I have a helpful suggestion. It happens that I was in a comparative religions class at the university with a girl from Meshkom. I asked after her in the village, but people claimed that she was living somewhere else, and no one would or could tell me where. But maybe we can trace her from the university's records office, since I know her name."

"A good idea," said Borko, and the others nodded their approval, less Deb, who merely looked away.

Christianity in its expansion among various peoples and cultures was generally flexible and tolerant about many older pre-Christian customs, successfully incorporating them into its ceremonies. In some cultures there are even customs with a distinctly anti-Christian character that are tolerated, Christian leaders choosing not to oppose their continued practice. This is not due to indifference, but because these leaders are aware of the fact that they cannot persuade people to abandon these deeply rooted customs…

– from *The Descendants of Alexander the Great of Macedon* by Aleksandar Donski

Chapter 6 – on the road for answers

So the next morning Borko, Deb, Sasho and I took the van into Skopje. Joel had volunteered to oversee the younger members of the crew in our absence. Everything seemed to irritate me that morning. The first thing that set me on edge was Deb and Sasho. Granted it was a bit hot and stuffy in the van, but why in the world every time Deb would open the window, Sasho had to complain about the wind and shut it again, I'll never know.

After they'd both tired of that game, they moved on to seeing who could be rudest to the other without being too obvious about it.

Deb said, "You're obviously not used to fresh air."

To which Sasho replied, "You mean fresh car exhaust!"

They're like a couple of little kids, I thought, as I turned around and gave them a scowl, in the hope that they might take the hint and just shut up for a while.

Then there was Borko, the Boar, or was it the Bore, as I'd begun to think of him, back to his old self. As we approached the city I had casually remarked, "There seem to be signs of 'spring cleaning' on the streets and in the city parks."

Men and women in blue work coats were busy raking up trash and planting flower beds in strips of ground adjoining the broad boulevards.

"Skopje has seen many renewals in its long history," said Borko, driving with one reckless hand and gesturing broadly about him with the other. "The entire Roman city, called *Skupi*, was destroyed by an earthquake in 518 AD. The Emperor Justinian, who was born in a nearby village, then had the entire city rebuilt. That is the city that a Slovenic people, a tribe called the *Brziti*, conquered and occupied in 695 AD and renamed Skopje."

He waved his hand again in a broad gesture to indicate the city around us as the van swerved dangerously in the narrow lane. "Many armies and invaders have fought over and occupied the city since then, but none did so much damage as another earthquake. This one struck on July 26, 1963. Over a thousand people were killed and many more injured, and over three quarters of the city's buildings were destroyed."

He was jabbering on, totally oblivious to everything and everyone around him. The man's in love with the sound of his own voice, it occurred to me. But at least he'd recovered from whatever happened to him back in that village.

"The half-demolished old train station over there," and the van weaved predictably as he pointed and spoke at the same time, "has been kept as a monument to the earthquake victims. The hands on the old clock out front are frozen at 5:17, the time the quake struck on that morning."

The man is impossible. He endlessly spouts these maddening encyclopedic monologues. How long, oh Lord, I thought, must I endure this. I nodded sleepily and said, "That's interesting." Though I'd tuned most of it out.

"And down there." He pointed down a broad boulevard opposite the old train station. "That is where our former President was almost killed by an assassin's bomb a few years ago. The blast killed his driver and nearly blinded the President."

Now he had my attention. I peered down the street where he had pointed. "Did they catch the assassins?"

"No. They didn't. Though there have been the usual suspects. Bulgarians, Serbs, Greeks."

"Greeks?" asked Deb.

"I'm not sure," said Borko, frowning. "Maybe not Greeks."

He parked the van in a lot reserved for it next to the city museum. Sasho headed for the university in order to obtain information about the girl from Meshkom. Deb accompanied him, though I couldn't imagine why on earth she preferred Sasho's company over ours. Or for that matter, why

Sasho had even invited her to accompany him, after the way they had treated each other in the van.

Borko suggested that we stretch our legs a little after the long drive. He led the way down a narrow, little cobblestone side street off the old market district, known as the *charshiya*.

Suddenly he grabbed my arm and pulled me after him, up a set of steps, and then he quickly darted into the open gate of a courtyard to our left. Once we were inside the yard, he seemed to relax a bit.

He guided me through the small crowd as if nothing unusual had happened. I gave him a puzzled look, as if to ask, what the heck's going on? But he chose to ignore it.

We had entered a cool, pleasant little courtyard with flowers and shade trees and several benches arranged in a row along a covered wooden veranda that ran the length of the high stone walls of the compound.

A whitewashed little church with a weathered orange tile roof occupied the far corner of the yard.

The Orthodox church appeared rather small and unimpressive from the outside. Borko beckoned me to follow him inside. The interior of the little church contained wonders to behold. Colorful frescoes in the style of Byzantine church art covered the walls.

"This is Macedonia," said Borko, waving his arm in a sweeping gesture over the entire church. "Not that strange, little mountain village we've been visiting. I don't know who they are, but this is the cult Macedonians traditionally dedicate themselves to - Orthodox Christianity."

The iconostasis, a thin wall that separated the main church from the sanctuary, was some twenty feet long and maybe ten feet high. It consisted of hundreds of small, intricate figures carved in almost three-dimensional relief out of the thick walnut wall panels. There were scenes from the Bible, a detailed depiction of the beheading of John the Baptist. Jesus's entrance into Jerusalem on a donkey, all interspersed with images of native flora and fauna, everything from grapevines to perching birds.

"It is the inspired work of many years by master craftsmen of past centuries from the Mijacha region of western Macedonia," explained Borko.

This is precisely the kind of historical treasure that so easily perished in the fighting in the former Yugoslav republics to the north, I mused. Craftsmen who would or even could do such work are almost impossible to find today, which makes such works almost irreplaceable.

"Someone from Meshkom must be capable of the same fine craftsmanship," I said. "How else to explain the quality of the forgeries they left us with?"

Borko merely grunted acknowledgement.

After we had satisfied ourselves with viewing the treasures of Sveti Spas, the Holy Savior Church, we stepped back out into the courtyard. It was such a peaceful place, after the turmoil and traffic jams out on the streets. Birds chattered away from the upper branches of the trees, and bright sunshine glittered on boughs heavy with leafy spring greenery.

Borko took me by the shoulder and guided me over to a flower-decked stone sarcophagus in the center of the courtyard. It was about six feet long and three feet wide, composed of slightly mottled cream-colored marble, the sort so familiar from Greco-Roman ruins. Fresh yellow roses and red poppies and some flowers I couldn't identify lay strewn across the lid.

"This is dedicated to a man who symbolizes the best in our people. Gotse Delchev, a teacher, and revolutionary, who died in the struggle to liberate us from the Turks, May 4th 1903." There was a reverence in Borko's voice that I hadn't heard before.

I was about to say something, when Borko continued. "The man showed great wisdom in his speech and enormous courage as he traveled about the countryside in disguise, organizing the people for an uprising against the *Turtsi*."

He paused again, but I didn't even consider trying to get a word in this time before he continued. "He was our George Washington and Abraham Lincoln all in one. His fate, like so many of our leaders, was to die at the hands of foreign assassins."

I shifted uneasily under the weight of Borko's big arm on my shoulder. So much Macedonian history seemed to consist of ash that hid red hot embers just waiting to burn anyone foolish enough to touch them.

"Now let me show you the old fortress across the roadway from here." And he led me out across a broad avenue, though not before cautiously peering up and down the street in search of something or someone. We proceeded up a grassy slope until we were standing at the foot of a tall stone fortress at the top of a hill.

"What is going on, Borko?" I demanded. And I stopped where I was, in order to force an answer out of him for my further cooperation.

"I think that we are being followed," he said in a hushed voice.

"Who?" I asked.

"I don't know, but I don't like it," he answered. "There was a car back there on the way to Skopje, too. But I didn't think much of it at the time. And now I keep seeing these same people everywhere we go."

"The original wall probably dates back to the 6th century," he continued in his normal, rather booming voice. "This commanding hill by the river has been a strategic point for many centuries for settlements of the Skopje Valley. Ancient Macedonians, Romans, Slavs, the Byzantine Greeks, and the Ottoman Turks all centered command of the valley on this piece of earth." He made another sweeping gesture with his hand as he spoke.

"And now it's just a peaceful park where grandmothers bring their grandchildren to play," I said as I gazed at the people around us.

"Not quite so peaceful," murmured Borko. He then quickly gestured off in the direction of a tall, imposing cream-colored mosque with a slim white minaret rising above all else in that part of the city. "That is the Mustapha-pashina Mosque. It was built in 1492, by a Turkish pasha."

"The same year Columbus discovered America," I commented. Why should I be amazed at the existence of a village that could trace itself back to Alexander's time, when so much here was already old when the Europeans colonized the Americas?

"And that old building with the courtyard near the open-air market," and he gestured to the north, "is the Kurshumli-han. It was an inn for several centuries, and then at the turn of the century it became a Turkish prison, where our revolutionaries were held by the Turks." He paused. His brows knit in a frown. "You know we were slaves of the Turks for five long centuries. Never again will we be slaves. We'd rather die than let our enemies ever subdue us again."

"And who are these enemies?" I asked.

"We are surrounded by enemies. All of our neighbors - the Serbs, the Bulgars, the Albanians, the Greeks, would like to carve up this last little corner of our Macedonia among them and disperse our people once and for all. They've done it before. Half of Macedonia is now Greek, our people driven out or bullied out of their identity. The Bulgars control another quarter of Macedonia, where the people live in daily fear of punishment if they dare lift their heads. And western Macedonia is slowly being overrun by the Albanians."

His eyes looked wild now. As if it were he personally who had been driven out of Greece and was forced to speak Bulgarian today or had felt compelled to sell his home to an Albanian in a town in western Macedonia.

"Any conquerors would forever after have to watch their backs here," I said. "This includes guests, such as the Americans who were here recently to patrol Macedonia's borders under UN and NATO command."

"Macedonians eventually cast off the Turks who had conquered their medieval ancestors," said Borko, ignoring my comment. "But our ancestors themselves had earlier conquered Romans, who had before them conquered the ancient Macedonians."

And no one apparently had ever totally disappeared from these mountains, I thought. They lie out there, hidden away in scattered refuges, just waiting to be stirred up by outsiders who stray into their territory.

I was reminded again of the pot always ready to boil over.

Borko led me across the lovely old stone bridge with its nine graceful arches that links the old market with the new business district of Skopje. The Vardar River was still a murky gray torrent, swollen by spring rains and snow melt off the dark, hazy mountains to the north.

As we crossed the main city square on the opposite bank of the river, Borko remarked, "This was called Marshall Tito Square for most of my lifetime, but since the fall of Yugoslavia it has been rechristened Makedonija Square."

I thought about that father of modern Yugoslavia, Josip Broz Tito. He was a father whose children had failed to live in harmony after his death in the house he had left them and according to the rules he'd laid down for them. Now they'd parted ways after a bitter quarrel among several of them over who would get what. Their poor half-brothers, the Bosnian Moslems, had taken the brunt of the beating, but much of what the old man had overseen - the construction of modern roads and buildings, and the like, now lay in shambles to the north. Only here in the south had they mostly been allowed slow stagnation and decay instead of the rapid destruction of war. There had been more limited death and destruction in recent times, when some Albanians in western Macedonia had resorted to terrorist-type violence, reportedly to force some political concessions on the Macedonian majority of the country.

"This is no easy place to live, Borko. Have you ever considered emigration? You would be welcome at any number of universities," I said as we crossed the broad, cobblestoned public square.

"Never," he said in a fierce tone. "This is my home. Our little *Makedonija* has both proud and noble history as well as tragic history of war and poverty and exile. She is beautiful, but long-suffering and much abused mother to we her children. At the time of the Albanian troubles here a while back, when some others stayed home, I volunteered and served reserve army duty on Shar Mountain above the town of Tetovo. What I wouldn't do for my poor dear!" declared Borko.

Does that include falsifying history? I wondered.

"*Na zdravje*!, to health!" Borko toasted us as we raised our glasses of wine. The four of us sat in a small restaurant near the river. The window in front of me faced into a small courtyard. The smooth bark of the plane trees and the gray paving stone of the yard shone dully in the fading light. The silhouette of an occasional passerby on the street beyond the entryway would appear for an instant and then be gone. Some were Albanian Moslems, the men in white felt skull caps and the women in grey or black flowing overcoats, some hooded, many with broad scarves, but all with their heads well-covered. Interspersed among them were bare-headed Slavic men and women in casual dress or sometimes more formal attire, if they were dining out or attending a play or concert after dinner.

"Do you like our wine, Jack? This is from the Tikvesh wine district, a sunny valley some 100 kilometers to the south," said Borko as he waved his glass of sweet white wine in front of my face.

I nodded my approval. I turned to Sasho. I'd been waiting impatiently for some time now for the opportunity to ask, "So what were you able to learn at the university about the student from Meshkom?"

"She is apparently living with an aunt and uncle about an hour away from the capital while she attends the university. In a village to the northeast, in the Tetovo region," said Sasho. "I have their names, so we shouldn't have much trouble finding them."

"If the *Albantsi* haven't already bought the house and the family isn't now in America," said Borko as he downed another glass of wine.

"If an entire village was unwilling to speak to us, why do you expect this one girl to open up to us?" asked Deb as she swirled the wine in her cup in a nervous gesture.

"She's a university student, after all, not an ignorant peasant, like those," responded Sasho as he smacked his wine glass a little too hard on the table top, spilling some.

"They were not such ignoramuses as you might think," said Borko, examining his wine glass thoughtfully.

"Well, we must hope that she shares our own dedication to science and scholarship," said Sasho.

"We certainly must," said Deb as she glared across the table at him. "I doubt that you'll charm the information out of her."

"Spoken, no doubt, as someone who knows a good deal about lack of charm," Sasho responded.

Their time alone with each other that day apparently hadn't brought the two of them any closer together, I observed glumly. So I was relieved when the meal arrived - spicy meat with potatoes, rice and green peppers and mounds of tasty wheat bread - putting a brief halt to all conversation.

For the first time in weeks that evening I felt an urge to call Jo again. "So I never read about the Alexander find anywhere," she said.

"You wouldn't, and maybe no one ever will," I said. "It's a long story that'll have to wait until I get back."

There was a pause, then she said, "I'm sorry to hear that."

"And I'm sorry that I didn't stay on the line to hear about your news," I said.

"Well, that's a long story too, that'll have to wait for another time."

The conversation only made it clearer just how bad things were here.

The next morning we were back in the van and on the road again as the sun peeked over the grey mountain ridge to the east. I sat silently soaking in all of the visual impressions of Macedonian life that passed by my window. The city again struck me as sleepy and provincial. But not provincial in the negative sense. Tree-lined streets and houses with flowers in window boxes and with cats perched on the sills, sunning themselves, can all seem so simple and untroubled on the crazy eve of the twenty first century.

The scenes shifted from moment to moment. Green boulevards made tidy by unseen hands, rows of small European cars parked on sidewalks, and a UN headquarters with a small fleet of white vehicles (ghost-like forces of the worldwide desire to promote peace where conflict is likely) all passed before my eyes.

The city gave way to village houses, each with its own gardened courtyard with a pleasing blend of fruit trees, grape vines, flowers and vegetable patches. American suburbanites with their obsession with boring golf course lawns could learn something from these residents of Macedonia's suburbia.

We soon broke out of settled lands and entered semi-wild ridge country. The dry, rocky hillsides were covered with scrub oak, only occasionally relieved by a small vegetable plot or pasture in the semi-fertile bottomlands.

We maintained a rapid pace for a half hour on smooth, paved highway. It brought us to the lush, fertile Tetovo Valley, bounded on the east by the dry Suva Gora mountains, and on the west by the tall, steep slopes of a rugged mountain range called the Shar Planina. We veered north, bypassing the center of the town of Tetovo. The roadway was narrow and winding and the rough cobblestone roads were lined with squat village houses with their characteristic orange tiled pyramid-like roofs.

The rich clay soil of the Tetovo Valley, on our right now, supported intensive cultivation of a wide variety of fruits and vegetables - apples, cherries, plums, pears, as well as wheat, corn, tobacco and green vegetables. The landscape was dotted with small plots enclosed by low stone walls, primitive wooden fences or thick hedgerows. Everywhere there were tractor or horse drawn carts that transported village men and women and their supplies to and from the fields. It seemed as if everyone in the valley was busy that day in those fields.

On the opposite side of the road, to our left, appeared the villages where most of these people lived. White-washed village houses with orange tile roofs were arranged one to the next in clusters that abutted the steep slopes of a tall mountain. The snow-bound, rocky, barren upper reaches of the Shar Planina mountain range were shrouded in a thin, grey mist, but the lower slopes, covered by a thick maple, oak and chestnut forest, shone brightly in the soft green colors of the late spring. The white spire of a minaret or the more blunted orange peak of a church roof occasionally rose amidst the cluster of roofs.

Borko eventually pulled the van into a narrow side lane leading up to one of the villages. The narrow, rutted lane passed between high stone walls filled with squealing pigs, clucking chickens and noisy children. The clutter and chaos of the scene on that street hearkened back to the Middle Ages. Life here seemed barely changed through many centuries of habitation. But could that other village, Meshkom, really be over twenty seven centuries old?

Sasho asked someone directions that eventually brought us to the high wooden gate of a particular house. He got out of the van and called up to the second floor window above the street. "Eh, *chichko*! Hey, uncle," he shouted.

An ancient, weathered old man in a patched and tattered old brown suit coat and with a blue beret on his head, peeked from around the slightly opened gate. He seemed puzzled at first, over who we might be. He asked Sasho a question, and when Sasho gave his answer, the old man broke into a wide toothless grin. As the two of them talked it became clear that he wanted us to come up to the house.

As we climbed the stairway up to a small balcony the old man said, "I knew that guests were coming today. A little bird flew in the house this morning and told me." That is what Borko said the man had said.

His wife was busily rushing to and from the balcony filling a table with little appetizers. Soon there were heaping bowls of white sheep's milk cheese, fried green peppers, shredded cabbage and bread, and of course, the usual bottle of home-made *rakiya*, grape or plum brandy.

But first she offered each of us a spoonful of homemade jam and a glass of cold water to wash it down, the traditional offering to guests in a Macedonian home.

This was my first visit to a Macedonian home. I watched the interactions of hosts and guests with an anthropologist's fascination. There were obligatory welcoming toasts. These were followed by a most oriental-feeling conversation, slow and meandering. In fact, I was later to learn that they have a name for it in this part of the world, a Turkish word, *muabet*.

Eventually though, Borko did get around to asking our hosts where we might find their niece.

"So where's the girl?" I asked Borko during a lull in their conversation.

"The old folks tell us that she's working in town at a restaurant," he answered.

It was a warm, sunny late spring day. The pungent smells of fresh farmers cheese, peppers and plum brandy filled the air. Flies constantly buzzed in a series of slow circles over our food. Their flight paths and landing plans were as constantly being disrupted by the sweeping hands of hosts and guests alike.

After an appropriate time Borko insisted that we must be going and thanked our hosts as we rose to leave. They urged us to stay a little longer. As we started to descend the stairs, the old man turned to us and said and Sasho translated again, "Excuse me for keeping you so long from your business. But as much as one ages, so much more of a stubborn jackass he becomes."

"No." Borko protested. "We're the fools for being in such a hurry. But `ludost, mladost.' Youth is foolishness, as they say."

"They were certainly friendly old folks," remarked Deb when we were once more under way.

"So now you know what is more typical of our village folk when guests visit their home," said Sasho. "That village, Meshkom, was not all so typical as you thought a while ago."

"Are you a typical Macedonian?" she asked.

Sasho frowned. He started to say something, stopped himself, then finally he said, "I have one small confession to make. We were made so welcome because I told the old man that we were friends of his niece. And I said that we had come from Meshkom to find her.

He immediately grew friendlier towards me. At that point, he greeted me with that same strange form of our hello that I kept hearing in Meshkom. Instead of saying *zdravo*, he said *zadravu*."

"Fortunately we were able to maintain the ruse," added Borko. "The old people assumed that we were friends of the family. And though I was tempted to draw information out of them about the strange people of Meshkom, I decided to save my questions for their niece. Though the old man let a few stray bits of information loose, in any case. He asked me, among other things, if we would be attending the <u>Lita</u> celebration next week."

"What do you think he meant by that?" I asked.

"I'm not totally certain, but I have an idea," replied Borko. "But it should wait until we've met with the girl."

We retraced our route back to the town of Tetovo. It appeared to be a busy, little city of low buildings and mostly old and narrow streets crammed with cars and with sidewalks filled with a bustling, colorful mix of people.

We proceeded south through the town, paralleling the Shar Planina mountain range, that loomed tall and white with snow at its summit, off to our right, until we arrived at the Baba Tekija. It was a complex of white-washed plaster and wood beam framed buildings that had once housed a dervish sect back in the days of the Turkish Empire.

One of the main buildings of the complex had been converted into a modern restaurant. We took a table in one corner of a pleasant, green courtyard and waited for service. When the waiter finally arrived, along with our order, we put in a request to meet with the restaurant helper, Iskra, during her next break.

The waiter suggested that that might not be any too soon, because we had arrived at the height of the dinner hour, when all of the restaurant's staff were quite busy. Eventually, however, a bookish-looking young woman with wire-rimmed glasses and her hair tucked back in school-marm fashion approached our table. Sasho and Borko introduced us and explained the reason for our visit.

The young woman backed away from us. She shook her head no. It was obvious that she was about to bolt and run, when Borko suddenly said something to her in a sharp, commanding tone of voice. "*Zadravu, dejche*!"

Whatever Borko had said, it apparently had tapped into some conditioning in her. It must have been difficult for her to defy an older authority figure, like the professor, Borko Milevski. Although the look of a frightened doe never left the girl's face as they spoke, I could tell that she was cooperating, despite my inability to follow their conversation.

They talked for a considerable time. It seemed longer to me than the restaurant management would have approved. I sensed that the student from Meshkom was being forthright in her answers to their questions. Not that it could have been easy for her to talk about some of these things. Several times she appeared on the verge of tears, apparently torn between their demand that she share her knowledge with us and her loyalty to family and community.

The conversation ended and she returned to her work. "She told us some truly remarkable things," said Borko. He hunched over the table and spoke in an almost conspiratorial hush.

"Like what?" I asked, eager for any shred of information.

"Like the fact that the village *kmet* is some type of high priest as well," he said.

"And what about Alexander's tomb?" asked Deb.

"She didn't know anything about that, or so she said," answered Sasho.

"What is important," said Borko, "is that she confirmed our suspicions that there is an ancient religious society in the village to which most, if not all, the village people belong."

"What does she know about it?" I asked.

"Very little really," answered Sasho.

"And what is meant by very little?" asked Deb.

"She only knows that many of the adults take part in strange rites on some regular basis."

"What kind of rites?"

"Seasonal festivals that correspond to the pre-Christian sun cycle of holidays - the solstices in summer and winter and the equinoxes in spring and fall and the midway points between each of these four," explained Sasho.

"Wouldn't that sort of thing have been frowned upon by the Orthodox Church?" Deb asked.

"It would, but it wouldn't necessarily lead to their end," suggested Borko. "There have been attempts at various times through the centuries by the church to root out paganism among the peasantry. But, as often as not, all it ever did was drive their activities underground."

"That being the case, the church would often choose to hold its own holidays on important pagan holidays," said Sasho.

"It makes sense that it was a way to supercede competing older religions," I agreed. "But it doesn't quite explain how this particular cult hung on the way it apparently has for thousands of years."

"No, it doesn't," agreed Borko. "The answers are back in Meshkom though. We must now go back there and confront that slippery *kmetinke*."

"Confront? No," I said. "The summer solstice is only a few days away. With the information supplied by our informant, we can catch him in the act. When I presume they celebrate this *Lita*. which sounds like the Celtic summer festival known as *Litha*."

"You're right," said Borko. "And perhaps our own word for summer, *leto*, is related to *Lita* and *Litha*," he added. He then looked at his watch and announced. "It is getting late. We had better get going."

As we stepped out into the dimly-lit parking lot, we were immediately surrounded by a group of six men in ski masks, brandishing pistols. They motioned us into a dark, windowless delivery truck that was parked alongside our van.

As the driver fired up the engine, several others trained their guns on us menacingly. No one spoke. Not even my garrulous colleague, who was rarely at a loss for words. Our captors made their wishes known chiefly through gestures.

We rode along in silence for what seemed like an hour. Eventually the driver pulled off the main road and guided the truck up a bumpy track in a wooded region far from any settlement.

When he finally drew the truck to a stop, we were ushered out into a dark secluded clearing in a woods. I trembled slightly and my knees felt weak as one of them bound the hands of each of us behind our backs and stuffed a cloth gag into our mouths.

We were led along a narrow footpath that led eventually to a wider path through the dark forest. I would occasionally stumble over an unseen tree root or stone in the path. Where could they be taking us, I wondered. I also experienced moments of regret that I hadn't resisted while we were still in the somewhat public space of the restaurant parking lot. But it had all happened so fast, and they had appeared so menacing with their masks and guns. Now it was too late.

After nearly a three hour climb we broke out of the forest and entered high mountain pasture land. Visibility was better here in the open. I could make out the dark, hazy outlines of clumps of vegetation, an occasional rock outcropping, and even small patches of snow that were hidden from the sun in shallow crevices.

Eventually we arrived at a stone-walled shepherd's hut with a corrugated metal roof. Other than the roof though, the structure could have been many hundreds of years old. The walls were low and thick. The mortar-less stonework was broken only by one narrow entrance way.

We were ushered inside. I had to stoop to avoid hitting my head. Once inside, one of them lit a kerosene lamp that flooded the small room with a pale, yellow light. It revealed a stone hearth and several beds constructed of woven willow branches and a small hand-hewn slab wood table.

Now I had a chance to study our captors a little. In addition to the woolen ski masks that hid all but their eyes and mouths, they wore baggy gray sweaters and dark blue work pants and military-issue black leather boots. Perhaps I studied them too hard for their liking, because the one assigned to me suddenly gave me a rough shove that sent me sprawling to the floor. When I tried to raise myself up again, he threatened to kick me as well.

The others were pushed into a circle on the floor alongside me. Then our captors left the hut. We sat there for some time, without a word. Though finally when our captors still showed no sign of returning, we began to whisper softly among ourselves.

My mind raced out of control as I considered our situation. It was possible, from some of what Borko and Sasho said, that this was some kind of politically-motivated hostage-taking. I couldn't help but think about the fate of the American hostages in Lebanon. Their years of confinement, often blindfolded and chained to some wall. Never seeing daylight or the outside world, or communicating with a fellow human being for long periods.

We made furtive attempts to undo each others bonds, with limited success. Eventually, however, over the course of the next several hours, we did manage to free each other.

Finally dawn arrived. Still, no one returned for us. But we were reluctant to venture outside the confines of the hut. One of us would occasionally risk a quick look around, out the door, but we were slow to venture any further.

Another hour passed and we heard the sound of approaching footsteps. Then a figure appeared in the doorway, brandishing an automatic rifle. Friend or foe? I had no way of knowing, but Borko seemed to know, because he began to talk excitedly to whoever stood over us with a rifle at the ready. A second man appeared and Borko, Sasho and the two men all engaged in a lively conversation.

The two were dressed in brown and grey-splashed military fatigues and caps. I was soon informed that they were members of a Macedonian border patrol, out on routine surveillance of the border with the adjoining former Yugoslavian province of Kosovo.

One, who held a small radio, had a brief conversation with someone over the air. I didn't understand any of what was said except for my name and those of my three colleagues. When we stepped outside the hut we were greeted by a grand view. Spectacular snow-covered peaks formed a wall to the west. To the east lay a vast meadow that sloped down and eventually ended in forest. Out beyond that lay a grand panoramic view of the broad floor of the Tetovo Polog Valley.

I could see half a dozen settlements scattered across the broad, flat valley. Each village was surrounded by a patchwork of garden plots, small fields, orchards and woodlots. The dull red tile roofs of individual houses could be made out in the village directly below, at the foot of the mountain.

The Macedonian soldiers guided us back down the mountain, until we arrived at another sheepfold, not unlike the one where we had spent the previous night. This one, however, appeared to be occupied. As we approached, two large, sturdy sheep dogs, nearly as big as wolves, with grey and black markings, rushed out to meet us.

Our guides halted, and one gave a loud call to the shepherd, who must have been somewhere nearby. The dogs had reached us by then and were barking and snarling at us rather ferociously. They circled the group of us, apparently looking for some opening for an attack. They were beautiful dogs, but we were in no position to admire them at the moment. We were each too busy following the dogs' movements in order to avoid getting bit. If one of the dogs approached a little too closely, one of the soldiers would threaten him, wielding his rifle like a club. Noble and beautiful perhaps, I thought to myself, but nasty beasts to intruders.

"These dogs are of a special breed, named after this mountain upon which they originate, the Shar planinec," explained Borko. "They have been bred specifically to serve as guard dogs to the sheep. They do not fear anything. They will fight off wolves and bears and human bandits, if need be."

Eventually the shepherd arrived and called off his dogs. They followed us at a short distance and continued to eye us suspiciously, despite our acceptance by their master.

The shepherd, a small, thin old man with a week's growth of beard, looked like someone out of a fairy tale. He wore the traditional grey felt skull cap of an Albanian Moslem man. He had a heavy grey felt cloak draped over his shoulders, and he wore baggy brown woolen trousers and a thick white homespun cotton shirt. He had rubber moccasins over thick hand-knit woolen socks on his feet. He leaned on a smooth, cream-colored wooden shepherd's staff with a crook at the end. One end of a hand-carved shepherd's flute poked out of one of his pockets.

Sasho noticed how Deb and I stared at the old man. "So you have never met an Albanian mountain shepherd before," he said. "They are one more somewhat mysterious ancient Balkan people. No one knows for certain just how long the Albanians, also known as Shiptars, have lived in these mountains. They have no direct linguistic or cultural link to any of their neighbors. Their homeland consists of rugged mountains that end in the jagged coastline of the Adriatic Sea. Unlike the Greeks, who took to the sea that surrounded them, reaching out to distant neighbors, the Albanians held themselves aloof from their neighbors. Their own mountain villages and families and clans preoccupied their attention. This has not always been a positive attention either, because blood feuds among rival clans have been common among them."

"Of more immediate interest to us, however," added Borko, "are the facts of their recent history. Two million Albanians in Albania proper, following World War Two, lived in harsh, Stalinist-communist isolation. The two million of their brothers who lived in neighboring Yugoslavia fared somewhat better, until the mid to late eighties that is, when President Slobodan Milosevic of Serbia made his career in politics by suppressing Albanian self-rule in Kosovo.

It was a center of medieval Serbian civilization, but few Serbs live there today, especially not since the time of the NATO war on behalf of the Kosovars."

"Yugoslav Albanians had the benefit of local political control of their communities, with much social and cultural freedom," added Sasho. "Unfortunately, they also have one of the highest birth-rates in all of Europe, thereby threatening their neighbors in Serbia and here in Macedonia with eventual population domination of the region. This has led to much ethnic strife. And this may very well account for our abduction yesterday."

After the old man had had a chance to stare at us, particularly the exotic *Amerikanci*, he invited us into his hut. Once inside he pulled out a large round of white, feta-type sheep milk cheese, a loaf of bread, some onions and a knife, and invited us to join him in a meal.

We ate ravenously after our long, sleepless night and the strenuous climb over the mountain. I don't know if it was merely the circumstances, my terrible hunger or what, but I've never enjoyed any meal, before or since, quite so much.

The old shepherd studied his uninvited guests carefully for a long time. Then he spoke, and Borko translated for Deb and me.

"There is a shepherd up here," he said, "who recently told me that a wolf came right up to the door of his hut. I suggested that it was probably just hungry and that he should feed it. The next day I saw him again, and asked him if he had taken my advice. He said, yes, he had. And? I asked. And today two wolves came to my door, he said."

We all laughed, and Borko murmured to me, "this old shepherd is crafty, I think."

After that we rose to leave. We thanked our host, and Borko received instructions from the soldiers on how to proceed on down the mountain on our own, and they departed in the opposite direction, the one from which we had just come.

As we walked I pulled up alongside Borko and asked, "Have there been other kidnappings here?"

He hesitated before finally saying, "There have been enough troubles."

"Tell me," I demanded.

At first Borko tried to ignore me, but finally he must have made up his mind. "Okay, I'll tell you," he said. "The old man back in that village yesterday told us a story I didn't want to share. It happened a while back. A very sad story."

He paused as if to collect his thoughts. "The old man said that Albanian men all clad in black and brandishing guns sent the poorly armed local policemen scurrying for cover. They succeeded in rallying the local Albanian young men to their cause.

They announced that all of the Macedonians must go, that this was now Ilirida, Albanian land, no longer part of "Slav Macedonia", as they call it. So the hundreds of Macedonians who lived there gathered up what little they could and fled on foot to safe refuges in the valley below."

I could tell that I was in for another one of Borko's long-winded stories about Macedonian victimization by cruel neighbors. An old story with hundreds of variations, as I had come to learn.

"It did not seem to matter" he declared in a voice choked with emotion, "that that village had been the site two years before that of a camp where ten thousand old people, women and children had found refuge after fleeing war-torn Kosovo. Nor did it deter these 'liberators' that a written document of that place, a Turkish census from the 15th century described a small Macedonian village, and that the first Albanian family settled there a hundred and fifty years ago. The Turkish census of 1900 showed over 80 Macedonian families and only 20 Albanian households. Large families had finally led to near equal numbers a hundred years later.

Some of the decent ones from among their Albanian neighbors tried to hide some of their Macedonian friends, but after a while they urged them to leave for fear of the consequences."

My mind was beginning to wander now, but I tried to listen to his long-winded recitation politely.

"A few people though, "he continued, "couldn't bear to leave. 'Better risk death' they said 'than to lose everything.' And it would only be years later that anyone would learn their fate."

Local tv and newspapers reported the news that their homes had been looted and burned along with their churches and their bakeries and small textile factories, and land mines laid in their fields."

Why hadn't I heard anything about all of this before? Wasn't it because after nearly a decade of ugly fighting in the Balkans few Americans paid much attention to news of fighting over there.

He turned to me then to make sure that he had my full attention, and when he continued, his voice had a strangled quality to it. "At that time we Macedonians thought that it would be enough to simply follow U.S. and Western European advice to open up our society, privatize state-run businesses and open a parliament and fashion a constitution to match that of our big brothers in the West. We had listened and had tried our best to learn from the several thousand American advisors, the economists, the agronomists and the parliamentarians, and most of all from the NATO military advisors, who had told us, 'You don't need an army, a few border guards will do, since you've got us to take care of you now.'

But it didn't work out that way when Albanian separatist guerillas decided to ethnically cleanse Macedonian villages in northern and western Macedonia. There was no Macedonian army to defend them. And when we turned to NATO for help, they supplied us with a couple of negotiators to see about coming to terms with the rebels."

He sighed, and then continued in a hushed tone. "And so they negotiated, Macedonian and Albanian politicians under the guidance of Francois Leotard from France and James Pardew from the USA. For several months they negotiated additional use of the Albanian language in public life, more Albanian policemen, and a constitutional change that made ours a state of all the citizens of the Republic of Macedonia instead of the state of the Macedonian people, unlike the constitutions of all of our nationalistic Balkan neighbors, and granted amnesty to those who took up arms for their cause."

His voice rose again. His anger barely under control as he continued. "We agreed to the changes, in the name of peace and maybe some social justice. Eventually people did return to repaired homes in many of the villages.

We accepted reality. There would have been no money or entry into Europe for the beggars of this one more broken Balkan former socialist state if we would have decided to use what little we had to buy more guns to defend ourselves."

He glared at me angrily now, as if I might be personally responsible for their misery. "Macedonian poverty and helplessness stood in such contrast to American superpower, and yet, Macedonian sympathy was sincere when your people suffered the attacks of September 11. The leaders of the Great Powers have never admitted to the ugly consequences, the collateral damage in Macedonia of their operations in Kosovo that had encouraged Albanian ambitions to create a Greater Albanian state. As a result many village people have suffered and some have lost their ancestral homes forever in northwestern Macedonia. That couple we met were two of just a few elderly Macedonian people who remain in that village."

I tried to ignore his accusing tone and move the conversation along. After all, I hadn't been anywhere nearby at the time or even been aware of any of what he had just described. There must have been at least a dozen similar ethnic religious conflicts going on in the world at the time. How could the average American expect to keep track of them all? And if they had been spared the terrible war devastation that had occurred to the north by agreeing to even a peace plan with flaws, weren't they far better off than Jews and Palestinians or Iraqis or Afghanis who had not proven so capable of compromise? But I didn't say any of this to Borko. "Do you have any idea what our abductors may have wanted from us?" I asked.

"No, I really don't. And I'm not so convinced that they were Albanians in this case."

"Why not?"

"Well, there are others who are interested in us. As I told you earlier," he replied. And again my normally long-winded colleague had no more to say on the subject.

We finally made our way back to the van in the parking lot of the Baba Tekija Restaurant by late morning. The sun was already beating down on us rather unmercifully. We were all tired and dirty and drenched in sweat, as well.

Borko paused to think for a moment, then he said, "I know a short-cut back to Marvintsi from here."

Instead of heading east again toward Skopje we drove south, passing through the predominantly Albanian towns of Gostivar and Debar. The road wound through narrow mountain gorges. Borko executed the numerous hairpin turns at break-neck speed.

I was so tired by then, however, that I slept through most of it. Yet, I wasn't the only one feeling more than a bit queasy when the mountains finally gave way to a broad plain that ended in the towns of Struga and Ohrid on the shores of Lake Ohrid.

"It's getting a bit late," said Borko as we approached the town of Ohrid. "We'd better find ourselves a place to stay for the night."

Some short-cut I thought, as we searched for a hotel. Fortunately it was not the busy season yet, so we readily found rooms for the night at one of the numerous hotels.

After a quick shower and a change into some clean clothes, I almost felt human again. I could have easily collapsed into bed about then, but we decided to go off together in search of a meal. Borko led us down a pleasant, tree-lined boulevard that followed the waterfront to the old town center. We found a little restaurant there that served the local specialty, Lake Ohrid trout with rice.

After the meal Borko proposed that we take a little shortcut back to the hotel. I was beginning to suspect that Borko and I didn't share the same definition of the word "shortcut." He led us up a narrow cobblestone street that continued to follow the coastline. It was lined with houses built in the style of the old Macedonian town architecture. The stuccoed walls, framed by wooden beams, hung further out into the street with each successive story.

We passed the 10th century Orthodox Church of Saint Sophia, a large, weathered gray stone building with the usual red tile roof and graceful low bell tower cupolas at each end in the traditional Byzantine style. Then we climbed a small, rocky promontory, past a lovely but much smaller medieval Orthodox church, this one dedicated to Saint John Kaneo, that perched on a narrow ledge some hundred feet above the lake.

The blue water of the broad lake sparkled in the late afternoon sunshine. A distant, smoky range of blue-gray mountains circled the lake. The far shore, the property of Albania, some thirty miles away, appeared only as an indistinct line that faded into the gray mists.

We climbed from there up a steep hillside through a pine grove that contained the excavated remains of a Greco-Roman palace. Portions of stone walls and sections of decorative mosaic floor tile with figures of deer and fern fronds lay exposed to passersby. There seemed to be no foot of ground in this land that didn't bear some evidence of long, successive ages of human habitation.

By the time we reentered the uppermost reaches of the town, I was feeling nearly bone-tired. How I ever got talked into a second one of Borko's short-cuts in one day, I'll never know. But finally we arrived at the grassy crest of the broad hill-top. An old stone fortress encircled the crest of the hill. We climbed the earthen berm that had accumulated at the base of the crumbling walls, and scaled the ragged, half-tumbled southern-most wall.

My legs felt like leaden weights by the time I finally managed to pull myself up the last few feet of the wall and stood alongside my colleagues. The view that greeted me almost made up for the pain in my calves and feet.

From here we could see the entire town spread out below us and most of the valley and the lake ringed by mountains.

"This fortress was built by Tsar Samuel at the end of the tenth century," explained Sasho. "But he and his army came to a bad end at the hands of their Greek enemies." And he looked in Deb's direction as he said this.

"There are quite a few churches down there, aren't there," I said, in a deliberate attempt to steer the conversation in another direction.

"I suppose there are," said Borko. "But in Tsar Samuel's time they say there were 365 churches in Ohrid. One for every day of the year."

"Too bad his soldiers could no longer see the beautiful churches," said Sasho.

"Why not?" asked Deb.

"Because the Greek Emperor Basil the Second had ordered that fifteen thousand of Tsar Samuel's soldiers that he captured should be blinded before being sent home!"

"A grisly act committed over a thousand years ago, and you tell it as if it were a crime committed by your neighbors last week!" said Deb as she put her head down and plunged on down the hill ahead of us.

That monstrous crime may have occurred long ago, but recent events suggested that the Balkans were still a place where groups engaged in fierce and often brutal competition. What on earth had made me think that an archaeology project would somehow be immune to the Balkan disease?

I was awakened the next morning by a god-awful pounding at my hotel room door. The next thing I heard was Borko's cheerful voice calling me to come down to breakfast. When I finally dragged myself downstairs, there was Borko, chipper as ever, even after our late-night boozing in the hotel bar.

I decidedly was not. I ate my breakfast in sullen silence. Though finally I asked, "And where are our colleagues?"

"Oh, I thought I should let the young people rest."

"You what?" I gasped.

"But it's Sunday morning and you and I should go to church. So hurry up and finish your food, so that we can get going."

"Church?" I repeated, as Borko led me out the hotel door.

The air was cool and sweet, with a faint breeze off the water. The lake birds were noisily cackling over their breakfasts. We proceeded up the main street, then up a steep side street to the gates of the little fourteenth century Church of Saint Nicholas. As we passed through the narrow portal of the church and entered the main room I could see about seventy five of the faithful of all ages, though many more women than men, participating in the Orthodox church service in progress.

The priest, who stood on a slightly raised platform before the assembled throng, was a bearded old patriarch in a purple and gold trimmed robe of white satin. He chanted in a deep baritone that was answered by a chorus of harmonious men's voices, somewhere up front. The Church Slavic used in the service, an archaic church language like the

Latin of the Catholic Church, put me in mind of ancient mysteries beyond easy comprehension.

Were the people of the village of Meshkom really a party to ancient mysteries? Or merely to uncommon thievery? Who could really say. Here today I was witness to rituals and ceremonies that were nearly two millennia old, so what made me so sure that even older traditions weren't alive and well in at least one remote mountain village of this ancient land?

But another part of my brain was urging caution. If something seems rather unbelievable about it, it probably is. After all, what did I really know? Only what my Macedonian guides chose to tell me, and I suspected that they might have reasons to perpetrate an elaborate fraud.

How certain was I that any of the ancient treasure was real. That the objects we first encountered weren't also manufactured recently? But why? For money? For fame? To bolster tenuous national claims to an ancient name?

As I looked around me now I could see that the church was lit by hundreds of small beeswax candles burning on metal stands. They provided a gentle illumination for the native earth colors, the umbers and ochres of the frescoes of Christ, His apostles, and Christian saints in the performance of miracles, that adorned every inch of wall and ceiling space.

"Our Moslem neighbors regard all of these portrayals of the Saints and Christ as heretical," Borko whispered to me as we worked our way toward the front of the church. "Because the art of the Moslem world consists only of geometric patterns," he furthered explained.

It was not hard to imagine that such naive extravagance as these wall paintings was the work of people related to my colleague, Borko. They somehow matched or fitted his own colorful style and guileless nature. Did I really imagine that Borko was capable of some grand deception?

Occasionally the priest would wave his censor and little bells would chime and a wave of sweet incense would pour across the room. The service was a divine feast for all of the senses.

Though I must admit that I had a bit of trouble at first getting used to the spontaneity of the church-goers. At any given moment various members of the congregation might decide to go pay a visit to the icon of a favorite saint in some corner or other of the church.

Borko surprised me when he too joined the restless congregation roaming about the church. He lit a candle and carried it over and placed it in the stand in front of an icon of Saint Nicholas. He made the sign of the cross, murmured a little prayer, then kissed the glass that protected the saint's image, before returning to my side. Was this a man who stole ancient treasures or who was capable of such artful deception?

After the service we returned to the hotel where we picked up Sasho and Deb and the van. Borko headed us south again, along the shore of the lake.

I assumed that we were finally headed back to Marvintsi as I watched the dry, rocky, steeply sloping shoreline skim by out my window. Somehow the local village people managed to coax a remarkable variety and abundance of fruits and vegetables out of the poor soil here. All along the way I could see little pastures with small, sun-bleached haystacks and orchards with apple and plum trees, grapevines and plots of tomatoes, cabbage, potatoes and onions. Small herds of cattle, goats and sheep, with an occasional horse or donkey, roamed the sparsely vegetated brown hillside meadows dotted with scrub oak and weedy herbs.

The road ended abruptly about 30 kilometers down the lakeshore at the Albanian border. A monastery had been built here at the site of a cool, shaded mouth of a clear mountain stream. Why did Borko insist on stopping at every religious shrine in Macedonia before returning us to Marvintsi?

He urged us out of the van and led the way into the monastery. It was cool and dark inside the old church in the center of the monastery compound. The thick stone walls kept the heat of the bright Mediterranean sun banished to the out of doors. As my eyes finally adjusted to the dim light, I had to grudgingly concede that this church contained some of the finest medieval frescoes I had ever seen in the Balkans.

Vivid scenes from the 'medieval' version of the life of Christ and imposing figures of church patriarchs greeted us at every turn. Borko guided us to a small chapel that had been erected in a small room in one corner of the church. There was a weathered gray marble sarcophagous in the center of the room.

"Here lies one of Macedonia's most important early church fathers," said Borko as he waved his arm in a broad flourish at the grave site. "Back in the year 860 AD the Byzantine Emperor Michael sent two monks, brothers from Solun, the Greek Thessaloniki, to convert the heathen Slavs to Christianity."

"I'm afraid they missed a few over in the village of Meshkom," said Deb.

Borko frowned at the interruption and, almost without missing a beat, he continued, "The brothers Cyril and Methodius, whose father was Greek and whose mother was a Slav, were well-educated for the times. They were able to devise an alphabet suitable for the Slavic tongue, and they set about translating liturgical texts from Greek into Slavic. Versions of this alphabet are today known as Cyrillic after Saint Cyril."

Now Borko circled the room pointing at various pictures of bearded patriarchs. "The two brothers gathered a small circle of Slav disciples around them and set off to convert the heathen Slavs," he explained. "But almost immediately they ran into great difficulties in their work. The Slavs were willing, but they had competition from the German clergy, who thought that the sacred texts should only be available to believers in the traditional Latin, Greek or Hebrew. The brothers and their disciples were hounded and persecuted and eventually, upon the deaths of their teachers, the disciples were driven out of more northerly Slav lands by the Latin clergy."

"Several of those disciples of Cyril and Methodius ended up in Bulgaria and Macedonia. And among them were Kliment and Naum, who came to Ohrid and settled. Here they founded a monastery in 900 AD, and a school to train priests. It had some 3000 students."

"So how come they didn't succeed in converting the people of Meshkom?" asked Deb.

"Good question," said Borko. "Though we don't know for sure that they are not also practitioners of Christianity."

"Oh, you mean pagans only in their spare time," said Deb.

"You might say that," said Borko with a scowl. "As I was saying, now, this is the grave of Naum." He pointed at the grave again. Then he swept his hand across the room. "And these frescoes painted on the wall behind the grave depict scenes from the lives of Kliment and Naum and miracles that they performed that earned them sainthood."

What is more miraculous, I wondered, that the two churchmen managed to convert so many heathen Slavs or the fact that a few managed to survive the process? As we finally drove east again in the direction of Marvintsi, I thought about the past day and a half. We had probably needed that little vacation in Ohrid. But I also had a feeling that we were on the verge of entering a world that was alien to the traditions that most Macedonians were raised with. Perhaps Borko had wanted to return for a moment to his Orthodox Church culture and its deep roots in his society, in order to get his bearings, so to speak, before we embarked on a journey in to the strange world of those pagan mountain folk.

Who were the Pelasgi, from whom according to Herodotus the Greeks borrowed the gods? The ethnic origin of the Pelasgi has not been determined. Herodotus, who was their contemporary, firmly believed that they were not Greek and spoke a language unfamiliar to the Greeks. Herodotus also wrote about the hostilities between the Greeks and the Pelasgi. According to Herodotus, the Pelasgi also lived in Macedonia, in the region of Crestonia.

from *The Descendants of Alexander the Great of Macedon* by Aleksandar Donski

Chapter 7 – some answers at last

Borko and I and our assistants rose before dawn. We ate our breakfasts in the van on the way to Meshkom. Still under the cover of darkness we hid the van in a small wood on the edge of the village and made our way to the top of a hillock overlooking a small open air amphitheatre. The student, Iskra, had described how she and other village children had spied on their elders from this same spot in the past. It was an ideal place to see without being seen.

Perhaps another hour passed before our sleepy crew was startled into wakefulness by the appearance, out of the hazy gray pre-dawn light, of a line of ghost-like figures. At the head of a long procession was a figure dressed in white robes and a dark crown of leaves. He carried a pair of short, stout pieces of wood that he would strike together every so often, creating a rhythm for the pace of the procession.

The hundred or so people who trailed behind him also had summer foliage, and some of the women had flower blossoms woven into their hair as well. The entire procession, once they had completed their entrance, numbered several hundred. They assembled themselves in a semi-circle around a great flat stone before the figure in white.

The white-robed priest had stationed himself in front of the stone, and he was now busily arranging a set of smaller stones into some kind of more or less symmetrical pattern atop the larger stone. After he had completed this task, he stepped back from his "altar" and simply waited in silence along with the others.

About ten minutes passed before the first rays of the rising sun glinted on the uneven surfaces of the stonework. At the moment of their arrival the priest gave a shout that was taken up by the others. The eyes of our hidden crew of observers widened at the sight of the priest, now clearly fitted with a glittering golden mask with a set of spike-like rays framing his round face. It dazzled and nearly blinded everyone who gazed upon it, just as it would if they had stared directly into the rising sun.

The priest then proceeded to chant something, first while facing into the dawn, then he did the same while facing west, then south, and finally north. At each direction he held his arms aloft in a gesture of greeting as he spoke.

"What did he say?" I whispered to Borko.

"I'm not quite sure," he whispered back. Then he turned to Sasho. The two of them conferred for a moment, and he turned back to face me again. "Sasho thinks it is that language again, on the scroll. He thinks it was some kind of calling of the spirits of earth, air, fire and water, each associated with one of the four directions."

"I feel like I'm right there at Stonehenge, three thousand years ago, witnessing the summer rite," murmured Joel as he took a series of pictures through a break in the foliage.

"Keep your voice down!" I hissed at him. It would be just like Joel to screw things up, I thought. And just when we seemed to be getting somewhere.

I thought that I saw the priest look our way momentarily, but as quickly, he returned to his duties before the assembled.

Our crew remained hidden until the ceremony concluded and the people returned to their village by the way they had come. Then we returned to the van and drove back to camp.

That evening as the sliver of a waxing moon rose above our heads, we sat around the campfire and discussed our next move. As the fire died down and the crew lingered for a last while, I couldn't resist saying, "It seems so utterly fantastic." I shifted my gaze from one person to the next around the circle as I spoke. "That these people have apparently maintained some unbroken tradition of pagan rituals that date back who knows how many thousands of years."

"So do you still think that this is all some elaborate hoax?" Sasho asked Deb, point blank. His chin pointed at her like an accusing finger as he fixed her in a steady gaze, awaiting her answer.

She was momentarily taken aback, since neither of them had ever acknowledged Sasho's eavesdropping on our conversation. But she finally said, "Whatever gave you that idea? Have I ever said any such thing to you?"

Sasho's eyes shifted slightly to left and right to see if his credibility with the others had suffered as a result. "It's no secret is it?" And he glanced over at me as he said this, as if I would want to corroborate the truth of this.

"I admit that some incredible things have happened since we've been here, as Professor Starkweather just said." She nodded in my direction as she said this. "And some of these things have strained my belief."

"Then you should go home. Where life is not so incredible. In the shopping malls and ranch homes. Where everything is simple. No doubt about who is who, or what they know or have done," said Sasho as he rose from the circle, apparently in pursuit of the last word before retiring for the night.

Deb flushed. It was the first time Sasho had ever alluded to the doubts she had confided to me a while back. And it stung doubly so because he had been one of the few who had shown her some degree of sympathy when Borko had unjustly accused her. She struggled to hold back a tear. She was determined not to make a show of her distress, that was, in any case, obvious to all.

Borko acted as if he hadn't noticed anything unusual about her behavior. Who could be sure with Borko? Maybe he simply didn't notice anything not directly concerning him. In any case, Borko announced, "It's time that we got to bed. We have made our plans for tomorrow. So til tomorrow, *dobra noch*, good night." And he rose to go and others slowly followed his lead.

One by one they drifted off, receding into the dim rectangular shapes of their tents that glowed dully in the colorless moonlight. Eventually only Deb and I remained by the dying fire, our features blurred and softened by the pale moonlight.

I had sensed that Deb was lingering in hopes of a private talk between us. She spoke first. "Professor Starkweather. Maybe I should return to the states. We're no longer involved in an excavation, and I really don't seem to have a role to play in this drama with the people of Meshkom." She shrugged her shoulders and kept her eyes fixed on the fire. "I don't even know their language. And it seems as if I've stirred up some things I shouldn't have."

I searched her face for clues to her state of mind. Discouragement, obvious distress, but there was the usual intensity to her gaze. This young woman had her power. I avoided thoughts that might cast doubts on my professionalism or dedication to my work.

"I hope you'll stick around, in any case," I finally said, averting my own eyes to the fast-fading embers of the fire. "Who can say where all this may eventually lead, or who will or will not be needed before its over."

I hesitated, searching for the right words. "If you decide to go, I'll understand, but I hope you won't be chased away by some of the insensitive things some of the others say. If you really intend to survive and thrive in our profession, you'll need to have a pretty thick skin. Hopefully not as thick as Borko's... but you know what I mean."

It appeared as if she might want to say more. I secretly hoped that she did want to spend a little more time with me here by the fire in the moonlight. But then she rose to go. I followed. Suddenly she reached out her arms and enfolded me in a hug.

She was considerably shorter than me, so her head nuzzled into my shoulder. As I felt her soft curves against me I moved to return the hug. But she as quickly broke away, smiled rather sheepishly and murmured, "Thanks," as she bolted for her tent.

I barely had time to say the words, "Good night," before she was gone.

I had been so tempted to try and draw her into something more intimate between us. But something made me hesitate. I didn't want to use my young assistant that way. "Damn scruples," I muttered to myself as I started for my tent.

Though another part of my brain told me that that had actually been about all the intimacy with her that I was comfortable with, another reason to be relieved at the time that she had bolted the way she did.

The next morning after breakfast, the crew again piled into the van and we headed for Meshkom, Deb included. "I almost feel like I'm part of a commuter van pool these days," declared Joel, as he opened a copy of the New York Times that I had brought from Skopje.

All of the sudden Joel let out an audible gasp. "Would you look at this!" he said. "Here's an article about us. It's entitled, 'Who's fooling whom?" And he proceeded to read aloud, "A joint US-Skopje archaeology team recently uncovered what they claim to be the long-lost tomb of Alexander the Great. Unfortunately, however, the entire contents of the so-called tomb of Alexander have been proven to consist of fakes of recent manufacture. The archaeologists in charge of this project have suggested that the original artifacts from the tomb were somehow spirited out and replaced by replicas during the early stages of excavation of the site. Predictably, this rather unlikely story has been greeted with skepticism by the scientific community."

He folded the paper on his lap. "Guess who wrote that." And he paused for emphasis. "Our journalist buddy, Mavros."

No one responded. What was there to say?

Upon our arrival in Meshkom, we dispersed in pairs to various parts of the village. Some crew members visited the grocer's shop, others sat by the village fountain, while others still went to the village church. When Sasho was paired up with Deb again, as usual, she showed no visible reaction. She's a survivor, I thought, as I watched them go off together.

Borko and I again sought out the mayor. This whole process was becoming almost routine for us, and the villagers were also almost coming to expect our presence among them.

However, this time when we regrouped at the van, later that day, we did have some things to report to each other. "The priest was really upset by our description of the ceremony yesterday," reported Rada. "He told us that he did not take part in it, and that he would not have approved of such things," she added.

Then she turned and looked to Joel, as if for confirmation of her words, since he had accompanied her to the church. He scratched his nose and appeared to fumble around for something to add. "Tell them what he said about local folk rituals."

She thought for a moment and said, "He said that he had only seen the usual little folk rituals and superstitions here. Those that survive from old traditions. You know, things like reading the coffee grounds, or wearing a garlic clove, or healing yourself with basil leaf."

"The grocer was not so quiet today," announced Sasho. "He reacted to our news by also denying that he had ever taken part in such a ceremony. And when I said that Joel had taken pictures that would help prove his story, he got very upset, and he told us to get out of his store."

"I've never seen him so angry," said Deb.

"I received the same reaction from the mayor," reported Borko. "It was the first time he failed to be calm with me. He denied that he had led such a ceremony, and when I said that we had taken pictures, he told me that they must be fakeries." He paused and glanced at me, frowned and continued. "I did not like the sound of his final words. When I suggested that he tell us who and what this cult is all about, or we would expose them publicly, he warned me not to threaten him, and he said that two could play at that game."

"Well, I would say that we have some movement, and we'll just have to see how it all plays out in the days ahead," I said.

That night I awoke from a deep sleep to the sound of footsteps outside the tent that I shared with Joel and one of the student crew members. Then I heard the sound of collapsing canvas and felt rather than saw the fabric enfold me in its embrace. The next moment I felt a heavy weight descend on my body, pinning me to the cot.

I fought with all my strength to break free, but it was no use. My arms were pinned to my sides and the weight on my chest made breathing difficult.

A momentary panic swept over me, and when I heard muffled cries from the neighboring beds, I too joined in, shouting for all I was worth.

Almost as quickly as it had come, the attack receded. There was the sound of ripping fabric and a clatter as someone rummaged through our possessions. This was followed by the sound of running and then of car doors slamming and engines revving up, and finally the squeal of car tires as they raced off. Now I could hear shouts coming from the other tents.

Suddenly the canvas rose up and Borko appeared at the entrance of our tent with a flashlight in one hand and a stout piece of wood in the other. "Are you alright?" he asked, as he and several others raised the tent poles back into place.

"I'm ok," I responded in a rather hoarse voice.

"Me too," said Joel, sounding winded, as if he had just run a race. "That was some nightmare I was having."

Only our tent-mate reported any injury. It seems he'd received a bloody nose during the attack. When Borko flashed his light on him, I could see that he lay on his back with a wad of tissue paper pressed to his nose.

Once we got a lantern going we were able to assess the damage to our tent and possessions. There was a gaping hole torn open in one corner of the tent. Joel's camera had been cracked open and the film was gone. So was the satchel that contained all of the film he'd shot in recent days.

We put things back in order as best we could, but no one was prepared to go back to bed right away. The crew members crowded into our tent and each one found a place, as best they could, to sit in the narrow space.

"So it must have been our friends from Meshkom," I said. "It was foolish of us not to take a few precautions. We should have kept our guard up."

"But we hadn't really stirred up the nest over in Meshkom until yesterday," said Joel.

"There is another thing I must tell you though," said Borko. "I recognized a car engine from among the sounds of your attackers running away. There is a certain Greek journalist who owns a car that makes that engine sound that I heard." He turned and glanced in Deb's direction as he spoke.

Deb was quick to respond, "Well, he's staying over at the Galeb Hotel over in Valandovo," she said. "So why don't you go pay him a visit, if you're so sure that he was involved!"

"A good idea," I said. "It's almost dawn. Maybe we can meet him for a little talk over breakfast."

"If he has been up to what I think he has, then he is liable to have built up an appetite," said Borko.

"You'll come with us, won't you, Deb?" I asked.

She hesitated at first, then nodded her assent. So it was decided that Borko, Sasho, Deb and I would set off for Valandovo and Joel and the others would watch over the camp in our absence.

As we drove, the yellow orb of the sun peeked over the distant ragged, gray ridge of the Belasitsa Mountains to the east. Deb appeared on edge. She stared out at the passing countryside and barely said three words the entire way there. I was relieved that neither Borko nor Sasho chose to make any references to her past history with Mavros.

The more I thought about it though, the more I was troubled by the raid on our camp. How did they know exactly where to find Joel's camera and film? Who had helped them? Mavros? Or did they have friends among Borko's crew, or more likely still, Dr. Misirkova's?

We reached the town just as the shops were beginning to open for morning business. In this warm climate shopkeepers preferred to start their day early, and many even took an afternoon break, and reopened again in the evening. But instead of stopping somewhere for coffee or food, we drove directly to the hotel where Deb thought Mavros was staying.

As we approached the hotel, we could see Mavros' VW parked out front. Borko felt the hood. It was still warm. He said to Deb, in about as casual a voice as he could muster, "When was the last time you saw Mavros?"

"I haven't..." she began, when I interrupted her. "She's been with us every day and every evening for the past three weeks."

"I just wanted to know if..." asked Borko. But again I broke in, "I know what you wanted to know, and she hasn't seen him. Isn't that right, Deb?" And she nodded her agreement.

"Well that's all I wanted to know," insisted Borko as we climbed down out of the van.

There was no one at the desk at that hour, so we followed Deb up to the room where Mavros had been staying. Borko knocked at the door and a voice responded from within, asking who it was. No one said anything, but a few seconds later the door opened a crack and then began to close again as quickly.

Borko wrenched at the door and managed with one great shove to thrust his considerable bulk into the room. The rest of us quickly slipped in behind him.

Mavros retreated from the door to the far side of the room and glared at his uninvited guests. Borko stood over him, clenching and unclenching his fists, menacingly. "So, have you been out recently, Mavros?" asked Borko.

"What do you want?" croaked Mavros.

"Did you visit our camp last night?" I demanded to know.

"Why should I do that?" asked Mavros.

"Yes, why should you do that?" demanded Borko as he began to close in on him.

"Yes, why should I?" Mavros shouted defiantly, though he retreated a step or two before Borko's looming form.

"Don't play with us!" roared Borko. "We know that you drove to our camp along with the people who attacked Professor Starkweather and his students."

He drew even closer to the Greek journalist now, who braced himself for an imminent blow.

"Stop it!" shouted Deb. "Leave him alone, Borko! You don't know for sure that he had anything to do with this." This caused Borko to back off a bit. It was not lost on him that this was the first time Deb had ever addressed him by his first name rather than the courteous title "Professor Milevski."

Mavros turned to Deb now, "Okay, I will tell you what I did and didn't do last night. Yes, I did drive my car to your camp last night. But I was following the people who attacked you!"

"Explain!" I demanded.

Mavros glanced back and forth from face to face, to see if we believed him, as he recounted how he had followed our team to the village of Meshkom several weeks ago. And once we had departed, he had begun his own interrogation of the village people. Though they had apparently been no more forthcoming to him than they had been to our archaeology crew.

He described how he had tried again on several other occasions to break through their wall of silence, but with a similar lack of success. And last night he had managed to follow the mayor of Meshkom and his friends to our camp.

"If I were writing fiction, it would be a fine tale. Theft of all the authentic artifacts from the tomb that you've been telling everyone about. But since my field is journalism, all I can do is laugh. But I still don't understand how these villagers fit into all of this," said the journalist. "And that is why I have been visiting them."

"So tell us exactly what you have learned about them," demanded Sasho.

"After a good deal of effort, I managed to bribe one old fellow from the village into talking to me. But he told me an utterly ridiculous tale. Something about how the mayor's family is from an ancient people of Macedonia, those called Pelasgians. People who have been so lost to history that some say they are only myth."

Mavros seemed to relax a bit. He leaned an elbow on the desk to his side and gestured with his free hand as he spoke.

"He claimed that the tomb is real. That after the death of Alexander, his mother had brought her son's remains here in order to protect them from his power-hungry generals.

He also claimed that the mayor's ancestors had sworn to protect the tomb. He said that the mayor belonged to a cult, whose ancient secrets have been passed down from generation to generation. So he claimed, anyway. But this would mean an unbroken tradition of guardians, for almost 3000 years.

It was all so utterly improbable that I have not even bothered to transcribe the notes I took." Mavros laughed as he said this.

"So you assume that he was lying to you?" asked Borko, relaxing a bit himself now.

"Even if there are some shreds of truth to his story, do you really think that I could print such a story, without being laughed out of Greece?" He was smiling now.

"Probably not," said Borko, not exactly smiling, but no longer glowering now. But then he suddenly turned grim again. "I must tell you though. Your car was seen at the site of a crime. The authorities are likely to want to question you about this."

Mavros grew solemn as well. His smile gave way to a troubled frown. He searched for a cigarette in the desk drawer. Once he found one, he struck a match and lit the cigarette. He drew nervous puffs from it as he said, "I didn't consider that."

"I think that we can be of help," I said. "What do you say to coming with us to the village today to confront the thugs who raided our camp last night?" I looked to Borko as I said this, for some sign of his consent to the idea.

"Yes, I'll do that," Mavros agreed. And Borko gestured his approval at the same time.

We left Mavros to get ready for the trip, while we went off in search of some breakfast. Once we were settled at a table in a small pastry shop, with large quarter pieces of the local strudel dough cheese pie, called *burek*, and a glass of liquid yogurt in front of each of us, we began to discuss strategy.

"So you think that Mavros' presence in the village could make for better chances of cooperation from the villagers?" Borko said between bites.

"It might at that," I said. "The fact that he's an eye-witness to their attack might force them to cooperate."

"It might just mean that he'll have one more person they need to try and frighten away," said Sasho. "And how do we know that the Greek isn't lying to us? The villagers couldn't have known where to find the camera and film, without some insider help." He glanced over at Deb as he said this, who stared right back at him.

"It might just force the mayor to make a confession, once he sees us together with Mavros," I suggested, trying to direct the conversation away from the hotter topic Sasho had hinted at.

"But then again, he might have expected us to contact with Mavros. Maybe he wants us to see just how doubtful all of this will sound to people who don't know all that we know," said Borko.

"It's possible," I said. "But even in that case, he'll be surprised if we come to him in the company of this skeptical journalist." I paused to wipe a few crumbs from my chin, then continued. "But this is where things get harder to predict. We can't be certain how either man will act. They are both unknowns to us."

"Mavros is no stranger to her!" said Sasho, pointing to Deb. "She has even been to his room."

Deb glared at him. "What are you trying to say, Sasho? That I must have slept with him? Is that what you're trying to say?"

"I'm just saying that you know more about him than any of the rest of us."

"That's not all you implied," she responded with fury. "And one answer to your implied question is, better with him than you!"

There was an awkward silence. Finally I said as gently as possible, "It would be helpful to know, Deb, whether he really meant what he said. You know, about the story the village man told him. Does he really believe that it's all a fiction?"

She paused, then with a slightly troubled look, she said, "Yes, I believe he does. He suspects that this whole thing is a big hoax. By people who want to promote the belief that the present-day people of the Republic of Macedonia are descendants of the ancient Macedonians."

"That's a lie!" roared Borko.

"The disappearance of the artifacts," she continued in the same steady voice, "only fed his suspicions, because it meant that the whole story of Alexander's burial here depends on the flimsiest of physical evidence."

"Let the blind fool believe whatever he likes. Our people are already publishing photos of the tomb," said Borko.

"And then when everything disappeared from the tomb, it strained our credibility with people all over, not just in Greece," argued Deb.

"So you're one of those who think that we would create such a hoax in order to claim some false kinship with the first Macedonians," said Sasho.

"I have my suspicions, that that is possible, yes," replied Deb.

"It is not as if it is new to suggest ancient settlement of proto-Slavic people in the Balkans," said Borko. "The German linguist Passof back in 1815 determined that Homer's Iliad, in its oldest known text, contains any number of words of likely proto-Slavic origin."

"And a Russian scholar, Genady Grinevich, recently published a study suggesting a link between Old Slavic and the language of ancient Balkan peoples. And there is the recent work of a new generation of our own Macedonian historians who are finding some very convincing cultural links between present-day Macedonians and the ancient peoples- legends, customs and rituals and speech passed down through the ages. But we've never, until now, had such proof of the connections of the ancient peoples- the Pelasgians, the Brygians, the Veneti, and the others who lived on ancient Macedonian soil, to people of Macedonia alive today," added Sasho.

"You see what you're doing?" Deb wagged a finger that dripped oily bits of pastry shell at Sasho as she spoke. "You take evidence that suggests only possibilities, and you present it as if it were some sort of convincing proof of something!"

"And there have been others as well, who have suggested these things to us, even before our discoveries," said Borko. "But now we have the much more convincing proof."

'Had,' I said to myself. The two Macedonians turned to me now, as if I could be the wise arbiter. It was a role I'd rather not have thrust upon me. But I offered a suggestion, "Let's focus on the immediate problem. We want our visit to Meshkom with this Greek journalist to work to our advantage. Open doors. Loosen some tongues."

I seemed to have their attention now. All eyes focused on me, and no one else moved to speak. "Our problem, as I see it, is how to use his presence to show that we know all about their raid on our camp." I swallowed a bite of pie and continued. "We could include something from Mavros's interview with one of the villagers. To get them to open up."

I paused again and took another bite as I thought my way through this. "Then again, Mavros could work against this result if he decides to laugh in their faces at anything else they tell us."

"I could stay close to his side and keep him in line," suggested Borko.

"Yeah, threaten to beat the heck out of him!" Deb mocked.

"Perhaps you would rather seduce him out of problematic behavior," said Sasho.

Deb knit her brow in a quick frown. I braced myself for the inevitable explosion, but it never came. Instead, she just turned away.

"We'll all try to keep Mavros from saying or doing anything that would discourage our hosts from opening up to us. Agreed?" I asked. And the others nodded their assent.

Some of the characters from the so-called "Greek mythology" were Phrygians (descendants of the Balkan tribe Brygians in Asia Minor.) For example, the mythological character Pelops (after whom the present-day peninsula of Peloponnesus is named.)

The ethnic relationship of the Brygians (Phrygians) and ancient Macedonians have already been discussed. The core ethnic component in the ancient Macedonian ethnogenesis was the Brygian, and the name of the present-day Greek peninsula was derived from the name of the people who were their descendants (according to the mythology).

– from *The Descendants of Alexander the Great of Macedon* by Aleksandar Donski

Chapter 8 – the professors receive a challenge

We waited for Mavros at the cafe for nearly an hour. Just about the time I thought that he had lit out for parts unknown, he appeared at the entrance. We paid our bill and departed with him in tow.

He followed us in his car. We stopped off at our camp for a few things before proceeding on to Meshkom.

When we were just about to leave, Professor Misirkova arrived in the company of two policemen. She approached Borko, and without the least sign of greeting, she launched into a long, angry speech in Macedonian. Occasionally she would point to us and wag a finger in obvious disapproval.

When Borko finally had a chance to translate for us, he said, "Jovanka is all unhappy because we are no longer doing archaeological work at this site. But instead, as she sees things, we are disturbing the peace here with our 'brawls' with local people. She wants us to pack up and get off the site immediately, so that her crew can do their work without further nuisance."

"What are the police for? To evict us?" I asked.

"She has filed a complaint with them. She said that the brawl last night was the last straw. She has also been talking with certain people back in Skopje. Urging an investigation of our activities, particularly our claim that the forgeries in the tomb were not the same objects that we discovered in the first place."

"Well, can't you explain to her that we're trying to obtain proof of our claim."

"She says that it is something best left to the authorities."

Borko spoke briefly with the policemen, and after we had been issued a written warning, we were allowed to continue on our way. I was in full agreement with Borko's decision not to describe 'last night's brawl' to the police.

We took both the van and Mavros's car to the village. Borko and I rode in the van and Mavros, Deb and Sasho rode in the car. When Sasho had insisted on joining Deb and Mavros, Deb had quipped, "My chaperone, eh?"

When we arrived in the village we parked in front of the mayor's house. We got out and started walking toward the house. The mayor himself met us at the door. Almost instantly several village men appeared at the gate, blocking our way back to the van. I wondered if we were about to have another 'brawl' with the locals.

But the mayor ushered us all into his front room, where we were urged to take seats. Everyone waited in silence while his wife prepared coffee for the guests.

This was the first time I had had an opportunity to study the mayor up close. The man appeared to be in his early sixties. He was tall and slim with graying hair that was retreating from a high, domed forehead. He reminded me of one of the old icons I'd seen of Macedonian church fathers from centuries past.

I knew that his name was Stoyan Pelagonevski, but the name's possible connection to Pelasgians had never occurred to me until now. "Before we discuss the serious matters that bring you here, let us have coffee together," he said.

If our visit was much of a surprise, he didn't show it. When his wife arrived with the tray of small demitasse cups of steaming, thick black Turkish coffee, he helped distribute them among the guests.

Still, nothing was said. And Borko also demonstrated a remarkable control. He was waiting for something, it seemed. A signal of some kind from our host, or maybe just the right moment or word or something. So I just settled back in my chair. I sipped my coffee and waited out the silence that had descended on the room full of people.

Eventually the mayor turned to Borko and said something to him in a hushed tone. Borko nodded, got up and approached me. "The mayor says he will discuss the matter with you and with me, but he prefers that the others leave," said Borko in an equally hushed voice.

I thought about it for a moment, and said, "Alright." I turned to Deb and Sasho and said, "Why don't you two go ahead and return to Marvintsi. Mavros can probably drop you off." Deb and I looked to Mavros.

Mavros nodded, though he appeared puzzled as to why we had dragged him all this way, if all we were going to do is send him home without his saying a single word. Deb gave me a final questioning look as they left, as if to ask, are you sure that you want to do this without us?

Once they were gone, Stoyan looked Borko and me over carefully. He said, as Borko translated for my benefit, "Now let me understand, you insist upon answers from me, is that right?"

We nodded. "That is the case alright," I replied, as if he would understand, or as if Borko might translate for me, which he didn't.

Stoyan looked from the one to the other of us, studying each of us carefully. Finally he said, and Borko was kind enough to translate, "So we now have a problem, because I am a member of an ancient order that forbids me to reveal its secrets to outsiders."

"But someone among you talks to Greek journalists," I said, and Borko translated for me.

"We know that already," the mayor replied calmly. "But he apparently only told the journalist those things that you already know and that the world is unlikely to take seriously, as you have probably already learned."

"Do these ancient rules prevent you from explaining why you attacked us at our camp?" I demanded.

"That I thought was self-explanatory. You threatened to blackmail us with pictures one of your people took without our knowledge or permission. We felt that we had no choice but to respond to that threat as best we could."

"Someone could have been badly hurt!" said Borko.

"Yes, there were some risks involved," admitted the mayor.

"You promised us some answers," said Borko.

"You must know by now that we can't just leave you alone. We know too much for that to be possible," I added.

"So you have opened Pandora's Box and you cannot simply close it again?" said Stoyan. He took a long, slow, slightly noisy sip from his coffee.

"We won't stop trying to learn the truth about you and about the tomb of Alexander. You can be sure of that," said Borko.

Stoyan hesitated before he spoke again. He studied our faces carefully before he finally said, "Are you willing to undergo initiation into our order?" Several of the village men appeared agitated at this offer. The shopkeeper who'd had the run-in with Borko looked particularly upset. "If you will take that step, then neither I nor any of the others may refuse to answer your questions."

The shopkeeper started to raise objections, but Stoyan motioned him to wait until he'd received an answer to his question.

"What would this initiation require?" asked Borko.

"Courage and purity of heart," replied the mayor.

"Will you subject us to anything that you yourself did not undergo?" asked Borko.

"No," was Stoyan's terse answer, delivered with some conviction.

Why should we trust this man? I wondered. He had already plundered our archaeology site, probably had had us abducted in order to drive us away, and now he had raided our camp. But, then again, what discoveries might we make if he proved as good as his word? A living link to a past thought to be all but lost?

"I am willing to go through this initiation. But my colleagues must know when it is to begin and end," announced Borko.

Leave it to the Boar to make an announcement like that without even consulting with me. But I didn't want to miss out on such an opportunity to explore an ancient mystery religion, risk or no risk. "I also agree, on the same conditions that Borko just made," I said.

"Fine," said Stoyan, but he was immediately interrupted by the shopkeeper, who insisted that the others be consulted on such a serious matter. A lengthy debate ensued among the several men present. From what little that Borko was willing, or maybe able to translate, given the use of their obscure dialect, I learned that the mayor had prevailed in the end, but not without strong objections from some of his fellows.

"Now that it is settled," announced the mayor, "you should go home, get a good night's rest and meet us here at dawn tomorrow. You will be occupied with this process for two weeks. During that time you will be in certain undisclosed locations in these mountains. We will return you to this house at dusk on the fourteenth day, or sooner, if you are unwilling or unable to complete your initiation."

Borko and I returned to the camp and announced our plans to our colleagues. That evening as we sat around the campfire together, there was an air of excitement surrounding the two of us. Joel, however, was the only one who dared to ask, "Can I come with you? I'd love to go through this ancient druid boot camp with you."

There are a lot of things you seem to love. I thought as I observed the casual arm Joel had draped over Rada's shoulder this evening. Despite the fact that no one was altogether surprised when a romance developed on a dig, there were certain unwritten rules of discretion that Joel was violating at the moment.

I focused a searing look on that arm. There was a slightly harsh tone to my reply as well. "No, you'll stay here and keep things in order, and you'll work with Doctor Misirkova, if she'll agree to that, until we return."

Joel tried to appear casual about his removal of the arm from Rada's shoulder as he nodded his assent. Though he muttered something under his breath like, "Bet she'll just have us all arrested for trespassing."

"Are you nervous about this, Doc?" asked Deb, with a look of genuine concern.

"Why should he be nervous, men are initiated all the time into armies and societies," Borko answered for me, with obvious irritation at the boldness of the question.

I turned a stern looked on him, as if to say, Thanks, Boar, I really appreciate it when you speak for me. But Borko's remark did serve to condition my answer, "No, I'm looking forward to it," I replied, though I confess that my words lacked much conviction.

"Why do you trust them not to put you through some pointless hell?" she asked further.

"That's what initiations are usually about in manly company. It's all to see what we are really made of," said Borko.

"Hey, then maybe we could just stake you out here in the hot sun for a few days and feed you raw grubs or something. Save you the trouble of going off to the mountains with the Druids," suggested Deb, swiping her shoulder-length hair back from her face and eyes, that had a mischievous glint at the moment.

I made a sick little grin.

Borko simply frowned and looked away.

"What do you want us to do if we don't have any word from you by the expected date of your return?" asked Sasho.

"You'll find us at the mayor's house on the date arranged for our return, I'm sure," said Borko. "But use your best judgement, in any case."

We sat up for another half hour with the crew, until the nearly full moon began to rise over the dark mountains to the southeast and the song of crickets replaced the evening song of doves and nightingales.

Borko and I rose before any of the others the next morning. My head was clear and my senses sharp, despite a slightly troubled sleep. Neither Borko nor I had indulged in any alcohol the night before. We behaved as if we were preparing ourselves for combat or an athletic competition.

I washed my face, ears and neck thoroughly in a basin of cold water drawn from our stores. As the water dribbled down into the pan from my close-cropped beard, I took a full, deep breath of the bracing night air. I had wanted something more than the same old everyday routine back home, and I couldn't say that Borko and his crazy little country had let me down.

I could hear Borko heating up some coffee nearby, snuffling quietly like some early-rising wild beast in the pre-dawn dark. That crap about a manly initiation had left me wondering, what sort of silly-ass business I'd let myself in for. My own response yesterday had been right out of junior high school. "I'm looking forward to it." As if I were some pimply-faced adolescent looking forward to getting kicked and stomped by the gang so that he could be one of them.

"So are you ready, eh mori, Jack?" asked Borko as he handed me a cup of thick, black Turkish coffee, syrup-sweet, just the way Borko liked it.

I grunted something to the affirmative. The coffee, even ala Turk, was welcome. I liked the heat of it in my throat and chest. I imagined the caffeine surging through my bloodstream, laced with sugar, preparing me for our rush into the unknown.

Borko surveyed me and said, "Cheer up, friend, it's not as if we're on the way to the dentist to have a tooth pulled." He paused for effect, and added, "That, after all, only takes a day, we have two weeks to look forward to!" And he laughed at his own stupid joke.

I still said nothing. I just stared at Borko as if it had finally occurred to me that the man was probably certifiably mad and the asylum in this case was called Macedonia.

Borko and I were probably close to the same age, in our mid to late 40's. We were no longer kids. We certainly had nothing to prove anymore. Or so I hoped.

So why in the world weren't we sending Sasho and Joel on this ordeal instead of ourselves? What were graduate assistants for, after all, if not to put through hell? Those that survived field work in some remote hellish place got to launch their professional careers with the publication of their findings. Some few even got famous. How old was someone like Carlos Castaneda when he subjected himself to a rigorous initiation with a Native American shaman? Probably still in his twenties. And Professor Leakey sent a young woman out to live alone in the jungle with the apes rather than subject himself to that rigorous life.

There was definitely something wrong with the present picture. Borko and I should not be on our way to this two week initiation into the Druid's society.

When we arrived at the village, Stoyan and his fellows were there waiting for us out front of his house. Our party proceeded out of the village and into the countryside by car. After a time, we stopped at a remote farmstead, a place where sheep were apparently corralled in the winter time.

The shopkeeper, who looked every bit as unfriendly as he had the day before, approached Borko and me with blindfolds. "Forgive us for taking such measures, but if you fail our initiation, we don't want you able to locate the site of the initiation again," said Stoyan as the blindfolds were applied.

We were hoisted onto waiting mules and led up into the Kozhuf Mountains, in a remote southern region of the Republic of Macedonia, near the Greek border. I felt the steady rhythm of the mule under me and heard the occasional voice of one of the muleteers urging the animals on. Otherwise I was only aware of passing scents. Wildflower blossoms, freshly-mown hay, the distant scree of a high-gliding hawk, and the warning bray of a donkey at the approach of our little caravan.

By mid-day we were somewhere high in the mountains. When we finally halted and our guides removed the blindfolds, I saw that we were in a natural bowl or basin several miles across, bounded on all sides by rugged peaks with steep slopes. The basin was heavily wooded. Pine and spruce trees marched up the ridges until they met sheer rock escarpments that would no longer support life. The snow had retreated before the mid-summer sun, leaving the peaks barren and wind-blown.

We unloaded our provisions and carried them up to the entrance of a large cave partway up the steep rock face of one of the cliffs. Once again there on the rock face at the cave entrance were the same ancient runes, the crosses, dots, circles and squares, with occasional cupolas and other embellishments, etched into the rock, in what appeared to me to be similar, if not identical patterns to those we had seen near the entrance to the tomb and on the approach to the village of Meshkom.

Once the work was completed, Stoyan motioned for Borko and me to follow him. He led us along a narrow, little path to a place along the rock face some twenty yards away. "You will begin your initiation with a cleansing of body, mind and spirit," he announced. "There is a small waterfall behind that ledge." And he pointed to where it was, though we could already hear the sound of water splashing on rocks below.

"You will bathe yourselves thoroughly in its waters." He fixed each of us in a penetrating gaze, commanding our full attention. "For the next 24 hours you will drink from the spring whenever you wish, but you will eat no food. You will not speak a single word during that period. You will make every effort to empty your minds as much as possible of all thought. You may sit or stand or walk in the surrounding forest, but you must return to the mouth of the cave by sunset tomorrow. This time tomorrow we will begin your training."

Then he turned abruptly and disappeared into the cave, leaving us to begin our baths.

Cleansing of the mind, where have I heard of that before? I asked myself as I plunged my head under the bracing cold stream of water that tumbled down the edge of the rock overhang. It was a warm day, and I was gritty and hot from the climb, so the cold water felt good on my skin.

So far so good, I thought. No mutilation of the flesh or staking out in the hot sun just yet. Just going hungry for a day.

A few moments later the shopkeeper appeared. He gathered up the clothes we had stripped off in order to shower. After he'd collected our things, scowling all the while, he turned abruptly and left.

"Hey, what are we going to wear?" Borko shouted after him. But the man merely put his finger to his lip, which now held a slight smile, to remind us that we were not to speak for the next twenty four hours.

Borko and I sat on a soft bed of needles under a lone, tall pine tree and soaked in the last hot rays of the late afternoon sun. As the sun began to set, we felt the first chill of night in the high country.

My first impulse was to return to the cave and try and beg admittance to the fireside. But Borko motioned for me to follow him into the forest, where he began to collect pine boughs in order to create a bed for us. Then he gathered dry grasses to line our nest. Working together we soon had a passable nest to burrow into before the chill dark of night overtook us.

At first we couldn't help but glance enviously into the cave where the others sat at a distance around a fire, eating their evening meal. Their fire conjured up all manner of images. At first it was only a place for a spit for roasting meat or hanging a cauldron of boiling soup, or a place to bake potatoes over the coals. But then it became a lonely outpost of civilization for a small band of men come to the wild mountains. Finally I saw it as a link to generation upon generation of initiates in some similar first night of their passage. Others must have sat at this same distance and peered longingly toward that fire.

Still, it unnerved me, the way we had been so abruptly turned out onto the wild mountain, to fend for ourselves, hungry, cold and naked. Thanks to Borko's resourcefulness, we weren't as miserable as we might have been. But would we fare as well tomorrow or the day after?

Eventually we sat rather peacefully and gazed out at the outer magnificence of the surrounding mountains and the evening sky above us. We listened to the sounds of the night, the crickets and the night birds - doves, nightingales and owls. I also heard the first wild wolf's call of my entire lifetime. The long, slow howl of the great wild dog filled me with a sad longing for something lost to my race long ago.

It occurred to me that this mountain was probably also home to the big brown bears, related to the American grizzly, that still roamed the Balkan high country. How would we escape one of those great beasts in our present humbled state, sans clothing or even a cell phone, not to mention a high-powered rifle?

I took some comfort from the steady rhythm of Borko's breathing as he sat silently beside me. An occasional creepy crawler would disturb my peace, but I felt surprisingly snug and secure, buried up to my neck in grass and pine boughs.

Around midnight we were visited by the most splendid full moon I had ever seen. The sheer size and brightness of that ancient globe suspended in the dark heavens surpassed any moon I had ever known before. It bathed the surrounding mountains in an eerie silver glow. Again my thoughts turned to the thousands of years of initiates who had shared this night before us.

Just going hungry and naked began to take on more significance by noon of the following day. Borko guzzled copious amounts of water. Then he would have to hurry off to the bushes to pee it all out again. I dealt with my own craving for food by pacing restlessly around the site and swatting and scratching at the hoard of insects that appeared to be particularly attracted to my pale exposed flesh. By that afternoon I'd worked up quite an appetite.

Eventually Stoyan's lieutenant came out to us. That same shopkeeper with the same hostile gaze. But he carried a bowl of fresh fruit and clean, white linen robes for us to wear. I was a bit embarrassed by the single-mindedness with which Borko and I attacked the food.

The shopkeeper didn't try to hide his disdain at our lack of good manners. It also crossed my mind that the particular selection of fruits we were eating would likely lead to further cleansing.

I also appreciated receiving the robe to protect me from the fierce Mediterranean sun. I could already feel the slow cooking pain of a sun burn across the pink flesh on my thighs, neck and shoulders. Another day or two running around naked and I would have looked like a boiled lobster.

Ancient Macedonians regarded the snake as an animal with magical powers. It is known that Macedonians revered the serpent-like deities Draco and Dracena There was also a cult of the snake in Pelagonia (a region of Macedonia), where it was considered a symbol of eternal life and reincarnation (for more details refer to: Nade Proeva "Studies of the Ancient Macedonians," Skopje, 1997).

The Upper Macedonian tribe, the Peaonians, also had a cult of the snake. It was represented on many ornamental items. It was among the most frequently portrayed animals on the material artifacts of that culture.

– from *The Descendants of Alexander the Great of Macedon* by Aleksandar Donski

Chapter 9 – the real test

We spent that afternoon carrying copious armloads of firewood from the nearby forest up to the cave entrance. That evening Borko and I were invited to join the others beside the fire-pit in the large chamber at the mouth of the cave. Everyone wore homespun cotton robes, held tight at the waist by long cummerbunds. We also wore traditional peasant folk moccasins with straps that clasped at the ankle, after the fashion of peasants in this part of the world.

Stoyan appeared before us that evening dressed in the same robe and gold mask that he had worn at the solstice ceremony. He bent down before the fire pit, now filled with dry wood, kindling and tinder, and ignited it. Soon there was a roaring blaze that illuminated the high ceiling and walls of the cave.

He spoke again in the ancient tongue that Borko, even with his extensive training in Balkan and Slavic linguistics could barely make any sense of. "*Priziraonte ogan'ea...*"

Borko strained to make out the words and translate them for my benefit. "We look at, no, we acknowledge the fire within ourselves. Fire that is the energy of universal dimensions. Power and new life have their sources in it. In our thoughts burn fires from the origins of life. Lightning flashes in our emotions, in our love, new life is made, conceived. We participate with power. We are sharing with others the energy of the universe. It keeps us warm. It fires our bodies. It is fuel for our relation to others. We fire. Fire is our power. Welcome, gift of Prometheus, Spirit of fire to the circle of our making!"

The translation was a bit rough, but I understood. What he espoused was an ancient nature-based philosophy. So far, it didn't offend my own rationalist philosophical orientation. But I still felt uneasy about delivering myself into the hands of a cult priest, no matter how old and respectable the tradition.

The priest held aloft a bowl containing a large cream-colored mushroom of a sort unfamiliar to me. It had been sliced into sections. One for each of those present in the circle.

After saying a few words of blessing over the bowl, the priest took a piece and put it into his mouth and began to slowly chew and swallow the marshmallow-sized bite. He then passed the bowl to the next person, who did the same. Soon the bowl was passed on around to Borko, who hesitated for the briefest moment. But he too tucked the piece of mushroom into his mouth. The shopkeeper watched him closely from across the circle, as if he were thinking, this ought to be interesting.

I could smell the pungent, earthy scent as I lifted a piece to my mouth. The taste was at first familiar from other mushrooms I'd eaten. As I chewed the piece, however, I tasted a sharp, almost bitter quality, not familiar at all. I chewed a few more times and swallowed, as I'd observed the others do. "Anything for a weird life," I said to myself - a quote from the silly *Hitchhiker's Guide to the Galaxy,* as I passed the bowl on.

It was soon a weirder life than I'd reckoned on. The flickering flames began to literally dance to the rhythms of my heartbeat. The gold mask on the pagan priest's head burst into dazzling flames that arranged themselves in a wild, almost fiendish grin. I turned and glanced at Borko and noticed tusks protruding from my colleague's round pig-like jowls. I quickly returned my gaze to the fire. Better a dance with the flames than encounters with the hideous and distorted faces of my fellows.

I had no idea how much time passed before I again raised my eyes from the flames. It may have been five minutes or five hours for all I knew. I had, however, seen things. Beings of pure energy had danced in joyous abandon. This energy had washed over me in successive waves. Its light and warmth were transmitted from the fire sprites directly to some core of my being. It felt like some joyous communion had taken place within me, a harmony and oneness with the elemental energy of the fire.

For the longest time though, I was dreadfully afraid to raise my eyes from the fire, for fear of what else I might see. But when I did finally look up again, the golden mask had faded to a pale orange sunset. Borko and the others appeared as a set of silent, grey boulders, arranged in a semi-circle before the fading sunset of the fire. I felt as if I myself had grown terribly heavy and immobile. I too had become heat-soaked stone at rest for the duration of the cool, dark night.

With the arrival of dawn I awoke as the other sleeping figures around the fire pit began to stir. Stoyan's shopkeeper lieutenant offered Borko and me each a pomegranate and a cup of herbal tea. He seemed grudgingly impressed that we were both still here this morning rather than having run off in a mad terror during the night.

I gratefully downed the beverage. I couldn't remember when I'd been so thirsty. I greedily sucked at the sweet blood-red juices of the fruit as well.

Borko acted as if nothing out of the ordinary had occurred the night before. Maybe his greater bulk had absorbed much of the substance that had sent me into such wild realms. Perhaps it had left him with no more than mild hallucinations of the sort I had known in my pot-smoking student days.

He no longer had his tusks, but the nightmare image continued to haunt me. The communion with the fire had been a wondrous thing, but I shuddered at the thought of random play with such a powerful psychoactive substance, outside the sacred circle. Therein lay madness. Even with the priest's guidance, I had some serious doubts about getting mind-altered with this crowd. My critical judgement was clearly impaired, and who knew what thoughts their priest might be planting in me?

What if this really was no more than an elaborate hoax? Maybe Borko was even part of it. How far would a threatened people go in order to establish a national myth about their rights to an ancient Macedonian cultural heritage? In order to dupe an unsuspecting team of American archaeologists into supporting their claims in the international arena? US support was worth a lot in the post-Cold War era.

Stoyan now beckoned us both to the mouth of the cave. "Remove your robes and leave them here in the cave," he said.

It appeared that I was not going to get to protect my tender flesh from the elements after all. I considered raising objections, but I waited to see what he had in mind.

Once we had disrobed, he said, "Now come with me." The shopkeeper gave us a knowing little smirk as he watched us go to whatever awaited us outside.

Stoyan led us to the cascading little spring and ordered us to bathe again. The cold water felt soothing to my hot, stinging flesh. Although the sun was up and beginning to burn clear and bright, it was slow to warm us after the brisk chill of the mountain spring water. I tried to maximize my exposure to its rays as I shook as much water as I could from my hair and beard, and let the rest trickle down and off me. But I would soon long for that cool morning air.

Before the two of us had even begun to dry off, Stoyan gave us a strange order. "Do not put your clothes back on. Instead I want you to smear a heavy coat of the clay mud from the base of the spring all over yourselves."

Reluctantly we began to smear the steely grey mud over our arms and legs. It felt cool and slippery. As it dried it began to feel like a tight silken undershirt or stocking against my skin.

Stoyan kept urging us to spread it in thick layers over every inch of our bodies. I smeared dripping wet handfuls across my chest, down my belly and across my pubic hair and penis, and on up my neck and across my beard and chin right up to my lips. The excess water dribbled down onto my chest.

Then he urged me to work it into my hair. I rubbed big, wet globs into my shaggy mane. Borko rubbed more clay onto my back. Soon we were both a rather comical sight - clay men - life-sized figurines of the wild, hairy men who must have once roamed the continent.

Stoyan guided us to a large clearing. He instructed us on how to control our breathing and what poses or postures to assume for maximum comfort. We were to spend the day as clay statues fixed in the center of the glen, exposed to the sun and the other elements. "Remain as still as possible. Become baked clay men. I will send someone to fetch you at sunset," he said in parting, as he left to return to the cave.

The first few hours were merely a bit tedious. But then the full heat of the Mediterranean sun began to beat down on us. I truly began to feel like a baked clay man. The clay protected us from some of the worst effects of the sun, but I soon craved water and shade.

The longer I remained planted in the clearing, however, the more I began to feel like an extension of the earth, as if I were truly rooted there like some tree or shrub. Apparently that is how the wild beasts of the mountain perceived us. At one point a magpie perched itself right on one of Borko's shoulders. Later, a couple of wolf pups came to play in the small meadow. The magnificent, sleek, frosty-gray and brown wild dogs frolicked for a time in the tall grass and then lazed in the sun and even took a nap mere yards from us before continuing on their way.

A small, snuffling, hairy brown boar also passed through the clearing late in the day. I tensed a bit at his presence, knowing that these wild pigs could inflict a pretty nasty wound, if they chose to attack. Nothing served to provoke the animal in any event. I was particularly relieved, however, that no great brown bear had chosen to visit that day.

When our favorite Meshkom shopkeeper finally came to collect us at sunset, neither of us was able to readily follow. Only after several attempts did I finally succeed in getting my limbs to respond. Borko limped along behind us. Apparently his body was even slower to recover than my own.

The lieutenant led us back to the spring where I immediately plunged my head under the falling water. I held my mouth open to it like a baby bird's blind clamoring after food. Borko was soon pressed up against me, equally desperate to drink from the cool, sweet waters. The villager stood there and shook his head, as if to say, pathetic.

After we'd thoroughly washed the clay from our bodies, he handed each of us a dry towel and a fresh robe. The mud plaster appeared to be a great treatment for sunburn. I already felt somewhat healed after a day. Most of the sting was gone, and my skin had a healthier color to it.

Once we'd returned to the cave, he gave us each another cup of the herbal tea and a pomegranate. So the crash diet continues, I thought as I greedily sucked at the fruit. At this rate we'll eventually walk out of these hills looking like scarecrows.

If I thought that this was hard on me, one look at Borko, as he desperately dug at the tiny seeds with his big hammy fingers, changed that perception. The man probably had eighty more pounds of bulk than me, and that big frame and body probably required considerably more fuel to fire it. Borko was obviously hurting. The shopkeeper appeared to have less regrets at the moment, that Stoyan had gotten his way and extended us an invitation to this ordeal.

To his credit there was not a squeak of complaint out of Borko. He was apparently determined to play this game out. I just hoped that I would do as well when things got rougher for me.

That evening rather than a return to the fire circle, Stoyan led us all to a small chamber deeper in the cave with a woven mat door that sealed behind us. The room was no more than sixteen feet wide and about seven feet high. A small cairn of stones in the center of the chamber emitted a faint reddish glow, and an enormous amount of heat. The chamber was easily 110 degrees, in sharp contrast to the cool, comfortable constant of the main cave.

Again the dozen of us were arranged in a comfortable circle around the glowing, hot cairn. We each wore only a swath of cotton loincloth in this furnace. That evening Stoyan led us in a series of rhythmic chants that soon had me thoroughly mesmerized.

I again lost all sense of time or place. I drifted or floated in a tropical sea of dreams. Various people from the span of my lifetime inhabited these dreams. I saw my parents and aunts and uncles, cousins and brothers and sisters. I encountered childhood playmates, schoolmates from high school and college. My wife, Jo, and children, and even members of the archaeology team joined me briefly. Everyone floated lazily by in the calm, steamy waters of my dream.

Suddenly, familiar faces disappeared and I was in a long column of marching men. Trumpets blared, cymbals crashed, and there was an occasional shout from someone up ahead in the column, followed by a roar of voices in response. I could also hear the steady, rhythmic tramp of hundreds of leather-sandaled feet on the hard-packed earthen roadway and the clanking of swords and spears born by the troops. About twenty five feet ahead of me on the road, I would catch an occasional glimpse of the funeral cart of Alexander. As quickly as it had appeared, the vision faded, as I regained consciousness.

When Stoyan finally ordered everyone outside to bathe in the cold spring waters, I stumbled along in a daze. When we emerged from the cave, the moon had already set. We were greeted by a breathtaking display of stars and star clusters. I couldn't recall a time when I'd seen such a dazzling, star-speckled sky as this one. One of the special features of the Druid summer camp, held high up in these remote, unblemished mountains, I supposed.

When the cold water hit my superheated skin I let out a ferocious gasp. My head spun and I thought I might lose consciousness, but within a short time my breathing was back to normal and a feeling of peace and well-being settled over me. After returning to my sheepskin bed by the mouth of the cave, I slept the sleep of the dead for the rest of that night.

The next morning Stoyan again carefully explained our task for the day. We were instructed in how to walk and how to breathe. He also taught us a sacred song to repeat as we trekked. Then, he pointed to a distant mountain peak on the far side of the basin. He explained how we were to reach it, and what we were to bring back to him that evening as proof of our accomplishment. "Remember, you must carefully follow my instructions about how to journey," he cautioned us. "Otherwise it will not be possible for you to make it to the summit and return all in one day."

It was hard to say who was more startled, when we met Deb, Joel and Sasho on the trail to the mountain top. Borko and I were barely recognizable in our long cotton robes. We were considerably changed in other ways as well. We both had wild, unkempt hair and rough, sun-browned skin. I had abandoned my glasses, and Borko had a three day growth of thick, black stubble beard. The only familiar feature in our appearance was our work boots that we'd worn especially for this trek.

Our assistants were dressed in their usual blue jeans and flannel work shirts and boots. Joel had a pair of binoculars, besides his usual camera, strapped around his neck. After the initial shock came recognition, and then delighted smiles lit their faces as our assistants recognized their mentors.

"We thought we'd better check to see that you were alright, Doc," said Joel in explanation.

"Yeah, we didn't think that these Druids could be totally trusted not to do you some harm," added Deb.

Only Sasho had the sense to ask, "Did we do the right thing?"

Borko gave him a long black stare. Then he snarled, "Get out of here."

Deb and Joel looked to me now. "Yes," I said. "Go back to camp, and don't come back up here after us again. No matter how worried you get. You had no business following us up here in the first place. We'll see you at the end of next week."

Our three archaeological assistants stepped back from the trail. They allowed us to pass on down the trail, without another word. However, the look on their faces as we walked by them suggested that they thought they were being instructed by madmen.

I could imagine their conversation on the way back to camp. How their respected teachers had lost it, gone totally AWOL, and were fast becoming the irretrievable victims of cult manipulation, ripe for plucking in a Jonestown or in the service of the death-cult computer programmers or some other dead-end cult. But they saw no way to stop their teachers' tragic slide. It would simply be a sad tale to tell their own grad assistants over beer in a tavern way station on the way to a dig someday. How two fine men and scholars had succumbed to primitive impulses. "Mistah Kurtz, he dead!"

After we were well past our assistants I could no longer suppress a slight smile at the anxious expressions on our students' faces. But Borko, who glanced over at me at just that moment, and who must have picked up on my thoughts, shook his head and frowned, as if to say, what insubordination! Then both of us returned in earnest to our measured breath and pace and the silent repetition of the sacred song.

Despite the mental tools that Stoyan had equipped us with for this trek, it eventually proved incredibly grueling. The summit, predictably, appeared much closer than it actually was. As we struggled up the steep incline, winding our way past rock outcroppings that speckled the treeless upper zone of the mountain, the summit actually seemed to retreat in front of us. We were thoroughly exhausted and dripping wet from our climb in the hot midday sun, by the time we arrived on the mountain top

Borko and I found the cairn of green stone that Stoyan had said would be here without difficulty. We each picked out a stone to carry back as instructed. Then we collapsed to the ground, too weary to even speak to each other for a while. For the next quarter hour, I simply listened to the boiler factory in my head - the high-pitched ringing in my ears and an intermittent buzzing in my head that accompanied the pounding of blood to my temples. I wondered for a while if I was a candidate for heart failure.

After we had rested, when it came time to rise and go again, neither of us could muster the strength. We had been fasting for almost four days now, and it was obviously taking a toll on our energy. Stoyan had warned us that this trek would not be easy.

I finally managed to stand up on wobbly legs. When Borko still made no move to rise, I stood over him and gently prodded, "Come on, Borko, it's time to get going. We have to leave now if we're going to make it back before dark."

"No, you don't know how hard it is for me to lift my legs," said Borko in a pained voice. He didn't even raise his chin off his breast to meet my gaze.

I tried to think of what I might say to motivate Borko. I finally settled on a strategy. "There is a shopkeeper from Meshkom who'll be particularly delighted to hear that you couldn't do it. They all think that we're just candy-ass academic office-worker types. You can bet they'll all be laughing their heads off tonight when we don't return, especially that shopkeeper."

At this, Borko muttered, "I know about mocking. The chubby little boy from the Home for Orphans, October 11th in Skopje." Then he made a superhuman effort to get back up onto his feet. It appeared to require some tremendous effort of will on his part, to get his exhausted, depleted body to obey him. Once he was on his feet, however, he shook like an exhausted racehorse that had just run the Kentucky Derby. I couldn't imagine where the man would find the strength to make the walk home.

I began to rub the tight, trembling shoulders of the old boar. In all this time I had never bothered to ask Borko about his family. And he had never mentioned any. But I had never imagined that he might not have any. I knew he wasn't married, except maybe to his work. But it gave me a new perspective on the strange fellow to learn that that he'd been raised in an orphanage.

Eventually the trembling stopped and Borko regained control of himself. He grasped the smooth green stone in his fist and we started down the trail together. Soon we had regained the rhythm and cadence that had sustained us during the climb. Fortunately, the downhill hike required a somewhat different set of muscles and considerably less exertion than the climb. Otherwise, I can't imagine how we would have made it back that day.

It still amazes me that we did succeed, given our condition. About a half mile from the cave entrance, Borko faltered again. One moment he was marching at my side, and the next he was lying in a collapsed heap by the side of the trail. "Let me rest," he rasped in a hoarse whisper. "Just a few minutes."

I didn't dare lie down myself, for fear that I would fall asleep on the spot.

Borko confirmed my own fear when he suddenly began to snore. I gave him about five minutes, then I started to shake him. "Wake up!" I shouted.

He reluctantly opened his eyes.

"We don't have much daylight left to find our way back to the cave. Come on. Let's go," I said as I tugged feebly at the inert bulk of him.

Eventually he leaned into me and began to raise himself back to his feet. It's a wonder that we didn't both collapse under the weight of him. Somehow or other he managed to put one foot in front of the other and mechanically plodded along to the cadence of our chanted song.

My legs felt like lead weights as I approached the cave entrance. Borko made my progress even more painful by leaning an arm into me for support, as he limped along beside me in a semi-conscious stupor. We must have looked like a couple of feeble old men on our last legs.

Neither of us had an ounce of energy to spare. We dropped our stones at Stoyan's feet and hobbled off together toward the spring. This time we both plunged into the water at once, so that it took twice as long for either of us to get a decent drink.

The question kept going through my head, why were we letting these strange mountain people subject us to such abuse? They would probably just keep upping the ante until we could no longer take it, and then send us packing for home with no answers and no further right, in their minds, to intrude upon them.

The shopkeeper lieutenant came out to us with clean robes and some soap and towels and natural sponge to scrub with. This time there was no sneer on his face. I even thought I detected a hint of grudging respect. Perhaps we were making some progress after all, and my fears were unfounded.

After the two of us had scrubbed ourselves thoroughly and rinsed and dried off, he brought us each a bowl of yogurt to eat, in addition to the usual fruit. I am absolutely certain that it was the most delicious meal I have ever eaten. Borko swore, "I'll never take pleasure in food for granted, ever again," as he licked greedily at the last bits in the bottom of his bowl.

That evening as we sat with the others around the fire, Stoyan embarked on a new instruction, which Borko, as usual translated for me.

"It is time that you began to learn about Dionysos, to whom our brotherhood is dedicated. Legend says he was the child of Zeus and Semele. He goes by various names, as the god of the cultivated tree, he is known as Dendrites, and in an older incarnation he was the wild Thracian god, Sabazios. He is said to have taught us the cultivation of the vine and to watch over the fertility of our crop. He taught us other things as well, such as some of the rites and training of our initiation, things he supposedly learned during travels in India."

The persistent pain in my muscles and joints from our grueling climb were all that kept me from nodding off during his recitation. All the same, I heard Borko's voice, translating, as if out of a fog. The words entered my mind, but I couldn't quite piece their meanings together.

His stories of the deity, Dionysos, seemed to go on for many hours, lasting late into the night. "While it was true that the Romans had turned him into the drunken Bacchus," he explained at one point. "He had other and nobler faces. Dionysos had, according to legend, a wife named Ariadne. He found her on the Isle of Naxos after she had been abandoned by the cad Theseus. Dionysos, however, recognized her true worth. He honored her with a crown of precious jewels. And upon her death the god placed her in the heavens to shine forevermore as the constellation of stars that bear her name."

The stories had a particular charm to them. Stoyan could truly perform magic with word and song. The brotherhood acted as sacred chorus for his chanted tales, repeating certain lines, and thereby giving them some added force and meaning. Modern theatre must have grown out of such an ancient tradition of dramatic recital.

Stoyan told his stories in a rich, powerful voice. The volume rose and fell with the emotional content of the phrases. He took time between stories to explain the deeper significance of a tale. The story of Ariadne and Dionysos, for example, apparently illustrated something about conduct in relations between men and women.

He later explained to Borko and me, "The women have their own secret society with rituals and traditions that parallel many of those practiced by the men. Some rites date back to an even more ancient goddess-centered religion." He stressed the mutual respect that existed between the two religious societies. They took part at times in joint ceremonies and celebrations, such as the summer solstice that our archaeology team had witnessed.

Borko and I absorbed these words like little children listening to a bedtime story. Our minds and bodies were too exhausted to do more than passively accept it all. We hovered the whole time in that narrow space between sleep and wakefulness. The next morning I remembered it all, but there was some dream-like quality about those memories. I was a bit concerned that my critical mind never had an opportunity to function in that atmosphere.

Over time I began to understand some of the thread of connections that wove these stories together into a cultural tapestry stretching from ancient times into the present day. Certain symbols would reoccur in many of the stories. Borko explained to me that he had heard variations on many of these same stories from old people during his childhood. He had also noticed how certain ancient figures seemed to reoccur in so many stories. There was the lion that had once roamed this land in ancient times and whose memory remained alive even today in folk tales told in every village and home. These stories had been passed on down through a hundred generations of storytellers, long after lions had disappeared. Yet, these stories had persisted into the 19th century when the first modern folklorists began to record them in books, so we know that their recital pre-dated the arrival of printed books or film or the modern zoological park among the common people, things that could otherwise explain so many stories about a long vanished animal from the countryside. Others stories featured other figures from ancient memory such as the philosophers of old who counseled kings, and so many of the stories reminded the people of the exploits of their greatest ancient leader, Alexander.

Each day brought new trials and new revelations. I kept waiting for and dreading a moment when I thought I would not or could not bring myself to continue the initiation. It came in the middle of the second week of our initiation. Stoyan stood before us that day with his hands folded in front of him and spoke in his usual calm, matter of fact voice. "Courage is mainly a matter of training and awareness," he said. "It is not an inborn trait bestowed upon one at birth. For example, if you were to set me behind the wheel of your automobile and order me to maneuver it through the traffic in downtown Skopje, I would be a nervous wreck, even if, somehow, I miraculously brought the car through the experience in one piece."

We both smiled at this. Borko and I had come to appreciate the way the 'master' transmitted his wisdom, this use of both gentle and self-deprecating humor as well as references to modern life that would have more meaning for his latest initiates.

Stoyan led us out into a semi-barren, rocky section of the mountain basin, where he searched the ground until he found a branch that satisfied his requirements. He broke it to the length he wanted and fashioned a short set of prongs from a branching Y at one end. He then motioned for us to follow him at a short distance.

When he spied a stone that seemed to satisfy certain conditions, he took the stick and gently overturned the stone, until he finally found one that had what he wanted under it. I watched in horror-stricken fascination as he reached his hand down to the base of the stick, and as he lifted it, I could see the gleaming, steely-gray scales and the evil-looking red button-like eyes and blunt, round snout of the serpent.

The three foot long viper that had called that stone home was understandably upset by this invasion of its privacy. It thrashed its body to left and right, while Stoyan grasped it firmly just behind the the head.

"The snake cannot strike beyond a certain distance, so that if one always extends the stick rather than approaching the snake, there is less danger when attempting to snare one," he explained as he set the snake down again on the sandy earth.

He let it slither a few feet in our direction, which made us both begin to back away, before he again pinned the snake's head firmly in the small fork of the stick. And he reached down once more and grasped the snake at the base of the head and gently lifted it, all the while supporting its body this time with his other hand. I watched all of this with a certain awe, tinged with rising terror. No, I said to myself. It's impossible for me to do this- if this is leading where I think it's leading.

Borko and I continued to maintain a safe distance between ourselves and the snake, though Stoyan assured us, "It is perfectly safe to approach closer. I have the snake completely under control." He stroked the dry, scaly skin on the deadly serpent's back as he spoke to us, which apparently had a soothing effect on the snake, because it no longer struggled to free itself.

I had a really bad feeling about all of this. Fasting or pushing our bodies to their physical limits, and even ingesting psycho-active drugs were one thing. But playing with deadly serpents was another matter altogether.

I had always had a rather irrational, lifelong fear of snakes. I was sorely tempted at that moment to shout, "No, I've had enough. Let me out of here!" But I remained oddly silent. Was it simply because I had been through so much already, and our initiation was nearing its end? How could I balk now, after all we'd been through? But I still couldn't imagine myself handling one of the deadly creatures.

There were no pits on the sides of the snake's head to indicate to me that it was a member of the highly poisonous pit viper family common to the Americas. Since it didn't have a rattle on its tail, and it had broad swaths of steel-gray and black on its body, I imagined that it was probably related to something like the common viper or adder that I had heard about in England. And if so, it was not a snake to be messed with.

Stoyan also showed us how to safely release the snake again. Then he explained, "You will spend the day learning how to safely capture, handle and release the snakes. You need to get comfortable with handling the deadly snakes for a ceremony that will take place this evening."

As he said the words, I felt a terrible sinking feeling in my gut. My worst fears had been realized.

Borko, on the other hand, took to snake catching with remarkable ease. He was soon coaching me on some of the finer points he'd discovered about how to catch them. You'd have thought he was a kid out collecting nightcrawlers for a fishing trip, rather than deadly pit vipers. I watched Borko's easy way with the snakes with horrid fascination.

I, on the other hand, couldn't seem to get past the idea that these snakes were extremely dangerous. One slip-up could result in a nasty bite that could make you deathly ill, if not kill you.

As soon as I uncovered one of the deadly serpents, I would instinctively recoil from it. I couldn't get myself to touch the snakes, as much as I tried. Fear that bordered on panic would seize hold of me each time I would try to reach down and pick one up.

I observed how Borko, after a long day of catching, handling and releasing dozens of the deadly reptiles, appeared totally relaxed around them. As his concentration had improved, he had begun to treat this activity, just as Stoyan had suggested we could, with some of the same ease most of us regard high speed freeway travel. It's potentially deadly if you don't watch what you're doing, but you feel relatively relaxed most of the time, because you do feel in control of the situation.

However, I don't think Borko even noticed that I had failed to pick up a single snake that day. He was too busy chasing snakes around. And for some reason, I couldn't get myself to tell him.

Just before dusk, the brothers were all sent out in search of snakes for the evening ceremony. Borko and I joined them, although I had already resigned myself to the fact that I would soon be sent back down the mountain, in disgrace. As each one of them captured a viper, he returned to the cave, carefully bearing the snake in his arms.

Borko easily found himself a snake, and as he prepared to carry it to the cave, he noticed that I still had none. "What's the matter? Couldn't you find one?" he asked.

Then to my horror, before I could utter a single word in protest, he thrust his snake at me. "Here. Take mine," he said. "I know where I can get another."

The snake was in my hands before I knew what was happening, and Borko was off in search of another. I stood there, paralyzed with fear. My fingers felt frozen in place. I wanted to drop the deadly viper and run away, but I was afraid that it would bite me before I could make good my escape.

Moments later Borko returned with another snake, and I fell in behind him, gripping my snake with trembling fingers. As we took our places in the circle I tried not to look down at the vile monster in my hands. It felt cool to my touch and not really so rough as I'd imagined. And it was dry as a sun-bleached stone. Eventually my trembling stopped, and I even managed to occasionally relax my grip just enough to take the cramp out of my hands.

That evening Stoyan began by having us raise the snakes above our heads with one hand grasping the head and the other supporting the body about midway in its length. Then he had us bring the snakes down behind our heads so that the bulk of the body rested on our necks and shoulders and the head lay just beyond the left shoulder with the tail draped over the right.

Someone less terrified by these snakes might have thought that the whole thing was nothing more than cheap theatrics, a performance designed to evoke chills and thrills just because it looked death-defying. But I wasn't one of them at the moment.

Eventually I began to catch subtler nuances to the performance, despite my obsession with the deadliness of the creature in my hands. It seemed to involve a certain heightened awareness of the man-beast relationship. It had echoes, no doubt, back to the ancient ritual bullfights of Crete. Few creatures on earth, however, evoked such strong feelings of aversion for me as the scaly serpent that rested in my arms. I was reminded of their ancient association with evil in the Garden of Eden story in Genesis in the Bible.

There was beginning to creep into my mind, however, as the evening wore on, just the first hint of an awareness that the creatures might indeed possess a beauty of sorts. As I studied the deadly viper in my hands, I began to notice how its dark skin gleamed in the firelight. The snake felt pleasantly cool and dry to the touch. The one I held was easily three and half feet long and thick as my wrist in its middle.

Although the snake rested comfortably in my lap, as I sat in the circle by the fire with the others, if I moved it would tense and remind me of the strength in that body. I was, of course, most conscious of the deadly head of the creature. After my initial aversion to the unblinking eyes and hard tapering snout with its flicking tongue, I even began to see beauty there as well.

Stoyan told us a story that spoke of the eternal dance with potentially deadly forces of nature. "Each one of us," he said, "in the course of our lives repeats the lessons of the old stories. We are born to the Garden of Eden and we fall from grace and are banished to a life of hard times, trials and tribulations. But with luck, with hard work, and with courage and persistence, some of us, little by little begin to redeem ourselves. To redeem ourselves from the awful fall from grace that our ignorance, thoughtlessness and carelessness condemn us to."

He went on to talk about the ancient cult of snake veneration in Pelagonia where they saw the snake as a symbol of the eternal nature of life and its constant renewal and reincarnation. Borko whispered to me, "I have read the works of some of our scholars on this subject- there seem to have been widespread cults dedicated to the snake among Macedonians, Paeonians, Ilyrians, and Thracians, and elements of some of these practices have persisted in some Macedonian villages to the present day."

To my horror, at that very moment my snake, sensing an opportunity, slipped from my inattentive hands. It didn't try to strike at me or anyone else. It simply crawled out into the center of the circle and stopped some six inches short of Stoyan's feet.

He paused in his talk just long enough to take in me and the straying viper. Although he still held a snake of his own with one hand, he reached down and caught my snake just behind the head with his free hand. He gently lifted it off the cave floor and handed it back to me, all the while continuing his talk as if nothing special had occurred - as if I had dropped a pen or a book at his feet, rather than a potentially lethal snake.

I don't know how I did it, but I held onto that serpent for the rest of the evening. I lifted it above my head with the others. Or held it in front of me with those cold, gleaming eyes and deadly mouth facing me, when Stoyan commanded it. And I carried it back out into the wilds and released it along with the others at the end of the ceremony.

Nothing before or since that evening has produced such powerful emotions in me. At evening's end I was thoroughly drained of all energy or sensation. It was as if I had ceased temporarily to exist as the hungry, grasping and ceaselessly emotional creature of my physical self.

In the morning when I awoke, I mostly felt like my old self again. I say mostly, because there was no way I would ever be quite the same after what I had been through.

That next day Borko and I were sent out to collect firewood for the evening's fire. We hadn't gone far when we came across the fresh tracks of a man. "He's from the city, wouldn't you say?" I asked, as I studied the pattern of the shoe sole in the mud.

"He stood in this place last night and watched us," said Borko.

"Do you think it was one of our crew?" I asked the obvious.

"It could be," replied Borko. "But I would have thought that they got the message and stayed back in camp."

"If they could follow our party into these mountains, so could someone else," I said. "Though it seems odd, considering all of the precautions that the brothers took to see that we didn't know the way, that they couldn't prevent our assistants from learning it."

"I would not be surprised if we know this one, too," ventured Borko. "See there." He pointed to several cigarette butts on the ground near the tracks.

"You mean Mavros?"

"Yes, Mavros."

It would be just like the enterprising Greek journalist, to stick to this story and follow it, right up into the mountains. "We should let the others know," I said.

As we turned to go, Sasho appeared from behind a tree. Borko looked ready to have a fit. Sasho hurried to explain himself. "I know that you said not to come up here again. But I felt that you would want to know that Professor Misirkova was at our camp with the police again. Our site permit has been cancelled. The authorities say that we are engaged in an elaborate hoax. It will probably only be a matter of days before they come to arrest us if we don't vacate our campsite. What is your advice?" he asked.

"Hold on as long as you can," said Borko. "We will be back in a few days to handle things. Now go!" he barked. His answer sounded overly-optimistic to me, but I resisted saying so.

Sasho hesitated momentarily. He obviously hadn't come all this way just to be ordered back down the mountain after saying a couple words to us. "You are okay?" he asked.

"Yes, yes," replied Borko. "Now go. And don't come back up here again."

This time Sasho nodded in agreement and turned and started walking back the way he'd come. Soon he had disappeared back into the forest.

As we made our way back to the cave, we discussed whether or not to tell Stoyan about the tracks, or to mention our meeting with our assistant. We debated the subject all the way back to camp. On the one hand, we didn't want to have this alter plans for our final initiation rite planned for that evening. On the other hand, the Guardians probably already knew that our assistants, as well as the Greek journalist, had been roaming these mountains and snooping on our activities. After all, this was their homeland, and if we could detect signs of an outside presence, surely the Guardians could too.

Could it be that the Greek is somehow in league with these people? I asked myself. Why else were they so unconcerned about Mavros' presence in the village? And the journalist seems to turn up in the least likely of places.

I just couldn't see how the Greek journalist seemed to gain access to so many places where he should have been totally unwelcome. Had he been invited here? Or could it be that he was simply bold and persistent beyond all belief?

That evening, when we were all assembled by the fire, Stoyan began a story of the origins of the cult. It occurred to me as he spoke, that this ancient cult had strong links to ancient Greek culture and myth. Was that just one more good reason to think that there might be a possible link to our modern Greek journalist?

"According to our ancestors, in the beginning there was Chaos, the vast unknowable void. From out of Chaos emerged Love, and it was Love that created Gaea, the earth our mother. And the sky, the oceans, the mountains, and all of the green plants and all of the creatures that fly, swim, run or crawl the world over. Out of Chaos also were born Darkness and Night, from which sprang their counterparts - Lightness and Day."

Stoyan appeared this evening again in his golden sun mask and pure white flowing robes. He was an imposing figure as he stood over our circle of brothers sitting knee to knee on the packed earth floor surrounding the fire pit.

"Heaven and Earth," he continued in his deep, sonorous voice, "Gaea and Ouranos, gave birth to the Titans, the first gods to roam the earth. But eventually they too longed for company, and so the god Prometheus shaped the first man from the clay of the earth and breathed life into him.

Heaven and Earth's children, the gods and men, men-like gods and god-like men, have fought and played and loved and created until our own age, this moment in time, in which I speak. Now it is for us to tend to the eternal Now, here where we stand, though we and our actions be but one small strand in the great fabric of creation. We, the children of Dionysos, we honor his virtues, his patience and his perseverance and his promise of each new spring. We also honor his sister, Demeter, goddess of all the cultivated green. She it is who bestows 'the gift of the mother,' thus she is 'the mother gift-giver,' the *majka-don* from which this land of Makedon takes its name."

He spoke about a great many things that night. He told us a story of the origins of his people. How they were descendants of Temenus, the legendary founder of the first Macedonian state many centuries before Christ. How that legend passed down through the ages by Herodotus in his famous history was not mere legend, but based upon much that was true. But it was his concluding words that stuck most in my memory. When

Stoyan said, "Our brotherhood has survived through many long centuries. It saw the rise of the ancient Macedonian state and its fall at the hands of the Romans. It witnessed the wave of settlement of more eastern tribes, the Slav *Dragoviti* and the *Brziti*, and of the Turkic *Bugari*, and their allies the *Avari* and *Pecheneg*. And it survived the coming of the Byzantine Greek Christian state. It somehow survived the dark days of that church, when it mercilessly persecuted heretics, such as those lambs of God, the Bogomili, who suffered so terribly at the hands of the church state. They suffered because they would not hide themselves away as we did during those terrible times. Even though they, like ourselves, embraced the teachings of Christ, they were not so careful to conceal their other beliefs and practices that defied the rules of the established church."

His voice rose as he said, "Again, we endured the Turkish Moslem invasion and conquest of these lands. And we have survived, within living memory, the terrible wars of the 20th century, when the nation-states of the Balkans grew out of the break up of empires, and we survived the communist states of our lifetime, to this day and the new state that has risen from its ashes."

"We have survived through a combination of isolation in our remote mountain home and our veil of secrecy - even when we took part in the greater world around us, when our grandfathers joined the *komiti* who fought the Turks at the turn of the century, and our fathers fought against the fascists in the Second World War as *partizani*. And today as our sons serve in the Macedonian army of an independent Macedonian state, the first time since the Roman conquest of Macedonia over two thousand years ago."

His voice grew hushed now. "But we have always held this part of ourselves that we reveal here, our ancient tradition and spiritual practice, far from the public eye. And we have survived until today, through many long and often difficult centuries by this course of action. But I tell you, the days to come will hold their own trials. Now there are insistent newcomers on our territory. Newcomers that include the two you see before us today, whom we offer a place at our table, and they accept."

Stoyan beckoned the two of us to rise from the circle and join him. Borko stood and stepped forward. I awkwardly rose to my feet and followed him. Then Stoyan continued,"And now the moment has come to pronounce you brothers in our fellowship."

As I stood there alongside Borko and Stoyan, facing the assembled brothers, I had butterflies in my stomach. I instinctively knew that this was no small thing we were about to do. These rites and the oath of initiation would seal the bargain that we'd struck when agreeing to the initiation in the first place. All manner of possible unpleasant consequences raced through my mind as the moment to declare allegiance to the brotherhood drew near.

I would be binding myself to these near strangers in a way that I had only been bound to another through my wedding vows. Did that make sense? And would they ask me to betray any of my past loyalties? And if I failed to do as they asked, would they track me down and kill me?

"From this day forward you will carry the sign of the brotherhood, and you will hail a brother in the ancient speech and know each other by the greeting, *Zadravu*!"

Then one of the brothers brought Stoyan a special little tool that had been pre-heated on the fire. He lifted first Borko's and then my arm and set the strange little implement to the pale, soft skin on the inner side of our right forearms. I felt a moment of tremendous empathy with the bellowing cows I had once helped mark with a hot brand.

I somehow managed to keep my response down to a sharp grunt, though I felt more like howling the way those calves had at the time.

When I lifted my arm later to peer at it, the symbol engraved in my still stinging flesh looked to me like a v and an s superimposed on one another. Apparently the strange, rune-like little tatoo was the sign of the Druid ranch that now owned me.

Following the tatooing we swore a brief oath of loyalty to the brotherhood and promised to maintain its secrets. No one mentioned an 'or else,' and I was not inclined to ask. But I had no doubt that the brotherhood would take this oath rather seriously, and that I would be well-advised to do the same.

What had I gotten myself into? Fortunately, I didn't have time to dwell on this subject. The rest of the evening was spent in celebration. One that I would long remember.

Musicians from among the brothers pulled out traditional *kaval* flutes, *tapan* drums, and even a *gajda* or bagpipe with a goatskin airbag and a single drone pipe and began to play. The cave chamber echoed with the festive songs and dances from the distinct folk tradition of their region.

Rakija appeared on the table, and a series of toasts set the stage for the celebration that followed.

Everyone sang initially, but soon the entire band of guardians were on their feet, dancing. Their rather athletic circle dances would often begin slowly enough, but they would end in a mad whirling rush that left everyone panting for breath by the time the musicians brought their loud crescendo to an abrupt halt. Their ancient dances, some still common among Macedonian village people, echoed their ancient struggles and their joys and sorrows and their communal life.

The festivities ended with a special song and dance, an ancient warrior's dance, in honor of we two new brothers. Even the shopkeeper sang and danced the *oro* in our honor with genuine feeling. Borko and I stood in the center of the swaying circle of dancers, arm in arm, swaying to the rhythm and joining in on the simple chorus of the song.

For a time I simply lost myself in the glory of the moment. I was bursting with pride in my achievement and my new place in this ancient brotherhood. And from all appearances, Borko was reveling in this new-found fellowship, perhaps in ways that I couldn't begin to appreciate.

After the circle broke up, and the others prepared for sleep, Stoyan took Borko and me aside for a moment. He smiled and congratulated us again on our new status. Then his tone grew serious.

"Understand again that you are now our brothers, no matter where you go. And you will always be welcome in our village, in our lives, and to join us in all of our sacred celebrations."

He paused momentarily to emphasize the words that followed. "And you are now free to ask all of your questions, as well. And we must answer you." He paused again and fixed each of us in a penetrating gaze before continuing. "But you are not free to share those answers with the uninitiated."

"Is there a way we could get permission to share some of the answers with our colleagues?" asked Borko.

"Only if the high council, including the women's society, were persuaded to grant such a thing. But it is highly unlikely that they ever would."

Borko nodded in understanding. But when he translated what Stoyan had said for me, I couldn't hide a momentary look of disappointment. Stoyan seemed to sense the source of my troubled look.

"A day may come when we are hard-pressed to maintain our secrets. If and when such a day should come, I have staked much on the belief that you scientists become brothers will see that we come to no harm from the outside world from which you come to us."

It was now becoming clearer why we had been invited to join them in the first place. But it seemed like they were taking a considerable risk that we wouldn't betray their trust as soon as we were off the mountain. Then again, I had no doubt that we would expose ourselves to considerable risk if we were to do something so foolish.

Stoyan remained with us for another hour, in which he related some of the remarkable things that he had only hinted at thus far. I felt such a tremendous sense of privilege to have this knowledge shared with me. As we finally rose to go, it occurred to me to ask one final question that had been nagging at me for some time. "Did you arrange for our abduction from a restaurant in Tetovo a while back?"

The answer, by way of Borko, was, "Some things may remain a mystery. I don't know who abducted you."

As we rose to go off to bed, Stoyan startled me with his final words to me that night. "And may you encounter only the friendliest of snakes in your dream world, ones that respond happily to your touch, from this day hence."

"How in the world did you know?" I whispered in astonishment. But he just shrugged off my question with a dismissive wave of his hand.

I have no explanation for his knowing, and I've given up trying to explain it, even to myself anymore. But there it is.

The study "HLA genes in Macedonians and the sub-Saharan origin of the Greeks" is presented in the Danish medical journal "Tissue Antigens", February 2001, volume 57, issue 2, pages 118-127... abstract: "HLA alleles have been determined in individuals from the Republic of Macedonia by DNA typing and sequencing. HLA-A, -B, -DR, -DQ allele frequencies and extended haplotypes have been for the first time determined and the results compared to those of other Mediterraneans, particularly with their neighbouring Greeks. Genetic distances, neighbour-joining dendrograms and correspondence analysis have been performed. The following conclusions have been reached: 1) Macedonians belong to the "older" Mediterranean substratum, like Iberians (including Basques), North Africans, Italians, French, Cretans, Jews, Lebanese, Turks (Anatolians), Armenians and Iranians; 2) Macedonians are not related to geographically close Greeks, who do not belong to the "older" Mediterranean substratum.

– from *The Descendants of Alexander the Great of Macedon* by Aleksandar Donski

Chapter 10 – the return

At noon the following day, Borko and I climbed back into the van that had sat parked out front of the mayor's house these past several weeks. We were back in our usual clothes and I had taken to wearing my glasses again. Borko had shaved that morning, for the first time in weeks.

It took several hours to drive back to the archaeology site. And during that drive our talk grew serious.

"Well, what do you think, Borko," I began tentatively enough. "Can we resist the temptation to share what we've learned with the outside world?"

Borko glanced my way. "You had better hope we can. No doubt that the brotherhood considers the oath we took every much bit as serious as the oaths our grandfathers in the *komita* took when they swore on a Bible with crossed dagger and pistol, when joining the fight against the Turk."

When we stepped out of the van at the site, the crew crowded around us. Everyone seemed relieved to have us back and in one piece, and, in fact, looking more fit and trim than we had before we left.

"That must have been some health spa up there in those mountains, where you spent the last few weeks. You look real good," declared Joel.

"Getting staked out in the sun naked and being fed raw grubs seems to have agreed with them alright," quipped Deb.

"So tell us what you've learned about these strange mountain village people," demanded Sasho.

Borko and I exchanged glances. "Don't ask, Sasho," replied Borko.

I could see a hardening in the faces of our young colleagues. They were none too happy with his response. But neither Borko nor I intended to talk to them about our adventures or our new knowledge of the mysterious people of Meshkom.

We walked off to our tents to stow our gear and rest awhile. After supper we sat around the campfire with our crew, who once again broached the subject of our experiences with the brotherhood.

"There is nothing to tell you," said Borko.

"Maybe the time'll come when we can share some of what we've learned," I added. "But you'll just have to be patient about it. This is a very old and secretive sect that we're dealing with. We can only go at a pace that they're comfortable with. Borko and I will keep visiting them, and slowly maybe over the course of time, we'll get permission to reveal some of the amazing things we've learned."

"But it will take time," cautioned Borko. "Maybe years. We can only hope that it will be in our lifetimes."

"Oh great!" groaned Deb. "I knew it. Didn't I tell you. They've been totally programmed by the Druids."

"We have not been programmed!" I objected. "We're the same people we always were. But we're honor-bound not to reveal things about the brotherhood that they haven't agreed yet to share with outsiders."

Borko and I sat side by side in the circle, with the others surrounding us on both sides.

"And we're the outsiders, right?" asked Deb.

"You weren't there, so you don't know what we know," said Borko gruffly. "So you are in no place to judge."

"You know that we were there," said Sasho. "You know that we didn't experience all that you did, but we saw some things. In fact, you don't know all of what we saw."

I wondered whether they'd watched Borko and I the day we'd stood out in that clearing all day, buck naked and covered with mud. "Well, you'll just have to be content with whatever you were able to learn by sneaking around up there on your own," I said.

"I'm beginning to learn something new about objectivity and subjectivity, and the danger that subjective experience poses to scientific inquiry," said Deb.

"So you think that we have become dangerously subjective, is that right?" asked Borko, his voice rising a notch or two with his anger.

"Yes, I think there is some evidence of that," said Sasho.

I had never seen Sasho challenge his mentor this way before. What had we done? Instead of creating a bridge between two worlds, we had become additional stones to the wall that the people of Meshkom had erected against the outside world.

Members of the welcome home party were openly glaring at us now. The chill in the air around the campfire made the distant mountains look warm and inviting in compare. I was already beginning to miss the brotherhood.

"Oh, by the way, Doc," said Joel. "Professor Misirkova came by again today. She says that she wants to see you and Professor Milevski as soon as possible."

Great, I thought. Just what we need, one more unfriendly face to greet us on our homecoming. At least there were no policemen here to put us in handcuffs yet. "We'll talk to her," I replied.

After an uncomfortable interval of stone silence around the campfire, I got up to go off to my tent for the night. Though I couldn't resist a parting, "Happy 4th of July, everyone!"

How would we ever bridge the present gulf between us and our crew? I certainly wanted to share what I knew with them, but how could I? And these students clearly weren't going to take no for an answer from their teachers. After all, what is it teachers do, if not share their knowledge?

Borko left the circle when I did, but the crew members stayed on until late into the night. I was kept awake by loud, drunken voices laughing and talking over the sounds of a ghetto blaster belting out equally loud rock music.

When I stepped outside to take a late-night leak, I could see some heavy necking going on over by the campfire, and a few of the kids were passed out after too much booze. Joel had also informed me earlier that he was no longer sleeping in the tent with us. He'd traded around until he and Rada had a little tent all to themselves on the edge of camp.

The next morning Borko and I sat in the mess tent having coffee all alone. The others were sleeping off the effects of last night's party.

"What has happened to this crew?" asked Borko.

"It appears that they've turned into party animals in our absence."

"It sounded more like Sodom and Gommorah out there last night, to me," he said, shaking his head in disgust.

Eventually Deb emerged from her tent and joined us. "I heard what you just said," she confided as she poured herself some coffee and sat down at the table across from us. "And it's true. While you were off getting inducted into the Druid society this expedition turned into a summer beach party. Ands serves you right."

"How so?" I studied my coffee mug, avoiding her eyes. I knew I wasn't going to like the answer.

"You didn't help keep them focused. Instead you got busy with your own individual project, and they were forced to shift for themselves." Her teaspoon clattered in the pot of dirty dishes as she tossed it angrily among the other utensils.

"Well, you and Joel and Sasho were here. And you're not children, you know," argued Borko with a frown. "You were expected to be in charge in our absence. But as we know, you weren't here so much either."

"But we don't have your authority with these kids."

Eventually others rose from their beds, and when Rada appeared at the breakfast table without Joel, I asked, "Where's Joel, still asleep?"

"He wasn't there when I got up this morning," she answered.

"Where could he have gone?" asked Borko.

"Is Sasho gone too?" asked Deb.

"I haven't see him anywhere this morning."

"I think I know where they've gone," said Borko.

I had a strange feeling that I already knew the answer as well.

"Up in the mountains, beyond Meshkom, is my guess," said Borko.

I stood up. "So they've gone off to learn some of what we refused to tell them. Is that it?" I asked.

"I imagine so," replied Deb.

"Let's get some gear together and get going," I said.

"We should alert Stoyan and the others," said Borko.

"Yes, of course," I said as I hurried off to pack things I'd need for the trip back into the mountains.

"I'm coming too," said Deb.

I paused to consider this. "No, someone has to stay and look after the camp," I said.

"Look after what?" asked Deb, staring at me with raised brows.

"What difference does it make? If she wants to come, let her come," said Borko, as he too strode off to get his things together for the trip.

"Okay," I said. "Just get together a knapsack with everything you'll need for overnight."

The three of us arrived in Meshkom by mid-morning. We found the mayor at home. When we explained the reason for our visit, he immediately sent for several of the brothers.

When Stoyan saw Deb, he asked why we had brought the young woman along. Borko explained, "She is our assistant, and she also has some knowledge of the plans of the others who are on their way to the cave." He hesitated, then decided to also reveal that, "She has already been on the mountain. She was among several of our students who followed us up there two weeks ago, without our knowledge or consent." He frowned as he said the last words.

Stoyan gave her a long look. Then he shook his head in dismay. "What mischievous students you have taken on, professor. Don't you have any control over them?"

"Not much, it would appear," answered Borko, looking over at Deb. She was in the next room, sipping a cup of Turkish coffee and smiling amiably at her hostess, Stoyan's raven-haired wife. Despite the language barrier they appeared to have established genuine rapport.

Stoyan's wife hastily prepared some further provisions for our trip, and the group of us set off for the mountains. We traveled on foot accompanied by a couple of pack animals. It was a half day's trek up to the cave. But I had almost memorized the narrow footpath way up the ridges, that crisscrossed its way through a series of steep gorges with thick pine and fir cover before finally emerging in the high country basin where the cave was located.

It felt good to be back on our way up into these mountains again. The pure mountain air was sweet and pleasant in my lungs. The hike was good, even if it was in pursuit of our unruly assistants. And I had to ask myself if I would have behaved any differently if I were in their place?

Although the brotherhood didn't seem particularly prone to violence, it only seemed prudent for us to accompany them. We couldn't know for sure, how they might deal with trespassers on their territory. I knew that I would not have wanted to be the one caught up there by these tough mountaineers.

At one point in the climb, Stoyan turned his gaze to the tall, billowy, white thunderheads with angry-looking dark shadows that were gathering over the mountain peaks ahead. "We may not make it to the shelter of the cave before those clouds burst," he announced.

He was right about that. We were still a half hour away from the shelter of the cave when the rain began to pelt us like b-b shot. It was a typical summer cloudburst in these mountains. It poured by the bucketful for about 20 minutes, then stopped as suddenly as it had begun. But we were all thoroughly soaked when we finally arrived at the cave.

Stoyan examined the footprints in the soft earth at the entrance to the cave. "Yes, someone has been here recently," he announced. Then he looked back at us and said, "They have not yet exited the cave. It will be enough if we simply wait here for them. They will eventually have to come back this way. Go ahead and build a fire now, so that we can get dried out while we wait."

We set to work building the fire. After Deb had helped us work, she stood next to the fire and shook the excess water from her jacket and swiped at the wet hair that had fallen across her forehead. I could barely suppress a grin, because she looked at the moment like a wet mop with eyes, nose and a mouth. But my respect for her was growing, as I observed how hardy and resourceful she could be. I didn't doubt for a minute that she would have passed our recent initiation trials as well as we had.

Once the fire was crackling away and everyone was busy drying steamy outer garments by holding them near the fire, Deb turned to me and murmured, "You sure defer to their cult leader, don't you?"

I grimaced slightly. I turned my back to the fire in order to give my backside a chance to dry. I finally said to her, "So you think that Borko and I have become glassy-eyed underlings of the evil cult-master, eh?"

"Well, you sure seem to be in lock-step with their program since your camp out up here with the Druid scouts."

This young woman could certainly drive me nuts at times. "Borko and I are still scientists," I said. Maybe we had become a little more sensitive to native traditions. Deb was too young, in any case, to remember the bad old days in American archaeology when we used to dig up Native American cemeteries and put both the bodies and funeral relics on display in our museums. "Would you have approved of the plunder of your ancestors graves in the name of science?" I asked her.

"Hey, Alexander and I could be related for all I know. But I don't have any problems with excavating his remains and funeral relics and putting them on display."

"Well, I do now," I said.

About an hour later three figures emerged from the dark depths of the cave. The light from their flashlight beams preceded them. They had been talking excitedly among themselves, but they fell silent as soon as they realized that there were people waiting for them at the entrance to the cave. They hesitated momentarily, then thought better of retreat. They must have realized that they would, in any event, eventually have to face whoever it was that blocked their exit from the cave.

When they finally emerged from the gloom, Joel, Sasho and Mavros faced Borko, Deb and I and a half-dozen men from the village.

"Well, did you see what you came to see?" asked Borko.

Joel nodded, but none of them spoke.

"Ah, I see the first signs of Greek-Macedonian cooperation here. And there were those who said that our two peoples could never come to terms," said Borko.

This provoked Mavros to speak. "Now I have seen the treasure of Alexander the Great. I still don't know what to think of this Dionysian cult business, but the treasure is no fiction."

"You had no right to keep this to yourselves," said Sasho. "Even if your claims go back to orders handed down from that master schemer, Alexander's mother, Olympias. Her day is long past."

"Keeping faith for 2300 years is no small thing in our world. Don't be so quick. Consider the rights of the guardians," said Borko.

"But Alexander has always belonged to the whole world," argued Deb. "He said as much himself. When he was asked one time, because he accepted people of every nation and race that he met, 'What race are you?'

He answered, 'I'm of the human race.'"

"That silly quote again!" said Borko.

"Is it so ridiculous?" asked Sasho. "That a man born in Macedonia, educated by Greeks, who married a Bactrian Princess, and whose army and empire included people of every nation between the Adriatic and the Indian Ocean, should proclaim himself a citizen of the world?"

"That still doesn't give you any right to trample on the rights of the people who've guarded his tomb all these centuries," I snapped.

"The tomb and treasure would not even exist today for you to loot, if the guardians had not proven so faithful. It would have been plundered long ago by grave robbers," said Borko, as he blocked their further advance out of the tunnel.

"We have no choice now but to call a Council of the Elders of our Society," said Stoyan. "We must now decide upon the best course of action, given the fact that there is no way we can keep these young people from pursuing this. We'll post guards on the cave to see that no one else disturbs it while we deliberate."

Then Stoyan beckoned to Mavros to give him his shoulder bag.

Mavros shook his head no. He started to back away as several of the village men moved toward him.

"Give it to him," I barked. "He can't let you take those pictures back to your newspaper. If they were to publish those, it would send a wave of treasure hunters up this mountain that an army couldn't stop."

"But newspapers in Skopje already have published pictures of the tomb," said Mavros.

"But few, if any people, took the news very seriously in the absence of the treasure," I said. "It was the hope at the time that the release of those photos might help in the search for the thieves."

"Well, we now have the thieves," said Mavros, nodding in the direction of the villagers.

"No," said Borko. "We turned out to be the thieves."

"You have no right," Mavros continued to protest as Borko removed the camera from his bag and extracted the film from his camera.

"What will you do with them?" asked Borko of Stoyan, as he nodded in the direction of our assistants. I could see Deb's eyes widen at the thought that they would be delivered into the hands of the Guardians.

"Your colleagues have not taken anything that does not belong to them, only pictures so far. So let them be your responsibility," replied Stoyan. "In an earlier time, outsiders who tried to steal from the Guardians were condemned to death. We live in new times, requiring new, measured responses. But we will not allow anyone to loot the tomb of Alexander."

It was nearly dark by the time we arrived back at the village, and almost midnight by the time we reached our camp and Mavros departed for his hotel room in Valandovo.

The Council of Elders was apparently in no hurry to reach a decision. An entire day passed with still no word from them. "There must be a heck of a debate going on among them," I said to the others, as we sat around our campfire the following evening.

"I bet they'll just rebury the Big Mac in some remote place in the mountains and let us archaeologists and the grave robbers spend another 2000 years looking for it," said Joel.

"I think we should go back up in the mountains and watch to see that they aren't doing just that at this very moment," said Sasho.

"No!" shouted Borko. "You have no right to do that!"

"You have no right to stop us!" Sasho shot back.

"Yes," said Deb, "We should go up there and see that they don't hide him where we'll never find him again."

"You may not be so lucky the next time they catch you up there, especially if Borko and I aren't there to bail you out," I said.

The tension among us only increased as the evening wore on. Borko and I continued to defend the rights of the Guardians to dispense with the treasure as they saw fit. But our assistants remained unmoved by our arguments. They became ever more insistent on spying on the Guardians.

I finally stood up and glared at our young colleagues. "Any of you plan to sneak off up there again, you'd better get your things out of this camp for good. And plan to sell real estate for a living, because you won't be doing archaeology again!"

"We are now?" demanded Deb. "No. We're sitting here wasting time, while your brotherhood is busy hiding the treasure of Alexander."

"I'll bet it's already too late," lamented Joel. "Their Druid buddies probably started hiding everything again as soon as we left yesterday."

"You are all fools," said Borko. "That pile of old *djubre* up on that mountain is nothing compared to the treasures of the living people who guard it."

"So we would think differently about things if we'd had a chance to get programmed by the Druid Mr. Moon, like you and Professor Starkweather," said Deb. I noticed that she no longer averted her eyes at all, when she addressed Borko. Now she fixed him in a cold stare.

"I do believe that you'd see things differently if you'd experienced what we did," I said. "What does the treasure of Alexander really represent to the group of you? The chance as archaeologists to crow your discoveries."

Sasho stood up and faced us now. "It is a chance for present-day Macedonians to get more publicity for the fact that we really do live on land that was once ancient Macedonia."

"Was that ever seriously in doubt?" I asked. "But I'll bet the local chamber of commerce will want to milk the tomb for all its worth, the way the Greeks have the treasures from Philip, Alexander's father's tomb."

"Would it really be so bad if the Skopje Museum rivaled the museum in Thessaloniki?" asked Sasho.

"There are certainly worse things than that," argued Deb. "The whole treasure could be buried away again in the earth, so that no one gets to appreciate its beauty or its historical value."

"Alright! Go then!" roared Borko. "Sneak back up there and watch them. I won't stop you. But don't expect us to rescue you when the Guardians catch you sneaking around their mountain again!"

"Let's get going now, tonight!" said Sasho. "Who's coming?"

Joel and Deb both nodded their intention to go, so did several of the students. They quickly packed all of their gear and prepared to set off. There was one minor hitch, however, when they asked Borko to let them take the museum van.

"I said that I wouldn't stop you," he told them. "But I never said I would help you."

"I'll go call Mavros again," announced Deb.

"Yes, do that," said Sasho.

Eventually Mavros arrived, and as many of them as could, piled into his car, and they drove off. Since there was so little room in the car, Rada was the only one among the undergrad students invited to go along, due to her special relationship with Joel.

Those left behind remained sullen and distant, despite the departure of the ringleaders. The kids waited impatiently for us to go off to bed, so that they could crank up their ghetto blaster again and rock out til dawn.

When I heard the decibel level of their music rise as I lay in my bunk, I began to despair again about the prospects for this entire expedition. All of the goodwill that we had built up through our initiation into the brotherhood might be undone through the rash actions of the students who had gone back up in the mountains.

Finally I stuck my head out of the tent and shouted at the crew, "Turn that racket down!" Then I pointed to the beer and wine bottles on the camp table. "And I want those bottles!" I paused for breath and continued, "From now on there will be no parties til all hours of the night, and you'll all get up at dawn tomorrow to begin work at Professor Misirkova's site." I paused again and added, "Or you'll get out of here!"

The students sullenly complied and skulked off to their bunks. Borko and I exchanged glances as he also poked his head out to see what was happening. He nodded his approval. But how long would this antagonism continue?

Just as I was about to tuck my head back into the tent, Professor Misirkova emerged from the dark. And even in this bad light, I could tell that she was not a happy camper. "So you have now assigned your rowdy crew to my worksite. I heard you. You might have at least had the courtesy to ask me first," she shouted at Borko and me.

"We were intending to come to you first thing in the morning, to ask," said Borko. "So what is your answer?"

"I shouldn't, but I hate to see your students continue on this way," she replied.

"Fine, Jovanka, fine," said Borko, nodding his head in agreement.

"But you and your colleague, Professor Starkweather, have been called to Skopje, to report to the university administration immediately. To explain what you have been doing this summer. And don't expect them to listen to wild tales about ancient Pelasgians stealing the real treasures of Alexander from under your noses." Having said this she turned abruptly and retreated back to her own camp.

Borko shook his head in despair and disappeared back into his tent. I wondered how we would ever prove the truth of our story without resorting to the evidence that the Guardians had forbidden us to reveal.

On the evening of the next day, Mavros dropped Joel and Rada off at the camp and went back to his hotel room to get cleaned up. They looked tired from their hike down from the mountain, and they ate ravenously. Their food supply had begun to run out. So the three of them had come back for more supplies.

"So how goes the vigil?" I asked.

"No movement yet," said Joel. "The guards have remained at their post at the cave entrance. So we figure that they haven't tried to move the Big Mac anywhere else yet."

"Borko and I have decided to make a trip into Meshkom this evening. We'd like to make the Elders a proposal."

"Have you told them yet about what we're doing?" he asked.

"No, not yet," I said, though he didn't look as if he believed me. "Though I wouldn't be surprised if they already know. You forget that you're roaming around in their mountains. Do you really think much of anything happens up there that they don't know about?"

Joel shrugged. He yawned and said, "Got to get to bed, Doc. Getting up real early tomorrow to go back up with supplies."

When Borko and I pulled up in front of Stoyan's house later that evening and went in, we were not surprised to find a large group of men and women gathered in the parlor.

"*Zadravu*, brothers," we were greeted at the door.

"We have a proposal for you," said Borko, as we stepped into the room.

"Well, let us sit and have a little coffee together, and then you can tell us all about it," proposed Stoyan.

We found places to sit. I looked around me. Some of the people in the room looked familiar, others didn't. Then my gaze fell on the detective from the regional police station who had investigated the looting of the tomb two months before. He winked at me when our eyes met.

Borko nudged me and drew my attention to another man, sitting at the opposite end of the room. "I'd swear that that man sitting over there was one of the guards at the tomb," he whispered.

"I wouldn't be surprised," I whispered back.

Eventually we were served coffee and the conversation turned to more important matters. "Actually," announced Stoyan, "if you had not come to us, we would have come to you. We are almost in agreement on a course of action, but we need your advice."

"We need some advice as well," said Borko. "Our students are in revolt. You would not believe how determined our young archaeologists are to learn the secrets of Alexander's tomb."

"If we don't find some way to include them and to share some of what we know with them, we risk turning them into dangerous adversaries rather than allies," I added.

When we returned to camp later that evening, the kids were rocking out again. When they saw us coming, several of them signaled to the others to cut back on the volume and get the booze out of sight. I didn't make a scene this time. We merely passed among them quietly and went off to bed.

French academician Georges Cerbelaud Salagnac, …in 1992 in Paris published a book entitled "The Ethnic Origins of Europeans" ("Les Origines Ethniques des Europeens." Editions Perrin, 1992, Paris, France). In this book …the French academician wrote:

"Macedonians still exist today in Europe, divided into two parts. The Greek province in the south and the Republic of Macedonia in the north… Both have a clear notion of their common ethnic origin, and from both Salonica and Skopje they do not feel strangers" (cited work, page 96).

from *The Descendants of Alexander the Great of Macedon* by Aleksandar Donski.

Chapter 11 – back to the mountain

The next morning early, I was there when Joel and Rada crawled out of their tent. I had my gear ready for travel as well, and several of the students who had been left behind previously were with me with their camping gear.

"Do you mindjoin you on the mountain?" I asked.

Joel shrugged and said, "I don't have a problem with that. King Borko gonna make you walk, or do you have use of the van?"

"Borko will let us take the van."

After breakfast Mavros arrived and several of the students climbed into his car. Others, including Joel and Rada, joined me in the van. Borko stood by the door in the company of the remaining students. He had chosen to stay behind with the remainder of the crew and await further news from the council. As I prepared to drive off I asked him, "Do you have any plans to make the time pass a little easier while you're waiting for news?"

"Yes, I do," he answered with a slightly mischievous glint. "I think I'd like to go find a few local friends to help in the education of the young people."

While I was still pondering this, he turned to the students at his side. "I believe that we can make some good use of our time while we wait," he announced. "I will need a branch about five feet long with a fork," he explained to them.

I gave a nod of approval as I put the van in gear and we drove off.

We stopped in Marvintsi on our way and picked up extra provisions for our stay in the mountains. During the drive, Joel turned to me and asked, "Your Druid friends aren't planning to jump us somewhere on the trail are they?"

"No, not that I know of," I answered cheerfully.

"You know, Doc, you sometimes act like you don't think I'm cut out to be a professional archaeologist. But the reason Deb and Sasho and Rada and I chose to defy you is that we care about archaeology, and we're not all that sure that you and Professor Milevski do, anymore."

"Yes, I think we figured that out. But maybe we've learned some things recently that made us think about what we were doing."

Joel didn't seem impressed. "Is this the same prof who likes to scowl each time he sees me with my arm around a friend, talking about other values besides archaeology?"

The hike up into the mountains took most of the afternoon. When we arrived at our assistants' camp, Deb and Sasho were startled to see me with the others, but they were more immediately interested in the food that our party had brought them.

"Any activity up at the cave?" asked Joel, as his colleagues downed big hunks of bread with feta-type cheese and plump red tomatoes.

"None that we could see," said Deb through a mouthful of food.

Joel picked up the binoculars and strolled over to a nearby ledge, where there was a gap in the brush through which he could site in on the cave entrance about a half mile away. He peered through the field glasses for a time and returned to the others. "Looks pretty normal to me," he said.

"Can you take the first shift this evening, Joel?" asked Deb. "I really need a break."

"I'll get Mavros to spell me," said Joel.

Sasho turned to Deb. "More bread?" he asked as he held out a hunk he'd sliced off.

"No thanks, I think I've had enough for now," she answered. "But that sure was good. Folks grow some great-tasting tomatoes around here."

"We have a very good climate for them," said Sasho. "You won't believe the tomatoes my mother grows in her village. Wait til you taste them."

"Yes, I'm looking forward to that," she answered.

Nothing like common cause to bring people together, I thought. "Do you want me to take a shift?" I asked.

"How come? We more expected to see you down there at the cave entrance, protecting Alexander's treasure hoard from the marauding archaeologists," said Deb.

"Maybe I'll go down and spell one of the Guardians after I've finished my shift up here with my archaeology team," I said.

"Honestly. Whatever made you come up here with us?" she asked.

"I just thought maybe I'd been neglecting my students recently," I said. "And since you didn't choose to wait down in our camp for word from the Council of Elders, I thought I ought to join you up here at your camp."

"Well, I hope you're not surprised if we don't altogether trust you these days. You and Professor Milevski came back from your time with the Druids considerably changed."

"For the better, I hope."

"That remains to be seen," said Sasho. "And where is my esteemed colleague, Professor Milevski? He isn't over at the cave, is he?"

"No," I answered. "He's still back at our camp."

"Rocking with the kids from new Woodstock Nation?" asked Deb.

"No, not really. The last I saw of him he was showing them something he'd learned from the Guardians, and the kids seemed really interested."

"Isn't that liable to get him drawn and quartered? Once they find out that he's spilling his secrets to the uninitiated?" asked Deb.

"There are things we can share and things we can't."

"So when should we start worrying about what you intend to share with the Druids about what we're up to here?" asked Deb.

Mavros, who had been listening to everything we'd been saying, broke in. "Sasho, you should have appealed to the authorities, as I suggested earlier. The government in Skopje could have sent an armed unit to prevent this national treasure from being hidden away again."

I frowned at Mavros. "In answer to your question, Deb. There's nothing to be done until we hear from the Council of Elders. Until then, I'm content to watch the cave with the rest of you. And if they move the treasure before that, I'll help you track them to the new site. But I know they won't take action until the Council makes its decision."

"Will you help us after the Council decides?" asked Deb.

Joel came back from observing the site with the binoculars just in time to save me from having to answer her.

"Anything else happening over at the cave?" I asked him.

"Nothing far as we can tell," said Joel. "They look as bored as we are. But I'm beginning to think that they know that we're here. They're just not making any big deal out of it."

"Well, then, how about if we go over and pay them a visit?"

"You can if you want, but I'd like to stay up here where I have a good view of their every move," said Joel. "I do not want the Big Mac to disappear for another 2000 years. No way, Doc."

"That's fine. You want to come along, Deb? Any others?" I asked.

"I'll come," said Sasho. "I can translate for you, and I wouldn't mind hearing more of their speech. If it is possible, I hope someday to do a thorough study of it. Study of their archaisms may provide clues to meanings of some of the more obscure words in the manuscript from the tomb."

"I think they might welcome that," I said.

"But Sasho hasn't been hung by his heels and fed raw grubs for two weeks yet," said Deb. "Are you sure that they'd be so welcoming to him?"

"I think that Sasho would pass muster with them," I said.

"You providing character references for folks who would like a job interview with the Druids?" asked Joel as he poured himself some coffee.

"Maybe." I looked at Joel now, studying him carefully. "Why? Would you like a reference?"

"Maybe." He looked down at the cup in his hands. "You know, I wanted to be in the last graduating class at Druid High, but it seems that they weren't that liberal. Not quite ready for an integrated school, I suppose."

"Well, could be they're more receptive now," I said.

"Right now I've got to show some loyalty to my old school," he said as he picked up his binoculars and prepared to return to the ledge.

"I never thought of you as a loyal or dedicated to school," I said and regretted it almost before the words were out of my mouth.

"I was, but I had a strange habit of trying not to show it too much," Joel fussed with his coffee cup now. "Maybe so no one would notice if I failed. Make it easier if they didn't know I'd ever tried all that hard in the first place," he said as he got up to go back to observing the cave entrance.

"Are you sure you don't want to come with us, Deb?" I asked one last time.

This time she and several of the others, including Rada, decided to join Sasho and me. The Guardians proved to be as bored as our crew, waiting for some sort of decision from the Council of Elders. When I approached with my students, they immediately welcomed us to their campfire circle.

One of the men had a shepherd's flute, a *kaval*, that he began to play for us. Sasho and Rada knew the song. They began to sing the words, about dark Andja, kidnapped by a Turkish pasha who intends to force her to be his future bride. She swears she will never accept him. A stubborn song for a stubborn people.

"Ajde slushai, slushai, kalesh bre Andjo

Tamburitsa sviri, kalesh bre Andjo"[2]

One song led to another, and soon they had a drummer and a guitarist join the band, and someone else started a circle dance that nearly everyone joined in.

Deb, Sasho and I sat down by the fire to rest. "Just a few weeks ago we couldn't get anyone from Meshkom to even talk to us," I said. "Now they entertain us with their music and teach us their dances."

An elderly man from the village, weathered-looking, with snow-white hair, sat down beside us. Through Sasho, he said to Deb, "You look the very image of our Demeter!"

He asked Deb some questions about her life and her work. Deb told him about her ambitions to be a professional archaeologist.

"What is it that is so appealing about digging up someone's ancestors and staring at their bones?" the white-haired old man asked her, innocently enough.

"We're so ignorant about the past," Deb replied. "Those bones and the things buried with them can tell us so many things about the people who came before us. How they lived and died. What they cared about."

"But maybe it's rude to stare at someone's bones. Maybe they would rather you left them undisturbed in the ground," the elder continued.

"I'm not disrespectful of the dead," Deb responded, after pausing to think about what the old man had said. "What I really want is to ask them questions. I want them to tell me all about themselves. As much as their bones and all of the things they chose to take with them into the grave can

---

[2]   "Come listen, listen, oh dark haired Andja
    a tamburitsa plays, oh dark haired Andja."

tell."

"You already said that. But don't you have parents and grandparents you can ask about the people from long ago?"

"Yes, but they don't know that much either," replied Deb with a slightly pained look. "They've been busy with their own lives. They haven't been able to keep that many memories of the past alive."

"But did you think then that you have no choice but to dig up our ancestors and ask their bones to tell you their story? Why didn't you ask us first? Maybe we could have answered some of your questions," the man continued.

"I didn't know that there was anyone to ask," replied Deb. "Why didn't one of your people come tell us that you were the guardians of the tomb?" Deb challenged him.

"Perhaps we were afraid that you wouldn't believe us or accept our right to protect the tomb from thieves," the man said. "You seemed more like the kind of people who take whatever they want with little regard for others, and give little or nothing in return."

"No! That's not how we are!" shouted Deb, standing now and getting ready to bolt.

"Tell me, young woman," and the elder looked at her closely now. "Do you remember ever seeing me before?"

"No," said Deb firmly.

"But many times when you have driven through our village in your car, you've passed me on the road, walking to or from my fields," he said. "Why didn't you ever consider stopping to ask an old man if he would like a ride?"

Deb stalked away now, into the night. Sasho got up and hurried after her. Later that evening the rest of us returned as well. Everyone was laughing and talking and loaded down with fruit that the Guardians had shared with us.

"You all sure looked like you were having a good time over there," said Joel as we settled into our sleeping bags around the fire pit. "It made me sorry that I didn't join you. But nobody said anything about a party."

"I've had more fun," said Deb.

I was lying on my back now, inside my bag, staring up at the first stars that were beginning to appear in the night sky. "Do you see that cluster of stars there to the south?" I asked. "Just below the Evening Star. It's known as Ariadne. Stoyan told us a story about how the constellation came to have that name. Do you want to hear?"

"Sure. If you want to tell us," said Deb with a yawn.

"That's a fine old story," said Joel, when I'd finished. "Now how about telling us a little something about the folks down at the cave."

"Of course, you know that even though everyone calls these old Balkan myths Greek myths, serious scholars have known for a long time that they didn't originate with the Greeks, but have much older roots among the ancient Balkan peoples," said Sasho.

I paused a moment, then said, "I've had some time now to think about the tradition and origins of the cult in Meshkom. I suspect that the cult has roots in the Neolithic societies of Old Europe. You probably know what I'm referring to, those societies described in recent studies of prehistoric Balkan archaeology.

It's been established that much of Southeastern and Central Europe were once part of an ancient cradle of civilization rivaling ancient Egypt, Mesopotamia or India. Societies dating back nearly 9,000 years.

They've found evidence of advanced agriculture, pottery, stone and metal work, as well as goddess-oriented religious cults. And evidence of peaceful, egalitarian peoples, at a time in history when most people assumed that primitive, violent relations were the norm."

Unfortunately, my orations fell only upon sleep-deafened ears, because when I finished, there were only the sounds of slumbering bodies all around me. However, about four in the morning, just before dawn, we all awoke to a deafening roar from the sky. The trees above our heads began to whip madly about. Then an enormous searchlight beam flooded our camp with light and moved on.

After it had passed over, we scrambled out of our bags and peered out over the rim of the ridge, where we could see the craft move on in the direction of the cave entrance. We could see now that it was a large transport helicopter making all the racket. The powerful turbulence created by its blades had whipped the trees into a frenzy around us. The chopper had an enormous searchlight mounted on its nose that it used to illuminate the area in front of the cave.

The helicopter landed in a clearing some two hundred yards from the entrance, in an area that had previously been marked with flares. A dozen men in camouflage suits, wearing black ski masks and wielding automatic rifles, leapt from the chopper as soon as it touched down.

They immediately began racing toward the entrance to the cave as we stared with wide eyes from our perch a half mile away. As the intruders approached the entrance, the defenders from Meshkom fled into the surrounding woods, recognizing that they were no match for the raiders. There was the sound of a few bursts of automatic weapons fire, but after a few moments there was only silence as the commandoes swept into the cave.

"This is Mavros's doing, I'm sure of it!" said Sasho, crouched down with the rest of us, watching the scene below. "That must be a Greek army special forces unit. Who else would have such up-to-date weapons and a helicopter gunship. Not our pathetic little army. The Yugoslav army saw to that when they retreated early on in the break up of Yugoslavia."

"I'll bet they can be out of here with that big chopper with the entire treasure of Alexander easily," said Joel.

"How do they dare violate Macedonian airspace?" screamed Rada.

"Who's to stop them? Our army and border troops probably don't even own a radar system that can detect such an intrusion," said Sasho.

"The treasure will probably end up in the museum in Salonika, where it will now make the Greeks' reputation for Macedonian antiquities grander than ever," wailed Rada.

After what seemed like an eternity, but may have only been about forty five minutes, the raiders emerged from the cave and made their way back to the waiting helicopter. They were airborne again and completely gone within minutes.

"It's gone forever!" wailed Rada.

"Those Greek bastards! I hate them!" screamed Sasho.

Borko and Stoyan and a small party of others arrived at the entrance to the cave around mid-morning. When Borko couldn't find anyone, neither the Guardians nor his own people in the vicinity, he planted his feet firmly on the rocky ground, and with his back to the cave entrance, he took a deep breath. Then he cupped his hands around the edges of his mouth and let out a powerful echoing cry.

"Eeeeeeh moriiiii Saaasho! Eeeeeh Jaaack!"

About twenty minutes passed before we emerged into his view down among the trees on the valley floor. A few minutes later we slowly approached the cave entrance.

Although we looked utterly downcast, as if someone had just died, Borko didn't catch onto our mood. He shouted to us as we drew near.

"We have news from the Elders. A decision was made by the Council of Elders yesterday evening. We have some archaeology work to do. It seems that they want us to study the treasures from the tomb of Alexander."

He still hadn't noticed our somber mood. "And from our notes," he continued, "we will make further reproductions of every object in the collection in order to make the tomb ready for public viewing. The originals will be hidden away again for their safekeeping by the Guardians."

He looked so pleased, but I could see his expression beginning to change as he noticed that no one was shouting for joy at his news.

"It's gone!" cried Rada. "The Greeks came and stole the entire treasure. With a helicopter. Just hours ago!"

"No! It can't be!" gasped Borko.

Minutes later several of the Guardians who had been assigned to guard the cave emerged from the woods. When they heard what was taking place. They began to laugh.

"What?" asked Sasho. "They are saying that they hid the treasure from them earlier? I thought it seemed like the raiders left rather too soon and too light-handed!"

The Guardians nodded that that was indeed the case.

Mavros emerged from the nearby woods moments later.

"Did you hear, Mavros?" crowed Sasho. "It didn't work. They were too smart for you!"

"But why did you do it?" demanded Deb. "We trusted you."

"It was to save the treasure from being hidden away again," he said.

"But it was so unnecessary," I said. "We're going to get to study and photograph all of the pieces in detail before they're hidden away again. From this information it should be possible to verify the authenticity of the tomb near Marvintsi. The whole world will have access to our knowledge of the tomb of Alexander the Great."

"It's still a pity that the raid failed," said Mavros. "For it appears now as if there will always be a shadow of doubt cast on the authenticity of your discovery, because only the replicas will be available for viewing. You know, there is still something suspect about this whole business. Your primitive Dionysians are somehow too clever. And the fact that the treasure of Alexander always seems to remain elusively out of reach adds to suspicions."

"You are the one who is unbelievable, Mavros!" exclaimed Deb. "You mean to say, after all we've seen, that you could doubt the authenticity of the tomb and treasure of Alexander?"

"Things are rarely what they seem in this part of the world, Deb. You have spent so little time here, how can you possibly know," said Mavros. "Take the assassination attempt on their President Gligorov that occurred a few years back. To this day no one knows for certain who tried to kill the president."

"They suspected Bulgars, Albanians, Serbs, even Macedonian nationalists. And, of course, they would never rule out a Greek."

"No, we can never rule out a Greek," agreed Sasho.

"There is, as you can see, little trust among us," continued Mavros. "And if we show goodwill towards one another at times, it is usually little more than a convenient pose for the moment."

"What an awful way to live!" said Deb.

"But it is how we've been for as long as we've been neighbors on this peninsula," said Sasho.

"Our various tribes staked out their territories. But no one has ever been satisfied with what he has. We have pushed and pulled at each other ever since. For a time one side will have the upper hand, but then some new power will rise and take control. This has happened over and over here."

"So true," said Borko. "Here in Macedonia, ancient Macedonians conquered their neighbors the Paeonians, the Illyrians, the Thracians, and the Greeks. But they too were eventually conquered by the Romans in the 2nd century before our time. And they, in turn, were overwhelmed in the sixth century by Slavs and their allies, the Avars, the Pechenegs, and eventually by the Bulgars, in the 7th and 8th centuries."

I could tell that Borko was only beginning to get wound up. He took a quick breath and plunged on. "Bulgars controlled Macedonia in the ninth century, but by the end of the tenth century the Macedonian Tsar Samuel rose to power. But he was defeated by the Vizantin Greeks, who ruled here for two hundred years, before they were chased out by a Serbian king in the 12th century. And they, in turn, fell to the Ottoman Turks in the 14th century. Not until the 19th and early 20th centuries were the Turks finally chased out by new Balkan states, who have been fighting over territories ever since."

It was a difficult story to follow, with its endless successive waves of conquest and settlement. I doubted that anyone could make much sense of all the competing parties and forces in this part of the world. And now, here was a village of long-lost Pelasgians to further muddy things.

"Doesn't anyone ever rise above tribal loyalty and prejudices?" asked Deb.

"I suppose our former President Gligorov could be said to have tried," said Sasho. "But you heard about what it earned him, an assassin's bomb that killed his chauffeur and left the president partially blinded."

"Oh, what an awful place to live!" said Deb.

"Yes, you are obviously an American, no matter how Greek you may look or sound," said Mavros. "Only an American, living in that vast mongrel melting pot of yours, with its vast spaces to relieve pressures for land and resources, could be so offended by our Balkan mentality."

"You forget though, Deb, that our greatest curse, our various nations and tribes, is also our greatest delight," said Sasho. "There are few places on earth where one can go only fifty to a hundred miles in any direction and end up in a completely different world - a different language and culture, with its own distinct songs, dances, stories and traditions to marvel at and find beauty in."

"That is, when you're not busy butchering each other," said Deb.

"Yes, that, of course, when they're not butchering each other," admitted Borko. He paused to think, then added. "But who knows, someday even we may outgrow our more barbarous ways. Look at the wild Vikings today. The French and Germans are cooperating lately, and even some Macedonians and Greeks." He looked at Mavros as he made this last comment.

The Council of Elders proved as good as their word. Our archaeology team was permitted to study the funeral goods of Alexander in detail. We established a camp up on the mountain not too far from the new storage site for the treasures. And each day we were permitted to visit this site and pore over the artifacts.

Eventually Borko and I were summoned to Skopje, as Professor Misirkova had suggested would happen. And as we might have expected, with no more evidence than a tomb filled with obvious forgeries, and a reluctance on our part to reveal more than that we were studying the authentic ones at a secret site in the mountains, the special committee formed to investigate us recommended that our permit be suspended. Obviously our story sounded ridiculous to academicians who were not involved in it. We were ordered to pack up our camp and return to the capital, from whence the American team would return to the U.S. and the Macedonian crew would be dissolved and the students sent home for the rest of the summer season. On the return trip to Marvintsi we discussed our options and it was decided that we would stall for as long as possible, before finally breaking camp and returning home.

When Borko and I finally arrived in Marvintsi it was too late to set out for the mountain camp, so we settled in for the night in our old campsite down the road from Professor Misirkova's camp. Borko had no trouble falling right off to sleep, but I couldn't seem to get to sleep, so I got up and put on my clothes and stepped outside.

It was a cool, quiet evening, a little overcast with no moon, so the night sky was especially dark. I could hear the faint chords of a guitar from the quarter mile distant camp of our colleague. So I decided to go over and have a talk with Professor Misirkova.

I slowly walked across the quarter mile of field that separated our two camps. Crickets were busily singing their night song. The air smelled of fresh, wild herbs. Fennel and some scent that I couldn't quite identify. As I approached the camp, I could smell the smoke from a wood fire.

When Professor Misirkova saw me, she rose from her place at the campfire among her students and stepped forward to meet me. I hadn't really noticed how good-looking she was, before now. She was a full-figured woman of medium height with square shoulders and a slightly wild but pretty mane of dark brown hair, tinting a bit grey now that she was in her mid-forties.

The light from the campfire flickered over the soft smooth features of her slightly broad face and dark engaging eyes. I hadn't expected to be so taken with her appearance, and I tried to keep my gaze from roving too much over her. Yet, I sensed that she had noticed my new attentiveness. As she stepped up beside me now, she displayed a sense of pride, mixed with a bit of self-consciousness.

"Hello, Professor Starkweather," she greeted me in strongly-accented

English with a slightly mellow, musical ring to her voice. She tried to maintain the somewhat stern expression that I generally associated with her from previous encounters, but I detected something new in her gaze tonight. Curiosity, of course, but also a desire to show a certain hospitality to someone who had come to her as a guest.

"What can I do for you?" she asked.

I felt a little awkward now and averted my eyes from hers as I murmured, "I just thought that I ought to come over and try to explain things a bit to you."

Her eyes hardened a little at this, as she responded. "What is there to explain? You and your colleague got into some kind of intrigue with some of the local people, and you left me to see that your unruly students engaged in archaeological research in your absence."

"You don't understand," I began.

"I do understand some things" she cut me off. "I understand that you and Borko have no interest in the work that my crew and I are engaged in," she said in a slightly shrill tone of voice. "You consider our work somehow beneath you. Not worthy of your attention." She paused, then continued when it appeared that I didn't have a ready response. "You've always appeared totally self-absorbed in your own projects."

She was now leading me a bit away from her crew. Perhaps because she didn't want them to overhear her venting her anger on me. I followed along in silence. How was I to respond? After all, it was mostly true, what she said. But then she hadn't been exactly a saint either. Snubbing me and my crew that first day when we arrived here. After that it was true that I hadn't made much of an effort, until now, to communicate with her or her crew.

I chose to ignore her latest barb and move on. "You, of all people, should be able to appreciate the importance of the discovery that Professor Milevski and I have made. It may be the biggest find in archaeology ever."

She led me on over to a bench out front of her tent, a distance away from her crew and their campfire, and gestured fro me to sit down next to her. I could hear the pleasant chords of a guitar that one of her crew was strumming and smell the faint scent of rose that probably came from her hair and the shampoo or rinse that she had used. The scene might have felt downright romantic, if we hadn't had such a history that suggested things wouldn't likely go that way.

"You would be surprised at how much I know about your work," she said. "Did you imagine that we could sit here a half kilometer away and be blind or ignorant to what you have been doing?" she said.

"But what do you really know?" I replied, trying my best to keep my voice down and keep any trace of anger out of my tone. You think that its all a hoax, but after what Borko and I experienced up in the mountains these last few weeks, I know that it couldn't possibly be."

"So you have experienced something, but do you have any convincing proof for the rest of us? That tomb of yours. I have been there, in your absence. It is all very interesting, and all very false." She said this without sounding self-satisfied or as if she took any pleasure in saying it.

All the same, my head bowed slightly and my expression turned glum, despite my best efforts to hide my reaction. No point to be coy about it though, I said to myself. "No," I answered her. "I have no convincing proof."

"I'm sorry to bring you to have to admit that," she said with what sounded like genuine sympathy in her voice.

I expected her to ask about my experiences in the mountains, since that would have seemed the natural thing for her to do, to satisfy her curiosity. But oddly enough, she didn't ask. Instead she changed the subject. Which was a relief, since I knew that I couldn't tell her anything. All the same, I couldn't help but wonder at her lack of curiosity.

"Are you at all interested in what we are doing here at our site?" she asked. "We have made some progress in determining the stratigraphy of this site - delineating civilizations and periods."

"Oh, is that right," I said. I should have been more interested. After all, my adult life had been devoted to archaeology. But this recent business had made the work of my fellows seem so insignificant in compare. No doubt she could sense my lack of any sincere interest, but she plunged on.

"We have established clear evidence of the presence of Paleolithic peoples here, going back possibly 50,000 years or more. But some of the most exciting work is at depths where we have discovered evidence of the first agricultural communities - Neolithic farmers, whose village culture is anywhere from 5,000 to 10,000 years old. Objects similar to some of those uncovered near Bitola. You know, maybe, cult objects that are unique to this part of the world, made from clay, such as miniature altars in the forms of animals or two-headed beasts, and replicas of houses with the faces of people formed into them."

Her enthusiasm was indeed beginning to affect me. "Really," I said, with genuine feeling this time.

"Of course, we also have found considerable evidence of the later arrival, probably about 3,000 years ago, of new peoples and cultures. These people show evidence of advanced bronze, silver and gold working - both in weaponry and ornamentation."

"I've heard a little about the wealth of Balkan archaeology, but I'm still always amazed at it," I said.

"Here, let me show you some of what we've found." And she gestured for me to follow her. She led me to a large camping trailer that had been converted into a laboratory. After finding the key and unlocking the door, she searched around by the entryway until she found the lights, and then invited me to enter after her. We then followed a narrow , cluttered corridor that led to a locked cabinet. Once again she extracted her set of keys from a pocket and found the right key.

What she removed from a tray in the cabinet was a small stone ornament in the shape of the female form. Lovely in its simplicity and in its ability to convey the essence of all that is female. The goddess-mother.

"It is about 7,000 years old, we estimate, and maybe even as old as 9,000 years. From a time when men and women were more equal, recognized for their contributions, and they shared power in public life," she said as she held the small four inch figurine up to the light for me to better see it.

The implied criticism of our own time wasn't lost on me. Probably due in no small part to her own feeling that she had been unfairly passed over for the Alexander Project. Which might well be true. I simply nodded my head in agreement to what she'd said.

By the time we emerged from the trailer and she had shut off the lights and locked the door, her crew had all gone off to bed.

"What was it you came here to see me about?" she asked as we walked over to the glowing pit of embers. All that remained of the fire.

"It had to do with trying to explain to you that we aren't the wild crowd that you've taken us to be."

Her eyes flashed with a momentary anger. "What am I to base my understanding on? What I see are drunken fist-fights in the middle of the night and stories of theft and all sorts of exaggerated claims, obvious forgeries, and now some of your students tell tales of ancient secret societies among the mountain people. Who could possibly make sense of it all? And don't think that I didn't notice the unruly behavior of your students while you and Professor Milevski were away."

It seemed hopeless trying to explain. I simply stood there in pained silence. Finally I said, "I wish that I could explain things to you."

"So do I," she answered. And after a pause she said, in a more sympathetic tone, "Don't try to explain then. But please don't expect the rest of us to accept your claims on faith. It is all too improbable."

"I won't do that," I said. I was trying to see things from her perspective. I'm sure it all looked very different from where she stood.

"You seem to be a decent enough person," she said. "Though the fact that you associate with that arrogant, boorish Milevski doesn't warm me to you."

"He isn't really as bad as he seems," I replied. Then continued, "Well, he is and he isn't. Once you get to know him better."

"I don't really care to. Given what I've seen so far," she said. A silence followed between us that seemed to signal the end of our conversation, so I said good bye and departed for our camp.

Our team worked at full tilt for nearly a month. But by the end of August it was clear that we had only scratched the surface. Many more months of serious study of the artifacts from the tomb would be necessary.

"It could take years to complete a study of all the artifacts," Deb grumbled, as the group of us sat around a table finishing supper one evening, back at our campsite.

"Do you think that the Elders will permit future access to the artifacts?" asked Sasho.

"We can only hope so," said Borko. "But I would advise you to do as much work as you possibly can in the few days remaining before we must leave. We cannot assume that we will have more access to the artifacts. It is the elders' decision, after all."

"They have security considerations," I added. "After that attempted raid, they have to be more security conscious than ever."

Joel shook his head. He obviously didn't share our concerns.

"It's times like this that I begin to wonder who you are anymore, Druids or archaeologists. Neither you nor Professor Milevski seem to care much anymore about what happens to the artifacts," said Joel.

I was surprised to learn that the wall was still there, after all this time. "No, I suppose we have different concerns than you. We respect the right of the Guardians to determine the fate of the burial," I said.

"It's enough for us that they have allowed us to collect information on all of the artifacts from the tomb," said Borko.

"But the funeral cart alone could take months to fully analyze," said Sasho. "There are so many questions yet to be answered, concerning the methods of construction, the sources of materials, and other questions. If only we could dismantle the cart and examine the parts in detail. And x-rays of certain artifacts might reveal some truly remarkable things."

"So are we due for another round of battle in the debate of science versus the sacred?" I asked. "And will we now have to advise the Guardians to rebury the funeral goods with the remains of Alexander immediately, before you have time to hatch another plot to steal them?"

"No! Don't do that!" said Joel.

"Even a few more days will mean a lot to our work," added Deb. "Please don't let them cut it short."

"But how are we to know that you aren't already conspiring with Mavros?" I asked.

"No, never again. Not after what he did," said Sasho.

"Have you been in any further contact with him, Deb?" I asked.

"Well, I...it isn't as if I've told him anything about our work here, or even the location of the new site," she said.

"So you have been in contact with him during your trips to town, is that right?" Borko demanded to know.

"Well, yes, but..."

"And tell me that he has never suggested that he would not try to steal away the treasures of Alexander again?"

"No, he hasn't," admitted Deb.

"Why did you continue to see him, Deb? After what he did?" asked Sasho, unable to conceal his disappointment.

"I decided to continue to see him after it became clear to me that you weren't angry about the attempted raid, Sasho," said Deb. "You were only angry because it was apparently a Greek raid. If Macedonians could have staged the raid and succeeded, you wouldn't have objected at all if the artifacts ended up in your own museum in Skopje. So I really didn't see any reason to dump Mavros, any more than you."

"But he deceived us," said Sasho in a pained voice. "And the treasure was found on Macedonian soil, after all, not Greek soil. It should remain here."

"And it will!" declared Borko.

"You should just be glad that the Guardians embraced Christianity along with their pagan practices some centuries ago, or you wouldn't have been treated with such kid gloves when you went snooping around them," I added.

Neither Borko nor I said another word about the subject that evening. But the two of us remained up after the others went to bed.

"We need to talk to the Guardians again, soon," I said.

"You're right," he replied. "We don't want a repeat of the raid that Mavros set up last time."

"The fall equinox celebration is only two days away. Let's bring it up with them after the ceremony," I said, in a partial whisper, glancing around furtively, out of concern that our young charges might overhear what I was saying. We could, of course, expect that they would know where we were going the next day, but I still harbored the illusion that I could keep secrets from them.

"Fine," said Borko, and he rose to go off to bed, the matter resolved.

The fall equinox celebration with the Guardians was revelatory for me. During the summer solstice I had seen their rituals from afar, as an outside observer, with nothing more t6han a scientist's curiosity. But now I was a participant, fully engaged in each symbolic gesture of the ceremony that marked the shift in light, when the light would begin to fade in autumn and increasing cold would begin to replace the warmth of summer.

Stoyan again presided over the ceremony in his striking golden mask. However, there was a new figure, a priestess who wore a silver mask and bore sheaves of ripe grain and fruit to the altar for a ritual blessing of the harvest. Her robes were made of white linen, decorated with red and black embroidery of the kind seen on Macedonian folk dress.

She stood and walked with a proud and dignified air about her. Each step seemed an act of careful, conscious deliberation. She seemed to float along with graceful ease, in comparison to the heavier steps of mere mortals.

As she passed nearby me in parade between our double row of robed and sandal-shod Guardians, something about her struck me as familiar. Maybe at Stoyan's house at one of our meetings, or perhaps during a visit to the village, or on the street somewhere, I had made her acquaintance. That wouldn't seem surprising, but it nagged at me that I couldn't quite place her.

After the calling of the spirits of the four directions, Stoyan spoke briefly about the passage of the light. Then, he related a story.

"Demeter, the goddess of agriculture," he said as he gestured in the direction of the woman in the silver mask, who stood by his side. "In the springtime she watches over the seeds we sow in our fields. In summer she nurtures the growing fruit and grain. Then in autumn she bestows her blessing upon our harvests.

However, even the gods of myth did not dwell in perfect harmony, and their conflicts, according to the legends passed down to us, had consequences in the lives of mortals. One such conflict began when the god of the Underworld, Hades, abducted Demeter's daughter Persephone from the meadow where she tended the flowers that were her special charge.

When Demeter finally learned that Hades had made her daughter Queen of the Underworld, she implored the chief among the gods to assist her in obtaining the release of her captive daughter. As the legend tells it, because Persephone had compromised herself by eating a few seeds of a pomegranate, rather than refuse all that Hades had offered her, the Fates decreed that she and her mother must accept a compromise. They declared that she must spend six months of each year with Hades in his dark Underworld.

And so the legend tells us, Demeter rejoices each spring at the return of her daughter, and in her joy she bestows the blessings of the reviving earth upon us. But again, in the autumn when her daughter must return to the Underworld, she withdraws her gifts of flower and fruit. And so we must endure six months of cold and dark, without blossom or seed, until Persephone's return."

As I listened to Stoyan retell this ancient myth, that part of me that followed the path of science wondered why humans have had such a need to personify nature in order to explain its workings. But then again, is that what Stoyan was doing today? In fact, neither I, nor any of my fellow celebrants took his story literally. What he was doing was giving us a concrete image, through story, for us to better appreciate the emotions that we all felt at the dying back of nature in the fall. Through the symbols and imagery of the story our emotional reaction to this drastic cyclical change in our lives no longer would remain so vague and confused. Just as we mourn the even temporary going away of a beloved child, we mourn the yearly departure of the warmth and light and flowers and fruit.

As the ceremony came to an end and the celebrants prepared to return to the village for a special dinner in honor of the day, I scanned the crowd in search of the mysterious Demeter. When I spotted her some distance away among the people making their way back to the village, I tried to force my way through the throng in order to get a better look at her. But as I made my way through the crowd, excusing myself to people as I pushed ahead, just when I thought that I might be getting close, I looked to where I thought she would be, and she was gone.

The next morning, when the others rose for breakfast, Borko and I were already up, though we both felt rather tired.

Once the entire crew was assembled, Borko made an announcement. "Our work is over. We've told the Guardians that they ought to rebury the Emperor and his funeral possessions without further delay. We won't be visiting the site today. Instead we will be packing to go home."

"So that's it," said Joel. "We've seen the last that we're going to see of the Big Mac and his gold?"

"Probably," I said. "Once it was clear that Mavros might still be on the scent of Alexander's treasures, we couldn't risk another attempted raid. We had to warn the Guardians. And they agreed that it should be hidden away immediately."

"So it will remain here," said Borko.

"Yes, it will remain here," repeated Sasho bitterly.

"But you should know," said Joel. "That your tomb filled with replicas will have all of the force of a cement dinosaur theme park out in the desert."

"Just as Mavros predicted," added Deb. "There'll be doubts about the authenticity of the original find. Our story is about as believable as a dime store novel, without the treasure to back it up."

"Baubles and trinkets of gold," I said. "That's all most of it was anyway. If you really want to understand the history of society, religion, culture, and language in this part of the world, I would advise you to take more notice of the living treasure we uncovered during this dig."

For some reason the words, "living treasure" triggered thoughts of my own neglected family, of Jo, of friends that I'd known over the years, and the way our lives were intertwined. Some of the new insights I had gained from my time with the Guardians might just be part of the key to preserving the living treasures in my own life.

We never really know what lies ahead, I suppose. But why should we be surprised though, by the unexpected turn of events. After all, that's what makes for adventure, for comedy, for tragedy, for romance and for high drama and the like. In other words, a good story, which is what we all yearn for in our lives, after all, isn't it?

"Good luck selling that argument to Professor Misirkova and her colleagues," Sasho awoke me from my reverie. "You know that they're already saying that our expedition is some kind of hoax," said Sasho.

"She and her friends may succeed for a while, but the truth will come out before too long," I said.

"Yes, the truth is out there," quipped Joel as he gazed up at the mountainside.

Yes it is indeed, I thought as I peered up at the dusting of snow on the distant ridge top, a herald of the end of summer in the high country.

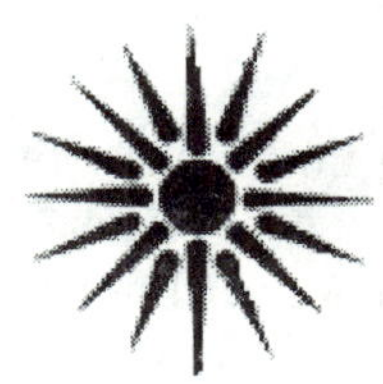

Epilogue

Sasho proved right about the unacceptability of our find in the absence of the genuine artifacts. The most open-minded of our colleagues simply adopted a wait-and-see attitude, while the vast majority dismissed us as brazen hucksters.

I couldn't altogether blame them. Our tale was rather hard to swallow. And when the tabloid magazines began calling me for a story, I knew that we were in big trouble. Like the study of crop circles or alien crash sites, the exploration of Alexander's tomb in Marvintsi would be shunned by the respectable scientific community. There would be no further funding for our work and no invitations to present our findings at the usual conferences.

Of course, we would be welcomed with open arms at fantasy-land conferences, where we would be encouraged to expound on Alexander's tomb and more, right after the latest alien abductee and before the reincarnated King Tut.

As a result, I fell into a serious funk for a while. Borko kept reminding me that we knew what we knew. There was no sense in letting the skepticism of others get us down. Besides, as we kept reminding each other, the truth would eventually come out. I just hoped that I would still be around to bask in some of the glory that would come our way on that day.

I stayed on in Macedonia until nearly the beginning of fall classes at the U. Borko had decided to cancel his own fall schedule at Skopje University in order to spend more time with the people of Meshkom. There was a good deal that he still wanted to learn from them, and I suspected that for the first time in his life he had found the family he had always yearned for. While some of their pagan rituals and ceremonies seemed at odds with his Orthodox Christianity, he was finding ways to reconcile the two. Not surprising really, the Unitarians in America had been hosting neo-pagan celebration groups in recent years, and it hadn't apparently interfered with belief in Christ among their membership either.

My last day in Marvintsi, I surprised everyone when I announced that I wanted to go say good bye to Professor Misirkova. Borko had slept through my last visit with her, and others were camped up in the mountains at the time, so there was more than one puzzled look as I strode off to visit her camp.

I found her working in a trench alongside some of her crew. When she saw me, she pulled herself up out of the excavation and extended a dirty hand to me in greeting. Her hair was tied back in an austere bun today. But I could still easily imagine that lovely wild mane of hers blowing in the breeze.

"So you've come to say good bye, I assume," she said in a mild friendly voice. Her eyes slightly averted from my own.

I took the soil-encrusted hand that she offered.

"Bye, and good luck with your work," was all I could think to say to her, before awkwardly shaking loose of her hand and abruptly turning and heading back toward our own camp.

"And best wishes in your own work, Jack," she replied with what I wanted to believe was sincerity in her voice.

The first morning back in my office at the university, I hung my coat on the coat rack and opened my briefcase and removed some papers and laid them on the desk. Then I sat down at the desk and began to go over my notes for my first lecture of the day.

After a few minutes I glanced around the room. There was the picture of my family. I had a note from the department informing me of the time and place of the next faculty meeting. It appeared as if nothing much had changed since I'd been gone.

I went back to my notes. I worked for about another forty-five minutes. I set my pen down. I undid my tie and loosened the sleeve of my shirt until I could roll it up enough to see the small bluish tattoo on my arm. I examined the strange little rune for a time.

There was a knock at the office door. I hurried to roll down my sleeve and readjust my tie. "Come in," I finally said.

Deb peeked her head around the door. "Dr. Starkweather, when you have a chance, could I go over some of my notes with you from this last summer's research?"

I nodded my head yes, and she continued. "I also think I have a topic that I'd like to research for my dissertation. It involves the continuity of a cult to the goddess Demeter." She paused and looked down at the notes in her hands. "And I was kind of wondering if you might use your influence with the Guardians to get me acquainted with the women's society in Meshkom."

"I'll do whatever I can," I said

"I'll spend this year preparing myself and arranging the funding for some field research next year," she said. "I'll also be preparing by doing some intensive Macedonian language study."

"Good," I said.

There was another knock at the door. This time it was Joel. "Hello, Doc," he said cheerfully. "Are you coming next week to my presentation to the Michigan Archaeological Society?"

"I wouldn't miss it for anything," I said.

"Do you think you'll stick around here next summer or are you coming with us when we go back to Macedonia for some field research?" He nodded toward Deb as he said the word "we."

"So you've got the bug too?" I asked. "You're not planning to camp out on that mountain again and spy on the Guardians, are you?"

"Nah, they can put the Big Mac anywhere they want. Won't bother me."

"Then what is it you intend to do over there?" I asked.

"I was thinking I wouldn't mind a crack at earning my own Druid tatoo, like the one you and Professor Milevski got."

"So when does this class in the Macedonian language meet?" I asked. "I believe I'd also like to attend."

"We don't have an official class just yet," said Deb.

"But the Slavic Department is processing an exchange scholar's application right now. A young professor from Skopje by the name of Alexander Kitanovski," added Joel. "He could arrive by mid-November at the earliest, and offer us some lessons, along with his other duties."

"Yes, I've already heard something about the man," I said. "Apparently he has a rather impressive background in linguistics, anthropology, and some specialized training in the preservation of antiquities. We'll certainly want him to do some lecturing in our department."

"Hey, didn't he sound at all familiar?" asked Deb.

"No, why? Should he?"

"It's Sasho," said Deb. Smiling now. "There's somebody else coming too."

"A professor Boris..."

"No! Not Borko again!" I gasped. Love the man, but I really need a break from the Boar.

"Nah, just kidding," said Joel. "It's Rada!"

"That's great!" I said. "Now get out of here so I can go over my notes. I've only got about twenty minutes before classes start up again."

After they left the phone rang again. This time it was Jo. "I'm going to be late again this evening. Got another meeting. Can you pick up something on your way home for our dinner?"

"No problem" I replied. "How about a salad I learned to make while I was over in Macedonia? I think I can find all of the ingredients at the store. And maybe we can open that bottle of red wine that I brought back with me."

"Sure. Why not," she said. "See you then, dear."

Documenting the ancient history of the Macedonian people

A year ago I offered my help in the translation into English and editing for publication of Aleksander Donski's *The Descendants of Alexander the Great of Macedon*. I have followed Alexander's works on Macedonian history and culture over the years with great interest, and I have always been particularly impressed by his ability to analyze and clearly express the evidence of possible cultural links between the ancient and present-day Macedonians.

I began reading his arguments on this subject several years ago with a certain amount of skepticism. While his evidence was always interesting and intriguing, for me it only suggested possible links between the ancient and present-day peoples. His early evidence did not appear all that conclusive. However, after reading this most recent work most carefully as I helped Marijan Galevski refine his English language translation of the text, I have become convinced that Aleksander Donski has now accumulated conclusive evidence to prove claims of cultural continuity from ancient to modern times in Macedonia. If one, or two, or even ten of his examples appear weak or unconvincing to some readers, by the fifteenth or twenty fifth example the weight of his evidence should begin to convince all but the most rigid pan-Slavist that a mass migration from beyond the Carpathian Mountains in the 6th century never replaced the thriving ancient Macedonian society of the time.

The sheer number of his credible sources, both ancient and modern, and the scope of his investigation, ranging from the linguistic, to the anthropological, to the social, historical, geographic, and more, and with particular emphasis on the mythic and folkloric, cast serious doubt on the old accepted story of Slavic displacement of the indigenous population of Macedonia. While no one can question the obvious Macedonian cultural links with other so-called Slavic peoples, particularly the clear and close ties to the neighboring Serbians and Bulgarians, Aleksander Donski provides us with equally conclusive and convincing linguistic and cultural evidence of the links between the indigenous ancient Macedonian people and those who also today call themselves Macedonians and who continue to dwell on the exact same territory of northern Greece, western Bulgaria and the Republic of Macedonia that was once ancient Macedonia.

However, I must warn you that Mr. Donski's book, although it is not overly long, is dense in factual material. It is a valuable source and reference book on Macedonian history and culture, but it is not an easy storybook for light reading. I chose to introduce readers of my mystery adventure novel to some of the book's more important ideas through quotations that began each chapter, however, that effort only scratches the surface of much of the important factual material his book contains.

When I was completing my doctoral dissertation in Slavic studies at the University of Washington in Seattle in the late 1980's and early 90's one of my advisors was the now-deceased scholar Dr. Imre Boba. If I learned anything at all from my time with this respected scholar, it was the importance of questioning conventional wisdom, while basing that questioning on sound scholarship, careful study of original sources and in light of new evidence. This mentor at times incurred the wrath of those who had devoted their lives to erroneous theories when he presented his findings at international conferences. However, experience tells me that sound scholarship eventually prevails in the end, and so I have no doubt that my former professor's work will some day receive the recognition it deserves, just as I have no doubt that sound scholarship concerning the origins of the present-day Macedonian people will be accepted with the passage of time.

When I began my study of Slavic languages, literature, history and culture some forty years ago, it was accepted as fact that the great Slavic civilizations of the Middle Ages had their origins in the rapid expansion of a hitherto obscure Slavic tribe beginning somewhere in the southern Ukraine around the 5th century AD. However, Roman historians Plinius, Tacitus and Procopius mention related tribes of Veneti, Eneti, Sclavini and Ante living as far south as the Dnieper and as far north as the Vistula River in the first and second centuries AD. The Veneti are also mentioned in the writings of a number of ancient authors such as Strabo, Pomponius, Mella, and Cassius Dio which place this people in various regions in more ancient times all across Eastern Europe and as far south as Asia Minor. Quintus Curtius Rufus mentioned the Veneti as part of Alexander the Great's army in the 4th century BC. Herodotus in the 5th century BC mentioned a people of the Balkans he calls the Eneti. And an even older source, the Iliad of Homer, mentioned the Veneti as allies of Troy, pushing their possible existence in the Balkans as far back as the 8th century BC.

All of this information and more is collected in Aleksandar Donski's book, but he relies for much of his knowledge of this subject on recent scholarship such as Matej Bor, Josko Savli and Ivan Tomasic's 1996 book *Veneti- First Builders of the European Community*. These Balkan scholars and others such as the Russian Pavel Toulaev, author of *Veneti: Ancestors of the Slavs,* published in the year 2000, and respected European scholars such as Professor Emeritus Mario Alinei of the University of Utrecht, whose Theory of Continuity ascribes very ancient origins to present-day Indo-European peoples in their present homelands, as well as others, have accumulated convincing evidence of an older and much broader Slavic cultural influence than one was ever taught about in Slavic studies.

Linguists such as Anthony Ambrozic have also begun to solve mysteries concerning inscriptions from all over the ancient world that defied analysis using Latin or Greek, when they used Slavic as the basis for translation. Ambrozic, for example, renders a more convincing translation of the 4th century BC bronze plate found in the vicinity of Padua, Italy in the 1970's known as the Tavola de Este inscription, and he achieves similar results with the Dura-Europos inscriptions from a city of the ancient Macedonian Empire located in present-day Syria by using Slavic root words as his basis for translation.

Using modern DNA testing scientists are also finding corroborating evidence that Mediterranean peoples, including the Macedonians, are not relatively recent arrivals in the region from some great Slavic migration or barbarian invasions of the Roman Empire in the 6th century AD. DNA study indicates that they belong to an "older Mediterranean substratum" that includes Iberians, North Africans, Italians, French, Cretans, Jews, Lebanese, Anatolians, Armenians and even Iranians, according to researchers from the Department of Molecular Biology of the University Complutense of Madrid, Spain, and others.

It is, therefore, rather pathetic, as Aleksandar Donski points out, for scholars to explore remote Afghani or Pakistani villages in search of remnants of the ancient culture of the Macedonians left behind there by Alexander the Great and his army, when they have not bothered to search for such evidence in a thousand Macedonian villages in Macedonia, the home of Alexander and his army, which many of them seem to assume contain no such evidence. It is especially pathetic for anyone who grew up speaking the Macedonian language and who was immersed in that society and culture to accept the verdict of such scholars, foreign-born or domestic, that the present-day Macedonians have no connection to the ancients, rather than make the effort to study the facts now emerging from recent scholarship that contradict such a belief.

For example, there are numerous references in Donski's book from historians, beginning with the Roman conquest of Macedonia in the 2nd century BC and on up to the 20th century, to people living in Macedonia who identified themselves as Macedonians rather than as Slavs, Greeks, Romans, Bulgars, or something else. There was indeed a continuity of identity with the ancient Macedonians right through the period of national revival and revolution in the early 20th century, and it is all well-documented. In fact, there are so many references to Macedonians over the centuries that it becomes all the more perplexing why two brief quotations, one from Procopius and the other from John of Ephesus that document a Slavic invasion of Macedonia and parts of Greece in the 6th century AD, are assumed to be evidence of a thorough Slavic replacement of the indigenous Macedonian population of the time.

This assumption becomes even more doubtful when one begins to read Aleksandar Donski's review of some hundred Macedonian folk songs, tales, legends, rituals and customs from past centuries whose origins can be traced to sources from ancient Macedonia. These include numerous tales about Alexander the Great, stories of ancient Macedonian history, stories with ancient motifs, stories that refer to animals that only lived in Macedonia in ancient times, and folk customs, rituals and beliefs that appear to have originated in ancient times in Macedonia. The author does not remind readers of the obvious linguistic or cultural evidence of Macedonian links to other Slavic peoples, particularly the Serbians and Bulgarians, because so many others have already established those links. He provides new or reminds readers of neglected evidence that demonstrates that there was indeed an enormous influence on Macedonian culture from ancient Macedonian society.

Aleksandar Donski concludes his exhaustive review of Macedonian folklore with links to ancient Macedonia with a challenge. If the present-day culture came from a 6th century Slavic invasion of Macedonia from beyond the Carpathian Mountains, why is it so easy to trace so many old songs, stories and customs back to ancient Macedonian sources, while no one seems to be able to produce old stories and songs with obvious links to the former life of the Macedonian Slavs in their former homeland on the other side of the Carpathian Mountains? It is a very good question to ask all of those who would label the Macedonian people Slav-Macedonians or see them dispersed among the neighboring Albanians, Greeks, Bulgarians or Serbians as a people without deep roots or distinct culture in the region and, therefore, unworthy of any separate identity of their own.

When people of Macedonian ancestry identify themselves to others in the world as "Macedonian", the reply often is, "Oh, yes, the people who conquered the ancient world under Alexander the Great". Now, if you were raised under or influenced by the Macedonism of the former Yugoslavia, or if, like myself, you were a student in a Slavic studies department of a university somewhere in the world, you probably would then repeat the stock answer: "The ancient and the modern Macedonians are separate peoples. We don't know for certain who the ancient people were, but we know that the modern people are descended from a Slavic people who came into Macedonia in the sixth century."

It was a reply that satisfied our desire for simple answers, it also served to deflect Greek hostility to a Macedonian nation, and it gave us some sense of belonging to a family that included hundreds of millions of fellow Slavs who would supposedly come to our aid in times of trouble due to our kindred languages and cultures. However, the relentless march of time has rendered that response both false and pathetic. New scholarship has demonstrated the over-simplification of a Great Slavic Migration theory, and new political realities have left a fully independent Republic of Macedonia adrift in a hostile ocean filled with sharks, some of them Slavic.

Now the choices for Macedonians are fairly clear. They can crawl off in some corner and die in humble anonymity, much to the satisfaction of those who have always hated the existence of a Macedonian language, literature, culture and nation, or they can embrace their identity in its fullness and richness, and maybe still end up going down with the Macedonian ship of state, but at least have their pride and integrity intact. If Macedonians should choose the second path, they and their friends in the world will need to arm themselves with knowledge, and I know of no better source at the present time than the new book by Macedonian historian Aleksandar Donski, *The Descendants of Alexander the Great of Macedon.*

Michael Seraphinoff, 2004, Greenbank, Washington, USA

About the author

The author of *Macedonian Gold*, Michael Seraphinoff, is a scholar, teacher and writer with a background in anthropology, linguistics and literature. He wrote his doctoral dissertation (University of Washington, Seattle, 1993) on aspects of the Macedonian language, literature, history and culture, a life-long interest with origins in his own Macedonian-American family background and history. In the present work of fiction, his first novel, he draws upon both a scholar's knowledge and rich life experience. In addition to his more bookish pursuits, the author has traveled extensively, taught in the U.S. and Russia, worked as a farmer, forester, sailor and baker. He also took an active part in the social and cultural ferment and change that characterized the 1960's, experiences that included communal living, social protest and spiritual quest and that confirmed him in his abiding and life-long love for the natural world. The author today works as an organic farmer/gardener, a teacher, and as an examiner for the International Baccalaureate Organization from his home on Whidbey Island in Washington state. He is author and translator of a number of scholarly and literary works, including poetry, short stories, and scientific articles and books.

Southeastern Europe